PAYDAY

A Fiery Ending to Fast Paced Intrigue and Adventure in Guatemala

O. Lynn Justice

Order this book online at www.trafford.com
or email orders@trafford.com

Most Trafford titles are also available at major online book retailers.

Printed in Victoria, BC, Canada.

ISBN: 978-1-4269-2223-7 (Soft)
ISBN: 978-1-4269-2224-4 (Hard)

Library of Congress Control Number: 2009912981

*Our mission is to efficiently provide the world's finest, most comprehensive
book publishing service, enabling every author to experience success.
To find out how to publish your book, your way, and have it available
worldwide, visit us online at www.trafford.com*

Trafford rev. 01/12/2010

 www.trafford.com

North America & international
toll-free: 1 888 232 4444 (USA & Canada)
phone: 250 383 6864 • fax: 812 355 4082

ACKNOWLEDGEMENTS

To my sweetheart since childhood, Bonita Hedrick, who has stuck with me through thick and thin, and under fire, who taught me how to be a husband and father of eight children and numerous other important lessons in life.

I owe a special thanks to Sarah Anglesey and Rebecca Talbot, who in spite of family illness and busy schedules, completed the final review and editing in record time.

The story you are about to read relates some actual events that involved some real people, which inspired the author and is supposed to add a measure of realism to this work of fiction.

Introduction

Linda Stacy and Orville Fletcher grew up on opposite sides of the Ohio River, she in Kentucky and he in Indiana. They met on the Indiana side of the river in early 1957, when Orville was fifteen and Linda sixteen. After only a couple of times together, they knew they were meant for each other. They kept the flame burning through high school and for three years of studying in separate universities and were married in the summer of 1963.

Orville spent the year before marrying as an exchange student at the University of Puerto Rico, where he learned Spanish. Upon graduation in June 1964, he landed a job in Puerto Rico as a field representative for UltraChem, a Texas Chemical company that operated under several corporate names throughout Latin America. In his spare time, he took up flying and received his pilot license in 1967. Upon completing his pilot training he and Linda picked out their first plane, a well used Champion one-fifty. The plane came in handy for work too, so Orville was able to quickly build flying time.

Orville progressed well up the corporate ladder with UltraChem, first as Field Representative, then Area Manager and finally Regional Manager. He showed particular skills in trouble shooting and overcoming obstacles in challenging markets. He had opportunity to hone these skills when the company moved him and his growing family from Puerto Rico to war torn Central America in 1970. As the conflicts grew in Central America, business was difficult. Finally in February 1971, he flew to the company headquarters in Dallas where he met with his boss, the company's Director of International Markets and the Vice President of Operations. They asked him what he suggested. Even though it meant he would be without a job, he answered that the company should secure all capital investments and close operations, at least until the political climate improved. They had arrived at the same conclusion and were pleased that he could lay aside his personal aspirations to defend the company's interests.

They gave him an office and a secretary and asked him to stay for two weeks to work up a closure plan. They met frequently during those planning days. In their final meeting before Orville's return to Costa Rica, the President of UltraChem assured him that there would definitely be a place for his loyalty and talents within the company somewhere in the world.

In May, three months after the Dallas meeting, Orville was finishing the implementation of his plan, when the company approached with a request that he move with his family to Buenos Aires, Argentina. The company had large commitments in Argentina, Uruguay, and Paraguay. Argentina and Uruguay were in the throws of civil war and Paraguay was under a stiff dictatorship. The Manager for those countries had just suffered a nervous breakdown after a second attempt on his life.

The directors felt that the company was close to losing its foothold in all three countries. Their commitment in that operation was a little over forty million dollars; nearly double the Central American investment. They urgently needed a turnaround in that market, or lose it. The new job would represent a considerable promotion and salary increase for Orville, but the level of personal risk would increase considerably. It was not an easy decision for the couple, but they accepted the offer after Orville spent two weeks in Argentina appraising the situation.

Orville was successful in putting together a highly effective team. Under his direction they secured the company's future in the three countries, and were able to expand the company's operations to include Chile. In spite of the wars and unstable economies Orville and his team were able to show profit for the company by the end of the second year. Not all was positive. Two employees were killed in those two years, one accidentally in crossfire. For the other, it was never determined if he was a target, or merely incidental to the violence of the period.

The company was pleased with Orville's success and showed their pleasure by giving him a very nice bonus at the end of that second year. The area remained unstable economically and politically for two more years with regular nighttime battles, and disappearances. It was challenging to handle business during those tumultuous years. There were several occasions in which Orville narrowly escaped with his life.

Nevertheless, each year was profitable for the company and they showed their appreciation by adding to Orville and Linda's nest egg.

After six years, everything was under control and just the way companies want it, but Orville was unhappy just doing routine management. He missed the crisis management and troubleshooting and he felt there was a market for those skills. After talking it over with Linda, they decided it was time to leave the company in order to start up his company. Orville had done his research and felt that Central America would be a good place to establish his base of operations. It was close to the U.S. and many U.S. companies had considerable capital invested there. The area was still unstable, but that was precisely why there was a good market for his skills.

The Texans would have liked to keep Orville for a few more years as their top executive in that area, but acceded to his request to step down. They showed their appreciation for his achievements by granting him another sizable bonus and contracting him as an outside consultant for their security in Central America, where they had recently reopened. That contract alone provided a good chunk of the income needed to keep the family at a similar lifestyle to which they were accustomed.

Orville thought it would be better, work-wise, to be some-where in the northern part of Central America, but schools were better in the South, in Panama and Costa Rica. Linda didn't think that schools should be a basis for choosing where to live, since she planned to home-school the children, so they chose to live in Honduras.

They made their move to Tegucigalpa, Honduras in the last half of December 1976. A year later they were able to purchase 90 acres, an hour and a half South of Tegucigalpa. It was a farm setting similar to what each of them had grown up in, and there were no schools, which meant Linda could justify her dream of home schooling their children.

Orville was successful with his business and his flying and other skills were important to his success. His work frequently involved getting someone in or out of a tight spot in the middle of some war or natural disaster, which there seemed to be an abundance of in Central America. Being able to get someplace quick and knowing what to do, once he got there proved valuable to his clients, and there weren't many with his particular set of skills.

By 1984 the bulk of Orville's clients were in Guatemala. The family voted to move to Guatemala City. They left the ranch house furnished and in the care of their foreman. Orville planned to travel regularly to Honduras and could check on the ranch, and the family planned to return to spend holidays and vacations at the home-place.

In addition to the move, that year Orville traded his Cessna 206 for a faster more efficient Cessna Turbo Skymaster. He was instrument rated and had honed his pilot skills considerably. Although he had no desire to become a professional pilot, he was very professional about flying.

There are numerous stories to tell. This one took place in Guatemala during the month of August 1986. The decade of the 80's was tumultuous for Guatemala, with several natural disasters and the last convulsions of a long civil war. At the time of this story Orville and Linda had been living nearly two years in a 5-bedroom home in Zone 13, just off of Las Americas Avenue on the southern edge of Guatemala City.

In most regards, they were pretty normal middle aged parents. Although Orville looked his age with balding and a chest that was drifting to the mid-section, he was strong and healthy. Linda stayed on a demanding exercise program and her body exuded energy and health. She glowed with a mature physical beauty that did not evidence her to be a mother of eight children.

CHAPTER 1
SATURDAY, AUGUST 2, 1986
HOME SWEET HOME

As I remember, we arrived back in Guatemala City around 8 p.m. the night before, an hour later than scheduled. We had flown Delta from Cincinnati to Miami and then Eastern from Miami.

Linda and the seven youngest had left Guatemala the latter part of June to join our oldest daughter, Lynne in Utah. She had just completed her second year at Brigham Young University in Provo. I met the family in Utah in the middle of the second week of July and then all ten of us spent a week and a half visiting friends in Utah and Idaho before flying to the Cincinnati area to spend a like number of days visiting both sides of our families in the tri-state area of Indiana, Ohio and Kentucky.

When I went to bed, I was so tired that I had planned on sleeping in Saturday morning, but I awoke as usual, a little after 5 a.m. Linda and the kids were still sound asleep. As a farm boy, I had grown accustomed to getting up early to take care of the milking and feeding of the animals before boarding the bus to school. Once gone from the farm, I continued the habit and found the early morning hours important for starting my day right. I could think more clearly and frequently find the solution to a problem that seemed unsolvable the day before. I would plan the day ahead, in the quiet that ceased once the family was up and moving.

The bathroom-closet off of the master bedroom was a unique arrangement for one's private needs. When you first went through the door, there was a semi-enclosed area for the bathroom with all the normal artifacts, including a marble-topped double sink. The tub-shower was anything but standard. It consisted of a sunken rectangular enclosure, made of poured concrete and painted with epoxy pool paint. It had two showerheads and ample room for two adults to submerse in the tub, or shower simultaneously. Down the hall beyond the tub, was the exercise-dressing room, with closets on three sides. The only exercise equipment was a weight machine, so there was plenty of floor space between the closets. The whole complex was in a large room with a high ceiling and ample light and ventilation.

I usually took my shower after jogging, but I decided that I needed a 'waker-upper' that morning, so I jumped in for a quick shower. After the refreshing shower, I dressed in my running suit, but carried my shoes, as I exited quietly through the bedroom into the outer hall.

I headed to the kitchen to prepare my morning cup of mate. I was really looking forward to it, since I had been unable to drink any on Friday due to the full day of travel. I filled the teakettle and started the water to heating. Then I pulled down the plastic container where I kept my mate and filled the mate cup. I had several mate cups, but my favorite was made of vitrified bone-like material.

I hopped up to sit on the counter while my water heated. After being in several large country kitchens during the vacation, I looked around our kitchen and it occurred to me how small our kitchen was. Even after having moved the washer and drier to the outside patio, and putting additional counter in their place, the kitchen was incredibly small for a 4,000 square foot home. It barely met Linda's requirements. Our kitchen like many in Central America were designed for maids, not for the lady of the house.

I picked some flakes of mate off of the counter and dropped them on my tongue. It numbed my tongue a little and I spit it out. Mate is a strong herbal tea, grown mainly in one province in Argentina. The Argentine and Uruguayan gauchos discovered mate, while tending sheep and cattle out it in the Pampas. Mate is a ten-foot tall plant that grows naturally in a small area bordering both countries. The manner of preparing and drinking the tea was still being done in pretty much the same way that the early gauchos did it. They cut up and dried the entire plant, leaves and stems. The resulting dry powder and twigs were placed in a gourd cup, and then wet down with warm water. A few minutes after the first dose of water had soaked in, the tea was ready to be savored. Instead of brewing the tea and straining out the leaves or powder, one strained it while drinking by means of a metal straw with a strainer on the lower end. The gauchos would pour hot water from a thermal container over mate and then sip the tea through the metal strainer-straw while watching over their herds. They learned to drink it with their hard bread, wild berries, jerky and an occasional piece of fresh meat. Sugar was not readily available, so they learned to drink it un-sugared.

I didn't care much for mate the first times I tried it in Argentina. It has a strong flavor and I was used to sweeter drinks. I learned to drink it during a business trip through the Entre Rios Province of Argentina and the interior of Uruguay. A work companion and I were calling on paper mills, sugar companies and similar large industry. We got up early and drove late each day for a week. Frequently during that week the only breakfast we could find was a piece or two of bread. I started out eating bread and drinking water, but soon accepted my companion's offer to share his mate. After a week of sharing, I was hooked. I returned home with a supply of mate and the proper utensils. Years later I read that mate had all kinds of medicinal and health properties, but I figure I drank it for the same reason the Gauchos did. I liked it.

After the water came to a boil, I prepared my mate and carried it to my desk in the library. Let me clarify, the desk wasn't really mine. Every member of the family affectionately called it dad's desk, but that was just for name's sake. I never sat down to it without having to clear a spot to work. With eight children, I was lucky to reserve our bathroom. It was the family desk. In fact everything outside our bedroom was family owned and operated. It was mine that morning, because I was the first one up to claim it. The house was in the back half of a twelve hundred meter lot. The Library was located in the Southeast corner on the second floor. The bookshelves lined two and a half walls. On half of the East wall there was a built in cabinet, which included hook-up for sound equipment. The rest of the room was window. Windows took up half of the room on the East and half on the South. The desk was in that corner, facing the door. From the chair I could look to the right and view East over the front lawn to the mountains. The South window was good for light, but not a great view, since it happened to look into the neighbor's back lawn and some two-story homes beyond that. As I sat down the Sun was just peaking over the mountains. I just sat for a couple of minutes and watched the sun eat up the shadow in the valley. It was a beautiful sight, but so bright that I knew I would have to drop the blinds in order to work.

I dropped the blinds, and then sat down to start sorting through a sizable stack of correspondence and to organize myself for a meeting on Monday with the local representative of my new employer. Yaneth, my secretary, had put them in touch with me while we were in Indiana. I was glad to have something big on the burner. The regular security services we offered provided a nice income, but it took special contracts to pay for our accustomed life style. The summer vacation had caused us to dip into our cash reserves, which I felt better replenishing as soon as possible. We never touched the invested reserve, just the spendable reserve.

It was six thirty and I had worked my way through about one third of the correspondence when I heard Miriam and Rosita, our two maids stirring around in the kitchen. I decided I had better go down and ask them to walk lightly for a while and tell them I would be fixing pancakes for the family, before they started fixing something else. Sometimes I thought that their loud conversations and banging were to let us know that they were on the job.

Both of them greeted me with, "Buenos días, don Orville." *The "v" in Orville came out more like 'b'.*

"Buenos Días, señoritas. How have you been? How are your children, Rosita?"

Rosita was the number one cook and maid. She was all of 4 foot, 8 inches tall and maybe weighed 99 pounds. She carried a step up stool everywhere she went to work in the house. She was the older of the two maids. She had two children with her worthless drunk of a husband. He worked irregularly, but beat her regularly. When I first found out that he mistreated her, I went to talk to him in spite of her insistence that I not. I was sure that I could instill an adequate dose of fear in him. I merely taught him to be subtler. I was pretty sure he continued to mistreat her. She sometimes wore a sweater when it was warm.

She answered, "Fine, Don Orville. Juanito was sick for a week in July, but he is fine now. We missed you and Doña Linda and the children and are glad you are back in Guatemala."

"We are glad to be back, at least I am glad to get back into a regular routine. We missed you and our other friends and the climate. How is your family, Miriam?"

Miriam was 20 years old and single. I believe she had a boyfriend, but didn't say much about him, at least not to me. Miriam was not tall, probably five foot three or four inches, but she was long and lithe and seldom walked anywhere. Even if she was going to move ten paces, she did it pretty fast. If she were going anywhere outside, she would run it. Miriam was an evangelical, spiritual person and was always telling us she would pray for us. She would tell the children "bless you" for any sneeze, or cough. It wasn't just words for her. You could tell she meant it.

She answered, "Very well, thank you, Don Orville. What shall we fix for breakfast?"

"If the two of you will squeeze some fresh orange juice, set the table and cook some bacon, I will prepare pancakes for the family, but not now. It's only 6:30 a.m. I expect we will eat around 8:00. You could peel some oranges and if any come in before 8:00, give them some orange sections, or a banana. They will love the fresh fruit. How are Husky and Amy?" (Husky was not a Husky, but a German Shepherd and Amy was a White Samoan.)

Rosita said, "That Amy, she digs many holes. José is not too happy about filling in holes every week."

"I am not sure what to do about Amy. She doesn't stay very white with all the mud she makes. I will be back at 8:00 to start the pancakes. Try to work quietly 'til then."

Back in the library, I opened a letter from, Hugo Salinas, the President and major shareholder of Quimicas Salinas, and my newest client. A check for $20,000 unfolded with the letter, a pleasant surprise that would pay for a chunk of our past vacation. I read the letter.

Dear Orville:

I cannot thank you enough for your help over the past six months. I followed up on your suggestions of further areas to investigate and your intuition, again proved to be on the mark. On behalf of the Board of Directors, my family, and myself I want to reiterate my deep felt gratitude for your effective resolution of our problems. I appreciate your discretion in handling this situation, which could have been so potentially embarrassing to my family. I know that I can count on your continued discretion.

Neither words nor money can express my gratitude, but I hope that you will accept the small gift that I have enclosed. Please believe my sincerity as I tell you that if there is ever anything my company or I can do for you or your family, please allow us the opportunity to show our gratitude.

I would be very interested in having you regularly available to us for consultation on a retainer basis. Perhaps you could phone me at your earliest convenience and let me invite you to lunch at the club, in order to discuss this matter.

Warmest regards,

Hugo Salinas,

I thought: *I sure am glad that Don Hugo followed up on my suggestions. He must have caught the other scoundrels that I suspected were working inside the company with his half brother. They had taken the company for three quarters of a million green ones over the past three years, but we had caught them just before they made the big bite. Hugo was right in not trying to solve it through their contracted security firm. Some of their security people had bought into the swindle.*

In Guatemala and generally in most of Central and South America, only the poor that could not afford otherwise, voluntarily involved the police in any serious investigative matter. Hugo had found me through some others that I had helped. We discovered that his half brother was deeply involved, which was potentially embarrassing for the whole family. Also some trade secrets were in danger of getting into the hands of the competition. At my suggestion, Hugo quietly got the participants to sign very binding documents in lieu of criminal prosecutions. He retrieved his trade secrets and about half of the money that we could trace to local and overseas accounts. The money that was spent was gone, but the participants were forced to find very low-key employment and watch their step from then on. Hugo's half brother was left administering one of the family's smaller farms up in the Petén. He was granted enough salary to maintain his family, but he no longer had any growth potential.

When Hugo took over managing Quimicas Salinas, it was Cloro Salinas, and it's only product was liquid chlorine. Hugo's parents and uncles were mainly ranchers and farmers that dabbled in manufacturing. The Cloro Salinas had no distribution network and merely delivered Chlorine from the factory door. The family was going to sell the obsolete Cloro Salinas, when Hugo, recently graduated in Chemical Engineering from Texas A & M, begged them to sell him controlling interest. He gave up a small chunk of his inheritance to buy the company and reengineer it. He brought down some of his gringo friends from Texas A & M to help him. They were happy to have a summer in Guatemala before going off to work in big industry, and besides that, a glowing letter from a foreign enterprise for a few months of work abroad never hurt a new graduate's resume.

That was 30 years ago. Hugo converted Cloro Salinas into Quimicas Salinas, S.A. and about four other satellite corporations, of which by 1989, he controlled around 90 percent. By then, the corporate group was manufacturing over a hundred industrial and consumer products and marketing several hundred throughout Central America and southern Mexico with a combined gross of around seventy million dollars annually. In the early 1980's, two of Hugo's fellow graduates from A&M accepted his offer for them to join his management team in Guatemala. Each of them rose to manage a division of Hugo's company. They were both key in uncovering the recent fraud. Good guys! I reflected that they probably also received a bonus. One of them, Geraldo Jimenez, a gringo from Mexican parents, was the one that had set me up with the new client I was to meet with on Monday. I reflected a silent thanks to Geraldo, and thought, 'maybe I can return the favor some day.'

I took pleasure when things worked out well for my clients. Of course, they didn't always! Sometimes my best efforts failed to obtain the objective, since the results depended on my being able to anticipate and outmaneuver the moves of some very astute and determined swindlers. I always tried to explain up front to my clients about all of the possible risks, and I kept them posted as much as possible during every facet of a project. I had three very efficient and trustworthy employees that coordinated my research, my communication, and my travel and they kept track of the whereabouts of key people (including a few enemies) and in general, covered my tail.

Every contract was unique, depending on how and where my client needed me. I had been contracted to rescue victims from kidnappers, save individuals and families from the middle of war zones and natural disasters, escort and protect prominent dignitaries into and through high risk areas, survey and report the security risks in countries of region and a few less glorious tasks. I had worked for individuals, small companies, multinational corporations, and governments and on occasion when a problem needed solving and there is no one contracting me to solve it, I did it for society in general. At that moment in 1986 my company was retained as consultant on security matters by nine organizations.

We could have lived comfortably on just the consultant fees, but those would have dried up if I were not actively involved in the fieldwork. The consultation contract part of my work was a natural result of my ongoing short term service to new clients with serious security problems that needed immediate solutions. Unlike others in my line of work, I liked both facets of the job. I felt great pleasure in solving a mystery, or resolving a crisis for a new client and I also liked the feeling of helping an established client avoid crisis through good research and anticipation of potential security threats. I got excited when I saw where the numbers and the data were headed and I could realize that I was establishing a good foundation for giving sound advice.

For logical reasons, my most challenging exposure had always been the part of solving crisis for eventual clients. Even in my line of work, one could coast at times in the boardroom with theoretical scenarios, but outside, in the real world, anything less than total dedication became dangerous. In the field, things could look fine and then go wrong very quickly. One had to remain alert and stay attuned to the dangers. I had experienced a few close calls. I suppose that was the main reason that there hadn't been a whole lot of competition in my line of work. I usually didn't feel fearful when I was in a high-risk situation. I just felt alert, but then on occasion, I got the shakes afterwards! I would get through or around obstacles by focusing on the objective and constantly weighing the different paths to it, and I worked hard at solving each problem as it occurred, rather than letting problems accumulate.

I tried to thoroughly analyze each project before committing. I had made the rule that I would only work for clients indulged in legitimate activities. That, in itself required some research. I had found over the years that quite a few clean looking executives handled some pretty dirty money. I didn't allow anyone to pressure me into working for them, although some had tried in pretty devious manners. I picked and chose what I considered to be worthy causes for worthy people. Frequently there was not time, nor was it prudent to go through all the legal channels to reach an objective. I mainly tried to be on the side of right. When in doubt, I did some serious self-analysis, and then I consulted with my associates and occasionally with Linda to be sure that I was not fooling myself about my motives. I could count on my associates to give me an objective analysis and although Linda didn't understand all aspects of my line of work, when it came to people and causes she could add good insight.

By 7:00 a.m., I had made it through another third of the correspondence. I decided that it was time to go jog, with, or without Linda. I stood up, stretched, and then went on downstairs. I knew Linda had been exhausted the night before, so I carefully eased open the bedroom door so as to not awake her. The bed was made and I could hear her singing through the open door in the bathroom-dressing room.

She was coming out with her shoes in hand as I started through the doorway. She gave me a kiss and a big hug and "Hello darling! You ready to try to keep up with me?"

"Yep, I'm ready."

She sat down in the wingback chair to put on her socks and shoes, then jumped up and said, "Then, let's go!"

We did our stretching warm-up on the drive inside the front gate. Linda ran five days a week. I averaged three. I walked quite a bit in my work and probably would not have run at all if Linda hadn't been so gung-ho about it. I did manage to work-out on the weight machine three or four times a week.

We had two courses that we had measured. One was one and a half miles long, and the other was one mile. During our warm-up, we decided to do the mile run, since we both felt a little out of shape from having not been able to run regularly while on vacation.

When we first married and went jogging, I could always out distance and out run her. I could still out run her, but over the years she had developed her pulmonary-heart system and her leg muscles to where she could on occasion keep running after I was ready to call it quits. She remembered those occasions and frequently reminded me that she was not the weaker sex. We did it in twelve minutes that day which got us to breathing deeply.

We took our shower together. Each of us used our own customary nozzle, which remained adjusted the way we liked the shower pattern. She liked the whole head doing a rain like shower. I kept the outer ring doing a rain and the inner ring spouting massaging bursts. I lingered a couple minutes after she got out, so that when I got out, she was standing wrapped in her towel. She sure looked cute in a towel. She looked around at me as I smiled and said, "Hi Hon!!!" I wasn't covered with a towel, and she knew exactly what I was thinking.

We both had been exhausted the night before after our trip from Cincinnati, but by that morning, we were both so ready for each other that it took but a few short minutes to satisfy our hunger while wrapped in each other's arms. We were meant for each other, and only each other, and knew it. As we came out of our bliss, I changed position and happened to glance at the clock. I said sort of offhand, "Well it's ten after eight."

Suddenly we both realized that we were witnessing a miracle. We were naked in bed together on a Saturday morning without any children knocking on our door. We stared at each other in stark realization, and then as if on cue, we sprang out of bed. We knew that we shouldn't press our luck any further. A knock could come at any moment!!! We pulled the covers up, fluffed the pillows and headed to the bathroom to complete our cover-up.

CHAPTER 2
SATURDAY MARKET

I got dressed while she was humming in front the mirror, painting her already perfect face.

I said, "I planned on pancakes, I will get them started while you finish dressing."

"Sounds like a good plan. I love you."

"I love you too."

I gave her a pat on the rear, as I exited the bathroom. As I stepped out of the bedroom, heading for the kitchen, I saw Lynne coming down the stairs. She was all dressed and fresh.

"Hi Lynne. How did you sleep your first night back in Guatemala?"

She gave me a hug and a kiss on the cheek, as she answered, "Fine, except the last hour. I finally gave up and got out of bed and showered. I had forgotten how noisy the dogs and the buses are! It will take me a couple of days to adjust to the noise level. But I rested fine, and am ready to become part of the noise. Any idea what's happening for breakfast?"

"Oh, hungry are you? Pancakes! I was just headed to the kitchen to start them. I am not sure what we have on hand, but if we have some apples or bananas, should I make fruit pancakes?"

"Yea, I haven't had anything like your pancakes since I ate your pancakes at Christmas. I'll help you."

As we walked by the dining room on the way to the kitchen, Miriam was coming out from setting the table. Once she and Lynne greeted one another, I informed her that Linda was awake, and instructed her to knock on all the other doors and tell everyone that breakfast would be served in twenty minutes. Lynne and I continued on to the kitchen, where Rosita was finishing the bacon and squeezing fresh orange juice. We said our 'hi's' and started our part of the cooking.

Lynne loved to cook, as did all of our girls. She had a bubbly personality and enjoyed people. I was good at Spanish, but her Spanish was perfect. She grew up with both languages and spoke without accent in English and Spanish.

Perhaps because Lynne was the oldest child, she determined early in life to be in charge. I remembered an incident when she was only four years old and we had recently moved to Costa Rica. Linda and I were returning home after shopping, when we passed her walking several blocks from our home, with her younger sister, who was only a little over a year old at the time. We had them get in the car with us and continued on home. We had a new maid, so when we arrived at home we asked the maid why she had allowed the children to walk unsupervised along the streets in our area. The maid answered sheepishly, that she had told Lynne that she could not leave the house, but that Lynne had told her in clear Spanish and in no uncertain terms, that when her mother was gone, she was in charge and she didn't need a nanny following after her. She was convincing enough that the maid backed off.

I sent Lynne to locate some apples, or bananas, while I started the batter. I first had to put some milk to curdle. We couldn't get buttermilk in Guatemala, so I made my own by squeezing a couple of lemons into the milk. It would curdle after ten minutes and it worked just like buttermilk. The pancakes turned out light and fluffy. By the time I got the milk started, Lynne came in from the fruit and vegetable bins with four tart apples. She knew what to do, so while I got the griddle oiled and heating, she started peeling and slicing the apples real thin with a potato peeler. For normal pancakes I used a hot dry griddle, but when making fruit pancakes I grilled them at a slightly lower heat and applied some oil, or butter on the griddle. The hot oil combined with the sugar in the fruit, made it crisp around the edges, and it helped prevent the fruit from sticking.

Once that was set up, it was time to make the batter. I always made the batter a little thinner when using fruit. Once the batter was on the griddle and the bubbles showed pretty evenly, I would spread the thin slices of fruit on it just before flipping the pancake.

Linda was an excellent cook and all of the older children had learned from her and were good cooks, but for some reason they all thought my pancakes tasted better than theirs. I figured they just liked being served by me. All of our children, since the time they could see the top of the counter from a stool, had helped me make pancakes.

Lynne helped by spreading the apple slices on the pancakes while I poured the batter and flipped them. By the time we were on the last batch of pancakes, several of the children had showed up to watch. Some little hands were reaching for the tray of fresh pancakes, but Lynne shooed them away, saying:

"Hands off, critters! It hasn't been blessed yet!"

One of the little ones said, "But we're hungry."

I added, "We all are hungry and breakfast is just about ready."

I then turned to Rosita and told her to get the bacon on to the table, while I gathered the last pancakes off the griddle. Everyone, except Lynne headed into the informal dining room. She stayed behind to help me carry the pancakes. Our informal dining room had a round table that Linda and I had designed especially for our family and a couple of guests. It would seat twelve. In the middle it had a built in lazy susan that allowed 15 inches of usable table space for the plates, glasses and utensils around the circumference. It was definitely the way to go to feed a large family, but required a few ground rules on operation, or the kids would spin the food right off of it.

All the children were seated with forks in hand when Lynne and I stepped in with the pancakes. Linda came through the doorway right after Lynne and I. I called on one of the children to bless the food and then it was a flurry of knives, forks and hands reaching for pancakes, butter, syrup and bacon. You would have thought they were starved. What had I said about ground rules! The lazy susan was spinning from zero to sixty and back to zero every two seconds. Linda and I smiled at each other as she squeezed my hand. She was happiest when our whole brood was together. Everyone was just glad to be home. Vacations are fun, but home is home!

The phone and doorbell were ringing pretty steadily before we finished breakfast. Most of the children's friends were aware that we were back. I instructed Rosita to tell any young visitors to wait in the front lawn. Their friends didn't mind that. They were headed for the trampoline as soon as they came through the front gate anyway.

As we started to get up from the table, Linda laid down the law that no one would join the visitors until we had had family council and prayer. We retired to the living room to leave instructions for the children. In that kind of setting I was mainly a tag along. That part of running the family show was always Linda's operation. Once in a while I offered a suggestion, but mainly I shook my head yes like the rest of the crew. She asked what each one planned to do that morning and then told everyone what he or she had to do before doing his or her own thing. The main thing she wanted everyone to do was to unpack and get their dirty clothes into the laundry hampers. She also reminded them of some of the house rules, especially about jumping on the trampoline. She and I were headed off to the Central Market and invited anyone that wanted to accompany us. We got three takers, Lynne, and our two youngest, girls. The rest had there own agenda.

Linda headed to the kitchen to leave some instructions with the maids, while all of the children scattered for their chores except Susan, who had been sitting on the piano stool during the family council. She merely turned around on the stool to face the keyboard, raised keyboard cover on the baby grand and began to play, which was what she probably did for the next two to four hours. I was frozen in place as she beautifully played a melody by Mozart. A few minutes later I was stretched out on the couch in a nether world of music and peace when Linda came to ask if I was going, or staying. Momentarily I was tempted to stay, but I didn't want to miss the morning with Linda and Lynne at the market, plus I knew safety-wise they couldn't go alone.

I had missed Linda. Now that may sound a little strange, since we had been together most of the time for the past month, but even though we had been together, it hadn't been *our* time. During the summer vacations and on holidays, even though Linda and I were together, our energy and attention were outbound towards our friends and siblings that we were visiting and our children.

By 10:00 a.m., Linda, the three girls and myself had loaded into the Toyota Model F Van to head to the market. As I was backing out of the drive, I counted eight heads in the yard that didn't belong to our children. They came from good parents and lived in nice homes, but everyone preferred to meet at our house. Most of our friends, including our neighbors, had only one or two children. It was pretty logical that they migrate to the Fletcher home where the bulk of the crowd was already formed. During the daylight and evening hours, it seemed like we were never just our family. We didn't mind as long as they went by the house rules. When it got to be too hectic, we would send them home without any fanfare or apologies. They seemed to appreciate our talking straight with them, and I was sure they hadn't gotten offended, because they all kept coming back.

Before we got through the gate, Edna and Margaret saw their dear friend, Janie getting out of her car. They immediately jumped out of the car and abandoned our market trip. Linda, Lynne and I got out of the car to say hi to Rick, Janie's dad. He was the Assistant Head of the U.S. sponsored AID program in Guatemala. Rick was a decorated Vietnam war veteran and a kind man. He and his wife, Dawn, had been going through some differences over the past year.

When it came time for him to take his new position with AID, they had agreed that she would wind down her job in D.C., and join he and their daughters a month later. The month had come and gone and she had declared that she was unwilling to move. Rick felt that his work in Guatemala was important to the people of Guatemala and important for his career, so after a year, they were still at an impasse. Their daughter, Janie was aged ten, right between Edna and Margaret. She was a sweet, loyal friend for Edna and Margaret and she spent a lot of time at our home, eating about half of her evening meals with our family. Rick was so thankful for all Linda did for his girls that he almost worshipped her.

Frequently, when Rick came to pick up one or both of his daughters from our home, he would bring Linda flowers or Whitman's chocolates. Linda would sell her soul for a box of Whitman's. I confess that I seldom remembered to bring her flowers or chocolates, even though I knew she loved those little frills. Sometimes I would think of it as I was coming through the front door. I would have shown greater wisdom if I had just turned around and gone back out and bought some flowers, but I always thought, 'Oh well, I will do it tomorrow.' One day when Linda stepped into the living room and discovered a flower arrangement that I had placed there, she exclaimed, "Oh how sweet, I didn't know Rick had come by!" She was pretty embarrassed when she discovered that I had brought the flowers. I was more embarrassed to realize that a friend was more reliable than me about bringing flowers to my wife. I shaped up for a while after that.

After a brief visit with Rick at the gate, we were on our way to the Central Market. Linda said that she wanted to stock up on some of the spices and fresh fruit and vegetables. I knew that was just a cover. What she was always after was some artisan treasures. Our walls were covered with hand-woven tapestries, and our tables and niches were filled with vases and carvings. No matter how full our house seemed to me, Linda always found a place for more decorations and I have to admit that she did have a good eye for balance and color, and our home always had a warm glow about it.

We found a parking slot a block from the Central Market on Eighth Street, a half block South of Ninth Avenue. A shirtless muscled youth offered to watch our car. I gave him a Quetzal –around $.25 then, and promised a Quetzal when we returned. He and I both knew that I was paying him not to break into our car. We felt a little pressed for time since it was 11:00 a.m. and about half of the market stalls closed between noon and 1 p.m.

As we walked in the main entrance, several young men ran ahead of us to tell the stall owners that Linda was back in town. Most of the vendors recognized Linda as a serious buyer. Many of them would follow her for half a block beyond their stall carrying all they could carry to offer her. Wherever she walked she had a half dozen vendors tagging after her, shouting their wares. Linda usually recognized what she was interested in from a distance and the vendors would follow her eyes and seize the item to begin bartering. If she were really interested in something, she would point her finger towards the item so that the vendor would separate it for a better viewing. Her trips to the market were partly to obtain wares, but a big part of her motives lay in the action. How she got the wares was as important as what she got.

I wasn't much of a buyer, but I loved to go shopping with Linda. I would just stand back and watch the show that went on around her. Once a couple of vendors actually got into a fight over who had the territorial rights around my Linda. She looked like a queen surrounded by her subjects, begging for her attention and approval. As soon as she opened her purse and bought an object from a vendor, the other vendors would go into a feeding frenzy of shouting and begging. And to think, I was married to this Queen.

Besides the van we owned two sedans, a brand new Citroen CX 2400 that Linda used when traveling light, and a two year old Audi that was mainly for my use. Either would be easier than the van to drive downtown, but I would never have considered going to the market with Linda with anything smaller than a van. On occasion even the van had been insufficient and we ended up renting a taxi to carry the additional treasures to our home. We always ended up hiring two or three strong boys to carry the loot back to our van. I felt that that day was going to be doubly entertaining since I would get to watch both Linda and Lynne shop. Linda and Lynne's shopping styles were completely opposite. While Linda plowed through the market from stall to stall, Lynne spent most of her time in two or three neighboring stalls, shopping and trying on sandals, belts, necklaces and bracelets. Lynne was looking for leather goods and jewelry to take back to Utah.

I hung around with Lynne for a while. She would step into the stalls, picking up and studying the things she was interested in. The vendors usually just stood back and let her browse. They realized that talking to her would distract her and perhaps send her to the next stall. Lynne was in a safe area of the market and quietly looking over the wares. I was hanging too close to her and got in her way a couple of times as she backed into me. After about fifteen minutes of shopping and my third time of getting under her feet, she looked up at me and suggested that I go on and join 'mom'. I walked on ahead to find Linda.

After a half hour of following Linda with two of her hired helpers carrying the goods, I realized that we hadn't seen Lynne since I left her at the first stalls in the entrance to the market. I headed on back to where I had left her. Once I arrived back where I had left her, I got this fluttering in my gut that frequently signaled when something was wrong. It was an instinctive reaction that had often proven unfounded, but had saved me frequently enough that I had learned to give it credence.

Starting from there, I moved along the outer aisle of stalls towards the back exit to the market. It was pretty deserted back in that part of the market. I only passed a couple of vendors carrying large cartons along the backside. When I turned the corner by the back exit I heard Lynne, murmuring, "NOOO!" and recognized the sounds of a struggle coming from the shadows behind some vacant stalls. As I stepped into the area, I immediately focused on two men struggling with Lynne between them. Lynne was facing me with her eyes wide. One was holding her from behind while the other was in front struggling with her. Neither of them noticed me. The one with his back to me was the closest easiest to take down. With a kick to the groin from behind and he doubled over and fell into Lynne. She was forced backward causing her attacker to stumble. He dropped his hold on her and started to run behind the other stalls. I launched into the air as he attempted to make the corner to his right, and I caught his upper leg with my tackle. We both went down, but I was instantly on top of him. He tried to buck me off, but after two bucks, I had landed two or three solid blows to his face that left him slack. I was ready to give him more, when I realized that he was no longer feeling anything. I quickly turned back to see about Lynne and the one I had kicked. She was a little mussed, but intact and standing over him and he was also unconscious. She had a strong thirty-inch long two by two piece of wood in her right hand. As I started to lead us out of there, Lynne reached down and retrieved her purse and a couple of bags off of the floor. We didn't say anything; we just swiftly walked out of the area.

We located Linda and her helpers near where I had left them. I told Linda that we needed to leave immediately. She took a quick reading that something was amiss, and we headed for the exit and out to the car. A couple of vendors followed us halfway across the open patio area, before they finally gave up. We loaded the goods in the Van and I paid the helpers and the car guard. As I got in to drive, Linda jumped in the back beside Lynne, and we quickly drove out of the area. I didn't want to hang around for the police to arrive, knowing that some relative of the men we left unconscious could easily turn it around to where we were the criminals and they the victims. *So much for a fun morning of shopping at the Central Market! I will reevaluate my previous conclusion regarding the security there.*

I drove expeditiously out of the area towards home. Since Linda was in the dark as to what had happened she asked Lynne. While I continued driving Lynn told her what had happened.

"While I was shopping a couple of stalls down from where dad left me, this man approached me with a couple of nice silver chains. I bought one and then he told me that he had some really nice matching earrings in his stall. He led me to the back where dad found me and by the time I realized what was happening, I was sandwiched between him and that other slob. I had been struggling only a minute or two before dad arrived. I am not sure what their final intentions were, but I knew right away that they weren't good. How fortunate that dad showed up when he did!"

I added from the front seat, "One thing is for sure, they will think twice before they attack another 'gringa'."

I concentrated on driving through the Saturday noon traffic until we arrived at the southern edge of Zone 9 where I pulled into the parking lot of the Hotel Dorado Club off Reforma Avenue and stopped the van. I got out and went around to the other side of the car and opened the side door. Lynne was closest to the side door and Linda was sort of supporting her from behind.

I looked at Lynne a little more thoroughly than I had at the market and I asked, "Are you okay? Are you hurting anywhere?"

"I am okay dad, just angry. I am so thankful you showed up. They were too strong for me. I tried to scream, but they stuck a filthy rag or hanky in my mouth. I still have the nasty taste in my mouth. I need something to drink. I don't know what would have happened if you hadn't arrived."

"It looked to me like it will take a while for the one you hit to recover. You may have fractured his skull with that pole you were wielding."

"I think I lost some of my Latin street savvy while living the quiet student life at BYU. I feel foolish having followed that man away from the main shopping area."

"Well I equally feel stupid for having left you alone. I can't believe I did that, and I can't believe that it took me so long to think of finding you. Please forgive me sweetheart."

Linda and I both hugged her. Other than a bruise on her cheek, she didn't appear to have suffered much wear. She had her head back on the headrest and was starting to calm down. Linda went into the club, of which we were members, and brought out a bottle of water and a wet towel to clean Lynne's face and arms, which were streaked with soil and perspiration. Once she was settled down, I returned the towel to the club, and then we drove home in silence.

It wasn't until we got home and started unloading the van that I realized that I had done some damage to my knuckles and right knee. I later found a sore lump on the back of my head. No one was ever behind me and I don't remember ever heading backwards, so I wondered how the back of my head ended up with a lump. Oh well, it wasn't the first time nor the last time that I knocked a little paint off of the machinery. Fortunately all the cogs were still in working order.

CHAPTER 3
THE SHOOTING RANGE

The rest of the day went more like a typical Saturday. We had a light lunch and I took a short nap. When I awoke at around two-thirty, I got dressed in one of my flight suits, which I liked to wear even when I wasn't going to fly, especially on Saturdays. I liked the extra pockets and the loose fit. It was my escape from belts and suspenders. I found Linda in the kitchen, baking some cookies with the three oldest girls. I told her that I was going out for a couple of hours. She stepped aside and let the girls continue putting cookies on the tray. She smiled up at me and gave me a raised eyebrow question. I extended my thumb and forefinger like a gun. I didn't need to explain that I was going to the shooting range for some practice. She smiled an understanding. She gave me a hug and a kiss on the cheek before turning back to some dough on the counter.

First I picked the new holster off of the top shelf where I had put it when I emptied my suitcase in the morning. I had two old holsters, both made of leather. The one fit on a shoulder harness and the other on an ankle harness. Most policemen and guards either carried their weapons exposed in hip holsters, or in a shoulder harness, under a vest or jacket. Not many hard hitting guns, fit in an ankle holster, but mine did, and I preferred the ankle holster. Besides being more comfortable for me, I felt that it was less conspicuous. I also found the tropics too sweltering to walk around in a jacket, or vest.

I had purchased the new holster while in the U.S. I bought it especially for my gun. It was made of canvas, with Velcro placed in such a way to allow various configurations. The part that actually held the holster on my ankle was a wide strap lined with Velcro that fit around my ankle, from which extended an additional narrower strap up my leg that ended in a support piece also lined with Velcro that wrapped around the calf of my leg at an angle just below the knee. I arranged the harness so that the holster fit on the inside of my left leg. It really felt comfortable, and totally invisible with the kind of clothing I was accustomed to wearing. It wouldn't have worked with tight-legged jeans, but I didn't like a tight legged anything. I had a couple of pairs of loose-legged jeans, but I mainly used slacks, or my flight suit that gave plenty of legroom.

Next I retrieved my gun and a couple of boxes of ammunition from the floor safe, which was under a shoe rack. I could pull the shoes aside and open the safe in less than a minute, so there was no need to leave the gun out. With our high walls and security system, I didn't anticipate an emergency that would require the gun at home, but it was there in the eventuality of a worst-case scenario. Linda had shot it a few times and could use it if needed, but she did not like guns. She had made a truce with my gun and recognized my need to keep and carry it. Upon arriving home, my first stop was usually the safe to put up the gun.

I carried my equipment to the range in the canvas bag. It already contained a noise canceling head set, a small set of binoculars and a roll of masking tape. I placed the ammunition in the bag with the other things. Then I slid the gun into the holster and 'snugged' it in place with the narrow canvas strap that Velcroed in front and snapped in the back for quick release. Once I pulled my pants leg down, I jumped around a couple of times, just to see how it felt. I could feel the heft, but the holster held its position just fine. I took the back steps down to the garage and placed the tote bag on the passenger side floor of the Audi.

The range was a military shooting range called the Polygon located about two miles from home. It was almost exactly on the opposite side of the airport runway. There was no way to get there without going around one or the other end of the airport complex. Although the streets were unpaved and a little rough, it was about a quarter of a mile shorter to go around the southern end of the airport through Santa Fe, which was the route I took that day. Santa Fe was one of several pockets of poverty in Guatemala City. It had been government land that was invaded by squatters, who were allowed to stay. Much of it was on steep hillsides, with shacks that frequently slid into the ravines during the rainy seasons. It wasn't as much of a slum as other areas in the city, since it was surrounded by upper-class homes and numerous businesses, including the airport that provided employment for many of its inhabitants.

The Polygon belonged to the air force, but officers and retirees from other branches of the military also used it. I had seen a few that I thought were civilians, but I was the only foreigner that I knew of that had access. A few years prior I had saved a couple of army generals from a tight spot. They became friends and when they discovered that I had to drive for an hour to a suitable practice range, they were more than happy to arrange a guest membership for me at the Polygon. It sure made it easier for me to keep current with my weapon.

As I stopped at the gate, I reached for my identification tag in the glove compartment. When I looked up to show my card, the gates were already open. The guard had recognized me and was saluting. I saluted back and drove on through to the parking area. There were only three vehicles in the parking area, an army green troop truck, a brown Toyota pickup, and a black Nissan Patrol with dark polarized windows. I was able to park close to the building, which was good, since it looked like rain.

I picked up my canvas bag, locked up the car and walked thirty feet to the security booth at the gate entrance. There, the guard did require my military ID. I placed it in a tray that he slid out under his bulletproof window. Once he pulled the tray back inside the guardhouse, he laid my ID on his counter and wrote my name in large letters on a card. Then he reached over to a wooden tray with around twenty or thirty slots, where he simultaneously placed my ID in a slot, while removing a numbered tag that had a hollow plastic laminate on the front and a safety pin on its back. He then slid the card with my name inside the laminate and sent it to me through the tray. The gate buzzed open.

Once through the gate, I stopped and pinned the nametag on my breast pocket. Then I walked about two blocks down a descending path that ended at another door through a twelve-foot high wall. There was a sign above that door that said "Use Ear Protection Beyond this Door", and a small table on either side of the door. I laid my canvas bag on a table, zipped it open, removed my ear protectors and put them on. With the ear protection, one could still hear the shots, but with reduced volume. It was an isolated area, but I was sure that the sound carried a long way up and down the canyon we were in. Once through the door, to the right was a building, which housed an enclosed range that contained booths with individually controlled targets, mainly for pistols, and to the left was a series of open ranges of varying sizes and depths, for use with rifles and shot-guns as well as pistols.

I turned right for the pistol range and walked about a block to an enclosed roofed patio area that housed two galleries of eight individual firing booths each. The two ranges were set oblique to one another and there was a door and a large window off the patio for each range, so that one could look in and determine which spaces, were available before entering, or if one were looking to meet up with a shooting buddy, they could locate them through the window before going into the range. The booths were open in the back and front, but were separated from one another by walls, so that one was visually isolated from the neighboring booths. Beyond the booths it opened into a general shooting gallery. A shooter had control of his target by means of a movable metal target holder, where one attached a cardboard target. The target could be controlled and moved down the range by an electrical pulley to the distance each individual shooter selected. The range was marked in five-meter increments from five up to twenty-five meters.

I looked in the range on the right where I saw two air force captains practicing. Since I was looking at them from behind, I wasn't sure, but I thought that I had seen them before. The range on the left also had two shooters; one was an active army officer and an older man dressed in civilian clothes. I went through the door into the second range. As I shut the door, the army officer looked back and we recognized one another. We each acknowledged and waved. No one tried to talk on the range. A salute or hand wave was the only practical way to communicate. I started to head to an empty booth, but the officer held up his hand for me to wait a moment. He tapped the other gentleman who had just finished a round of firing. He said something to his friend, before pointing my direction. When the other gentleman turned my way, I also recognized him and waved.   A simple wave was not going to be enough for either of them that day.

They both walked over to shake my hand. We had met on numerous occasions at the range and a couple of times socially. Apparently each of us liked Saturdays for shooting practice. They commented that they hadn't seen me for some time and inquired if I had been traveling. I explained that I had spent the past few weeks in the U.S. The officer was an active Lieutenant Colonel and the one dressed as a civilian was a retired Colonel. I couldn't remember for sure, but I sort of recalled that they were related to one another, either that, or real good friends, or both. Anyway, we each did the handshake and pat on the back and a big smile. Not much talking. They walked back to their positions and I headed to an empty booth near the left side of the range. I stepped up to the counter and pushed the button to move the target holder and nothing happened. I moved to the next booth on the left and did the same with the same negative results. On the third try, I found a booth with an operable pulley system.

I pulled out my gun and laid it and the canvas bag on the counter. I used a German Mauser automatic 0.380 9MM. Most everyone in the military used army forty-fives. A few officers used standard 9MM. There were very few 0.380's in circulation. I was sure that there were others in Guatemala, since the ammunition was readily available, but I hadn't run into them. The Mauser Automatic is smaller and lighter than a standard 9MM. The standard 9MM has a slightly stronger impact than my 0.380, but the guns were bulkier and I had never been able to acquire the accuracy I could with my Mauser. I reasoned that force of impact didn't have much relevance if the bullet didn't go where one needed it, so I had stuck with my compact automatic for several years. Besides that, it was small enough to fit comfortably in an ankle holster, where I found it most comfortable to carry.

Not many people are accurate with a one-hand hold on a handgun. Generally speaking, if you want to do more than scare people, you will do better with a two-hand stance. The quick draw and one-handed shots looked good in the movies, but in reality, most accurate shooters developed a stance and aim. My Mauser was small enough that you had to be careful on how you placed your left support hand. If not the gun would bite the support hand, when the action moved back to reload. Instead of trying to get both hands on the stock, you had to place the right hand around the stock and the left hand merely cupped under the right hand. I only had to bust my thumb to bleeding once to remember where to place my left hand. Once I got used to it, it felt natural and comfortable.

The targets were of cardboard in a block shape of a human torso. The preferred areas were marked A. They were the center part of the chest and the head. The next most preferred area was the neck, which was marked with a B. The C area surrounded the A in the torso and the D was on the out fringe of the C.

I moved the target out to fifteen meters, equivalent to fifty feet, which was the optimum range for most pistols. My aim and my gun were consistent between fifty and seventy feet. I opened the canvas bag and placed the roll of masking tape, my binoculars, a box of shells and marker on the counter beside my gun. I only used the binoculars for the first shots. I preferred to get my bearing by checking the first shots with the binocular, rather than move the target back and forth. The gun was already loaded. I stood up to the counter and fired off three rounds, pausing to aim after each shot. I probably fired the three shots in six to eight seconds. I laid down my gun and raised the binoculars to check where my three shots had landed.

I quickly located two shots, high and to the left in the C. After a few moments of searching, I was about to declare the third round wild and off target, when I located it a couple of inches below and to the right of the other two, on the corner line of the A section. I suspected the last one I located was the first shot and the two successive shots were the high ones, which meant I had flinched or pulled on the latter two. I laid down the binoculars and picked up the gun and aimed again. I was a little more conscious on how I placed my feet that second time. I fired off three more rounds, then laid my gun down and reeled the target back to my counter. The second set of three were centered but in the lower part of the torso. This time one was firmly in the A section and two just outside in the C-section.

I put a piece of masking tape over each of the six holes and with a marker wrote the number one on each piece of tape. I reeled the target back out to fifteen meters. Since the Mauser held one in the chamber and seven in the clip, I had to reload the clip. After the first two sets of three, I started firing sets of five. It took me the two initial sets of three and three sets of five, a total of twenty-one rounds to finally get three out of five in the A center section of the target and two in the B or C sections. On my last sets I was squeezing off a set of five in about four or five seconds and grouped them in a two and half inch circle. I was able to keep it pretty consistent. I always planned on using a box of fifty cartridges during a practice session. Of the fifty shots, twenty-eight were in the A area, four in the B, fourteen in the C, and four in D outer area of the torso. None were off the target. My latter clips were more productive than the start, which meant I improved with practice. My hand and arm were a little shaky from having used some muscles that I hadn't, while on vacation. I was glad to get back on the firing range. My friends were folding up their equipment as I was leaving. We again waved to one another. There were three other men coming in to practice. I didn't recognize any of them.

I removed my ear protection as I went through the outer door. In spite of the protection, my ears were ringing, but I could at least hear. My friends came through the door while I was stowing my ear protection in the canvas bag. They invited me for a drink, but I begged off without telling them that I didn't drink alcoholic beverages. I merely said I needed to get home. As we said our goodbyes, the first large drops of rain started to fall. They headed down the path to the kiosk that sold snacks and drinks, as I turned to the guard station. I handed in my name card in exchange for my ID and was turning the corner to my car when the rain started in serious. I made it in my car door just as the skies opened and dropped buckets of water.

I slowly drove around the airport to home in the rain. I stopped to fill the car at the Texaco station just two blocks from home and by the time the attendant finished filling the car, the rain had slowed down considerably. It was just sprinkling with a little wind when I got out to open the gate at home. I drove on into the garage, walked up the back stairs with my equipment and headed straight to our bedroom. Linda followed me into the dressing room talking to me as I went in, asking me how my practice had gone and telling me how her afternoon had gone. Supper was about ready to serve, so I put all of my equipment in its proper place, deciding I would clean and lubricate the gun after supper.

The rest of the evening was a typical relaxing Saturday evening. It was great to be back home. Ho! Hum!

CHAPTER 4
MONDAY, AUGUST 4

Sunday was a good wind-down after a busy somewhat traumatic first Saturday back from vacation. By Sunday, Lynne had transposed her Saturday episode into a learning experience and bounced back to her normal cheerful composure. Sunday helped all of us make the transition to being back in Guatemala. After Church, the family surprised me with a birthday cake at lunch. My birthday wasn't until the following Wednesday, but Linda knew that weekdays were unpredictable and that it wouldn't matter when they celebrated. It would still be a surprise, even if they did it on the actual date. I never remembered birthdays, not even my own. Forty-four! I didn't feel forty-four, but then again, how was forty-four supposed to feel? I had never been there before!

I arrived at my office at twenty after seven that Monday morning, about a half hour before my staff arrived. I had leased an office on the fifth floor of the Etisa Building, which was an eight story semicircular building on the southeast corner of Seventh Avenue and Montufar Street, next to the Plazuela España. It was a long narrow semicircular building with a small tree shaded park in front of the building, street parking in the front and exclusive parking in the rear. It's twin, the Edyma building and park were on the opposite North-East Corner. Each of the buildings contained a bank and several consulates. Each of the other two corners off the Plazuela España had restaurants and parking lots.

My office consisted of 1,300 square feet on the western end of the building. The narrowness of the building allowed for all of our offices and meeting areas to have natural lighting. There were two offices and a small dining room on the south side of the building that had windows overlooking the rear parking area. The whole north side of the offices was all windows and sliding glass doors that allowed access to an outdoor patio ten feet deep that ran the full length of the offices.

On the front side of the building we had a reception area, a conference room and my office. The abundant natural light proved to be very handy during the frequent electrical outages.

There was a rather large reception and work area with one office to the left of the reception area, then a hallway that led to another small office on the left, a small dining room and two bathrooms. On the right side of the hallway behind reception was the conference room and lastly, my office, which was large enough, but not too large. I had a very comfortable desk and credenza with two upholstered chairs, a couch and two additional chairs that matched the ones in front of my desk. Everything upholstered was done in brocaded cloth, picked out by Linda. In addition to all the glass looking out over the patio to the north, I also had a corner window looking to the west where I could watch take-offs and landings at Aurora Airport. On the fifth floor there was no building close that blocked my view either North or West. The one nicety of my office remaining to mention, was my own private bathroom, with a shower included. I would frequently take an afternoon shower to erase any lethargy after lunch, especially during the hot months of March and April.

As I said, our building occupied the South East corner of Plazuela España. Plazuela España, was a traffic circle with a large fountain in the middle. The raised central fountain pool was surrounded by horse heads that apparently at one time shot streams of water into the larger pool at the base of the fountain. The horses no longer shot streams of water, they just sort of spit and drooled.

I believe traffic circles were the bright idea of some traffic engineer in Europe before the invention of traffic signals. The traffic circles filled two objectives. They were designed to allow the traffic to flow smoothly and the inner plazas provided visible locations for artists to express themselves in monuments and sculptures. The idea was for the traffic coming from four different directions to flow into the circle and out on one of the four options, without having to stop. It required some pretty skillful driving to make it work and only one overly timid or aggressive driver to cause chaos. The concept never caught on very big in the new world.

In Latin America, there were very few traffic circles outside of Buenos Aires, Santiago, Mexico and Guatemala City. They worked well in Argentina and Chile, but the drivers in Guatemala and Mexico hadn't demonstrated the discipline and skill required. In Guatemala a timid driver would remain frozen in a lane, while the aggressive drivers would cut across two lanes of traffic in the circle, without giving any signal of their intentions, other than laying on the horn. I liked my office and its convenient location very much, but after nearly a year of occupancy, I had considered moving to another office building because of all the shouting and horn honking. Then the problem was suddenly resolved when the Muni made Seventh Avenue a one-way street to the north and installed modern traffic signals. There appeared to be hope, after all. The thought occurred to me that perhaps some day in the future they might even get the horses to spout streams of water.

The Etisa building was not one of the newer ones, but it was right in the heart of the business and hotel district in Zone 9. My office was above a branch of the Bank of America, where we did most of our banking. The Piccadilly Restaurant, which served Typical Guatemalan food was just across the street and the Cebollines Restaurant, which served Typical Mexican Food was on the opposite side of the Plaza. My office was also within four blocks of numerous other fine eateries and the major hotels, and ten minutes from home and the east entrance to the Aurora Airport, where I hangared my plane. In addition, the Etisa Building was only two blocks East of the Aurora Airport runway flight path. I did a good bit of my problem solving, while gazing out my patio window at the planes landing and taking off.

I spent the half hour I was alone in the office organizing a few things. I was able to spend the rest of the morning in strategy and planning meetings with my staff; Yaneth Santilla, Roberto Rosales and Mike Cunningham. I had hired Yaneth the August before our move to Guatemala in September 1984. Roberto came on board two months later in November. Mike joined us nearly a year ago in October 1985. At the beginning there was a little sparring between Roberto and Yaneth. I watched the sparks fly between them for a couple of weeks and then sat them down and explained that I valued each of them, but was unwilling to work in the tension that existed between them. Somehow they got their act together and became models of cooperation and support. When Mike came on board, his transition onto the team was seamless. Each of us had unique talents and backgrounds, and we had learned to work well together.

Yaneth's father was of Spanish descent and her mother was indigenous from a small community near Lake Atitlán. She was born and raised in the Capital for her first five years of life. She was six when her parents were killed in the purging of the early sixties. Their maternal grandmother in the highlands near Sololá raised her and her two older siblings. Yaneth's tragedy was not over. Her two older siblings perished in the conflict when she was thirteen and her grandmother passed away when she was fourteen. She ran away, finding her way to Panama, where she gained employment as a maid for an American General's wife. Her employer took her under her wing and helped her finish her education. When the General was transferred back to the U.S., Yaneth had graduated from a top secretarial school in Panama and was perfectly bilingual. I met her while she was working as the secretary to the manager of a major hotel in Panama. She wanted to get back to Guatemala. Within the first month of working for me she showed herself capable of handling my correspondence, reports, appointments and general secretarial work and after a few months she took over the banking, travel arrangements, and all of my routine communications.

Roberto was full blooded indigenous from Momostenango, in the Western highlands of Guatemala. He was working as a guard while studying law at San Carlos National University when I discovered him. The politics on campus were becoming too complicated and he was having trouble making ends meet when he dropped out after four semesters. He had completed four years of military service, and two years as a policeman before working as a private guard. He understood good investigative techniques, was an excellent marksman and a superb driver. Half of the time he looked like he was asleep, but behind that sleepy composure was a quick mind and a very powerful man stuffed into a five foot five inch frame. He spoke Spanish, Quechi and Mam, and understood a few other indigenous dialects and a good bit of English.

Roberto handled the fieldwork for the government side of our research and investigations. He was my inside man into the Army, the National Police Headquarters, the Public Ministry, the Human Rights office and a couple dozen other connections in the middle levels of the government. Roberto knew a lot about what was happening in the street and who was causing it, or resisting it.

Mike was quite different from Roberto. He was born in Honduras of a Honduran mother and an American father and did most of his growing up in New Orleans. He spoke English, French, Cajun and Spanish. He studied a couple of years in a community college and was captaining a supply boat to the oil rigs, when he met Aaron White, owner of Confecciones Natalie, a medium sized maquila in Guatemala City. Aaron needed an able bilingual assistant and convinced Mike to move to Guatemala to work for him. Mike had worked with him for two years when White's nineteen-year-old daughter was kidnapped. I was brought in two days after they had paid a very sizable ransom without getting their daughter back. Mike was in our first meeting and I liked his perception. Once I decided to take the case, I requested that Mike assist me in my investigation.

Mike was observant and had a hunch that it was an inside job. He had noticed the daughter hanging around with some marginal types. Together we were able to track down two of the three perpetrators, most of the ransom money, and the daughter. We rescued her alive, albeit shaken and somewhat contrite.

As it turned out, the daughter was a participant in a self-kidnapping plan. She changed her mind about the time the ransom was paid and became an unwilling participant. The perpetrators were in a crunch, since the daughter was having a guilt trip for what her parents had been through and no longer wanted to be a part of the plan, but they were holding several hundred thousand dollars that they did not want to part with. The discussion had turned to getting rid of the daughter and from that moment she became a disposable hostage. Mike and I arrived in time to forestall any action on their disposal plan.

No legal action could be taken by the Whites against the two perpetrators, nor any request for police pursuit of the missing perpetrator, without sending their own daughter to prison. Aaron White's wife and daughter left the country immediately following the rescue and Aaron no longer had the heart to continue in Central America. He sold his company for less than the value of the assets and pulled up stakes. Mike had married a charming Guatemalan girl from Zacapa, and accepted my offer to stay and work with me.

Mike liked people. He was persuasive in a nice way. One never felt pressured by him, but nevertheless inclined to help him with whatever he was requesting. He was also an experienced pilot. He didn't have a multiengine rating, but he was very proficient in single engine aircraft and he did well as copilot in my twin-engined Skymaster on occasion. He handled all fieldwork relating to private industry and institutions. Mike also had excellent computer skills, and had been able to organize our research into a sortable database that made our work a lot easier and more efficient. In addition, he worked jointly with Yaneth to oversee the business side of our operation. He was a martial arts expert, but he lacked one skill that we wished he had. It seemed impossible to teach him how to fire a gun. He was so shy of the sound and the recoil that he could not keep from squinting and jerking. The last time Roberto and I had tried working with him had been in February and finally both of us concluded that he should not even pick up a gun. He would be at least as much danger to himself and his team as he would be to an enemy.

In addition to all the rest that they did, Roberto and Mike covered my flank when I needed them. All three of my assistants understood Central American politics and knew how to get things done there. They knew the interrelations of the major movers and shakers in society, both in government and private industry. We worked well together and we liked the kind of work we did. Although they all earned incomes considerably above the norm, I didn't feel that it was only the money that held them in their jobs. The four of us were personally involved in the success of our little operation.

During our meeting that morning, they were able to bring me up to speed on all pertinent events in the area. Then they briefed me on the latest happenings with our clients and sought my advise on how to resolve some issues. After any absence from the office of more than a week, I customarily phoned all clients that I had any direct dealings with. With the input from my staff during the briefing, I marked a couple of clients that I needed to phone that morning, including Eli.

Eli was short for Elio Navarro. Eli was a Cuban American and a very good friend. His wife, Amparo and Linda also hit it off well. The Navarros had two girls, the same ages as our second and third daughters. Their girls studied at a Catholic School and had a different set of friends than our girls, but they always got along well when the two families were together.

In addition to being a friend, Eli was also the General Manager in Central America for UltraChem, my former employer, and our oldest client. Eli was a friend, and an important element in my relationship with UltraChem on a local level. For a number of years we provided them with several routine services in Guatemala, such as background checks on potential employees and customers. We were instrumental in helping their personnel learn how to handle those routine matters and for the past two years they had taken care of it themselves.

After leaving direct employment with UltraChem, I had continued to maintain a close relationship with several of the company's top executives and any request for non-routine service usually emanated from UltraChem's Director for Latin America and on occasion from their Vice President for International Operations. I suspect that the requests may have started with Eli, but he ran it through them to resolve any conflict of interest, since everyone knew we were close friends. I had hired Eli as an assistant, two years before I left UltraChem. He and his wife were from amongst the numerous hardy refugees that miraculously escaped Cuba during the early years of Fidel's regime. Their escape, just like for many other Cuban refugees, focused their energy and purpose in life. After the Cuba experience, they never took anything for granted. They treated life as a gift from God, analyzing and savoring every detail with considerable passion and enthusiasm. If they were celebrating a happy event, such as a birth, or coming of age, they did it with lively dancing and loud conversation. A death would inflict deep grief on the faces of young and old for weeks.

For the past several years, UltraChem hadn't required regular service, but they regularly called us for special services, usually when there was a problem that their own personnel could not handle, or one that the management preferred that they did not handle. From the beginning, it was understood that I personally took care of their needs, no delegation. They never quibbled over fees. In fact, they nearly always added something additional to my regular charges. On the first two or three occasions, I phoned to tell them of the overpayment. On each occasion, Eli explained that it was intentional. From then on, I merely made sure I thanked them for the bonus. I never could really establish a relationship between the time spent, and the complexity of the job, with the size of the bonus. Sometimes when I felt the job was easier than others, they would give me a larger bonus. I found it more calming to not even think of a bonus. As a consequence I always felt thankful to get one and I always thanked them upon receipt. Perhaps that was their plan. Anyway, I made note and told Yaneth to remind me to phone Eli once we had finished the meeting.

The last item in our meeting was to discuss our newest potential client, Engineer Jorge Alfaro, the owner of Perfiles de Acero, S.A. and two other construction related companies in Guatemala. Yaneth confirmed that I had a meeting scheduled with him at 3:00 that afternoon at the Hotel Dorado. Then as previously requested by me, the three of them reported all the background information they had been able to obtain on Alfaro in addition to the preliminary report that Yaneth had faxed to me in July. In summary, we knew that in addition to his companies in Guatemala, Alfaro was part owner of a company in El Salvador and one or two in Honduras.

Jorge Alfaro was originally from an elite family in Nicaragua, but had been living in Guatemala ever since the Sandinistas took over his country in 1980. He was a Civil Engineer, graduated from Técnico de Monterey in Mexico. It probably was not by accident that when the Somoza regime fell in Nicaragua, his construction projects were spread in several countries of Central America, thus, a sizable portion of his capital was outside of the country. He staggered a little from his losses in Nicaragua, but with a lot of hard work and wise allocation of his resources he had been able to re-establish.

Jorge had become a major player in Central America in the construction of power plants, factory buildings and warehouses. He did most of his bidding on a cost plus basis and had been able to modify building designs so as to combine building materials in a way that was cost advantageous. By bidding cost plus, he passed any savings on to his clients. A savings of even four or five percent on a multimillion dollar project was always interesting to a client. He had always treated his managers and foremen with respect and professionalism. They responded with a high degree of on time performance, which earned bonuses for themselves and Jorge, and allowed their clients to come on line faster and start earning sooner.

I met Jorge briefly in Nicaragua during the last days of the Somoza regime. On one of my trips I was evacuating missionaries for a Church when I had a little problem with the fuel pump on my Cessna 206. I happened to be in Jorge's hangar soliciting the help of his mechanic when Jorge returned from a trip. We spoke briefly and exchanged cards. Since then I had crossed paths with him and his sons numerous times over the years as we each moved around in Central America. Jorge kept a tight rein on all of his businesses and was totally in charge of the operational aspects, but had handed over some of the administrative responsibilities to his sons. I had never met his wife and two daughters, but I had visited a few times with his sons, Miguel and Raul as we had run into each other at airports and restaurants. The older son, Miguel graduated in Engineering from the University of San Carlos. Raul was a little more of a playboy, but after a couple of false starts, was completing B.A. in Economics from Landivar University.

In spite of several phone interruptions, we managed to cover all of the important occurrences during my three weeks of absence. I informed them that I would spend Tuesday morning at the airport and we scheduled for all of us to meet again at two in the afternoon on Tuesday. Roberto stayed for a few minutes after the general meeting to fill me in on some specific assignments. They were all out of my office by 11:00 a.m.

I called some of the clients I handled directly to let them know I was back and then bring each other up to date on any pertinent occurrences. I reached half of the six, excluding UltraChem, whom I saved for last. For those I didn't get to talk to, I left word with their secretaries or wives that I was back in town and available.

I then phoned Eli. Alicia, his secretary informed me that he was in a meeting and would call me back. I had just stood up to stretch and look out my window when Yaneth rang in to tell me Eli was on the phone. He told me that he had just finished his meeting and was stepping out just as Alicia hung up with me. We spent the first ten minutes just on the friend side of our relationship. We filled each other in on our families, travels and lastly our work.

Then I jokingly asked if he was just calling to invite me out to lunch, or did he need something. He laughed and told me he had bought the last time and that I owed him lunch. Then he explained that his boss, Allen Farnsworth, the Director of Latin American Operations, wanted to make a quick oversee of some of their operations in Central America and that Allen had specifically asked him to try to get me to take them in my Skymaster. They wanted to spend most of Tuesday the 26th in Puerto Barrios which is on the north-east coast of Guatemala, then, time permitting, fly that afternoon to Belize, a British protectorate to the north. On Wednesday the 27th, they wanted to leave Belize in the afternoon and fly to San Pedro Sula, Honduras for meetings in the evening. On Thursday morning the 28th, we would return from San Pedro Sula to Guatemala City. I was taking notes as he talked. I figured the schedule was doable in my plane in the two and half days allotted. The problem was that Allen only had an opening for such a trip during that last week in August.

As soon as he started saying they needed me, I had opened my *Day timer* calendar, which I had just made some notes in during our staff meeting. When he told me the dates I noticed a couple of conflicting notations.

I said, "Eli, hold just a moment, so I can check my calendar with Yaneth."

"Sure, but you don't have to tell me right now. We can talk later this week. I know you just got back and have lots of things to get up to speed on."

"Well hold for just a couple of minutes anyway. It might be less complicated to look at this now than later."

"Sure. I'm here. Check with her."

I put Eli on hold and called in Yaneth and asked her if she knew of any other commitments for that time period. She checked her little book and came up with the same two that I had notated earlier. After some discussion, we decided that each of them was re-schedulable.

I flipped the phone off hold. The line was open. We had been cut off, or Eli hung up. I dialed his direct line. He picked up after a couple of rings.

"Hey Eli, sorry to leave you hanging on hold for so long."

"No problem buddy, after a couple of minutes I hung up and took a couple of calls that had been pressing. Do you know if you can do it, or do you need more time to look at things?"

"Yaneth says I can. We need to reschedule a couple of things, but nothing major. I haven't been back in town long enough for my life to get complicated. Most of my clients don't even know I am back in Guatemala and some of them probably don't even know I left."

"Great! I will let Allen know and start lining up the meetings and hotels. Tell Linda hi for me. I know that this week will be too busy for me and probably for you, but how about coming over for barbecue on Saturday. We have missed you guys."

"You know that Linda and I feel the same about you and Amparo, but this Saturday we are going to be in the Peten. How about the following Saturday?"

"That sounds good to me, let's run it by the wives."

"Good, I will talk to Linda about Saturday the sixteenth. I am also really glad for another opportunity to be with you and Allen. Thanks for thinking of me to handle this trip."

"Hey this time it wasn't me. Allen insisted that I try to arrange it, and you know as well as I, that we could not do such a trip any other way than with you. Have a good day Orv, I will fill you in as I get the itinerary more solidified."

"See you Eli, bye."

After hanging up, I thought of how good Eli's comment made me feel. I did realize that there was no other way they could do that kind of trip in the time allotted. If they flew on a scheduled airline, it would take them a week instead of the few days we had scheduled, to cover the itinerary we had discussed. My plane and I were the only pair in that part of Central America that held valid licenses and permits for all three countries. Eli and a few of my other clients knew that. I guess we all like to feel unique in a few ways.

CHAPTER 5
HOTEL DORADO
PLEASURE AND BUSINESS

At noon I left the office and walked the two blocks to the Hotel Dorado Club, where I met the family. I played some racket ball with Daniel, or better said, he played with me. He was so quick. I was running full court, back and forth after the ball while he covered a yard radius and defeated me while beading a minor sweat on his upper lip. I left him and Asher to play another round, so I could recover. My tongue was hanging out as I headed for the pool to swim for a while with the girls. I swam with Linda and the four younger girls, while the two older girls lay around the edges of the pool sunning themselves. I figured they were soaking up all the sun they could absorb before heading back to school. We all had lunch at the bar by the pool. Linda and I were able to sit on the deck chairs and chat a little between the shouts of 'watch me do this' from the younger ones. I remembered to tell her about Eli thinking of getting the families together for barbecue at their home on Saturday the sixteenth. I explained that Amparo wasn't aware yet. She said she had wanted to talk to Amparo, so she would phone her and talk it over and find out what she could bring if we did it.

At two thirty I showered and dressed and went for my 3:00 p.m. meeting with the Alfaros. Yaneth had arranged for us to meet in one of the Dorado Hotel rooms. Frequently in my line of work, I had found that my services could be more effective if less people knew that I was involved with a client. A room in a large hotel offers considerably more discretion for clients than an office. The hotel Manager, Mr. Maurice Staples knew about my line of work, since he had had occasion to make use of my services a few years back when I was traveling from Honduras and staying in the Dorado. He had ordered a special rate for me, since I was pretty regular and was only a daytime customer.

Although Jorge and his sons had known me cordially for years, until then, they really had no idea about what I did for a living. We had exchanged calling cards years before, but I had always used the generic term 'Consultant' under my name. The title 'Consultant' covered a world of activities. For me, calling cards were merely cordiality. I really never expected to catch a client with a calling card. It would have been impossible to describe what I did on the front and back of one of those little cards anyway. My clients found me just like the Alfaros had found me, through referral.

Yaneth had told me that Jorge and one of his sons would be meeting with me. I had frequently crossed paths with his oldest son, Miguel, and was sort of looking forward to seeing him, but as it turned out, Jorge showed up with his youngest son, Raul. When I inquired about Miguel, his father informed me that he was in El Salvador where he was heading up a major project for the conglomerate. Since I really didn't know whom Geraldo had talked to, or how much he had told them about me, I started the meeting by asking how much they knew about what I did.

Jorge's response was pretty much to the point as he stated, "Apparently Raul here commented to Geraldo Jimenez about some problems we are experiencing, and Geraldo suggested that we get in touch with you and that we could trust you. Orville, let me be frank. Miguel and I have known you cordially for years. I have seen you in places where the political climate was no less than hostile. We have run in the same circles and I have never heard a bad thing about you, but frankly I don't know what you do and until now I have not been interested in finding out. After Geraldo recommended that we get in touch with you, I called a few friends and found that their knowledge of you is at least as vague as mine, so would you mind telling us what you do?"

I started out by mentioning some of the consultant work I had done for two of my clients. Then I mentioned four high profile cases I had worked on during the past three years that were public knowledge, such as the rescue of Carlos Facussé and the return of the kidnapped Juárez child, plus a couple others that I was not directly involved in but had participated in an advisory capacity.

I explained in enough detail my role in the solution of the first two cases that Jorge and Raul could be left with no doubt as to my having been a key element in the good ending of both cases. I then offered the names of two prominent citizens that they could call that would vouch for my honesty and legitimacy. Neither of them seemed inclined to reach for the phone, so I asked them to tell me about their problem.

The first incident that they had noticed was in the second week of July. Raul had just finished night classes at Landivar University around 8:30 in the evening. About five hundred yards after leaving the university gates, on the narrow two lane road leading back to the city, he had noticed a car following with its bright lights on when a light colored sedan pulled out in front of him. Raul was quick in veering to the left and barely cleared the front end of the sedan by straddling the ditch by the embankment and accelerating back into the roadway. He escaped with some minor damage to the undercarriage of his BMW. A less astute driver would have been stuck right there.

Raul didn't think much of it. He borrowed one of the company cars while they repaired his and he didn't report the incident to his father. Jorge said that if Raul had told him, he would have likely just cataloged it as another one of Raul's frequent accidents, which according to Raul "were always someone else's fault".

The second incident had occurred the previous week on Monday, July 28th. Raul was again on his way home from evening classes. He was driving west towards Zone 10 on Vista Hermosa Boulevard, which is a four lane avenue divided by a wide median, a gray Mercedes passed him and then applied his brakes as soon as his car was in front of Raul's car. At the moment that Raul was considering passing the Mercedes, he realized that a pickup had pulled up alongside in the left lane. The pickup had begun to squeeze him to the right as a gunman waved his gun for Raul to pull off. Again Raul's quick reaction spun things in a direction that was not part of the plan. As soon as Raul saw the gun, he slammed on his brakes and turned towards the pickup. A car behind him, that he suspects was part of the ploy, hit him in the left rear quarter, as he was stopping and veering to the left. His turn to the left and the impact of the following car completely turned him around facing the opposite direction of traffic in the left inside lane. The Mercedes, the pickup and the car following threw on their brakes but continued beyond Raul's BMW. Raul had stopped. He flipped it into first gear, jumped the median and drove between two trees to cross over onto the opposite side of the avenue and head back east. As he was crossing the median, a bullet came through the right rear window and exited through the middle of the windshield. He discovered another bullet hole through the trunk lid when he got home.

Raul had no doubt that this most recent incident was not an accident, and he connected the dots between it and the first incident of two weeks prior. He reported both incidents to his father that evening. They both concluded the same as I just had, someone was out to get Raul and if they had been trapping someone with less driving skills, they would have succeeded.

Since that incident, Raul had been restricting his movement, while accompanied around the clock by a bodyguard. They were switching cars, times and routes, but still concerned as to who was after him and whether the pursuers would give up on their plan. Raul's bodyguard was part of a group they contracted from a local security company for security at their offices and steel fabrication plant in Zone 12. I didn't mention it, but I figured the guards were at best, one notch above standard issue. The Alfaros were silent as they waited for my response.

I told them that I would be willing to work on their problem. I asked a few questions regarding their intended itineraries for that week, the descriptions and license tag numbers of the vehicles they would be using, the safety of their homes and businesses and about the guards that had been hired to protect Raul. I gave them a few suggestions as to some additional precautions they should take, including an additional bodyguard for Raul. I asked if their guard service could provide an additional guard starting the next day, to which Jorge answered in the affirmative. I asked them to brainstorm and put together a list of known and possible enemies. I asked them to mark those that they felt might be more likely to take some action against a member of the family.

I explained that if they determined to contract me that I would require a retainer of $5,000 towards expenses and I explained the fee setup for my time and for each member of my staff's time. I explained that we would present a billing each Monday for the previous week of activity, unless expenses were higher than anticipated, in which case we would extend a special billing for expenses, or require an increase in the retainer.

I finally added that my effectiveness would diminish greatly if what I did became common knowledge. For that reason and for my security as well as the security of my staff and my family, I requested that my work for them remain anonymous unless I specifically authorized the release of any information. I told them that a sizable portion of the expenses would merely be listed and not have supporting invoices or receipts that could be submitted for accounting, and that in fact, I wanted no dealing with accountants or legal representatives.

Jorge responded affirmative that they wanted me to work on their case and that unless otherwise requested by him; all communications would only be with him or his sons. He then asked who would be the payee on the check. I told him to make it in the name of our corporation, SCOT, S.A. We decided to meet again at the Hotel on the following Thursday the seventh, at two thirty, unless either of us decided that we needed to meet before, in which case we would make contact by phone. We exchanged phone numbers. I gave them a picture of myself, Mike and Roberto and explained that they should show their guards and family members and make them aware that we three were involved in protecting them, but that if they happened to see us, or run into us, to not even nod or acknowledge us.

We finished our meeting at 5:30. I walked back to the office. Lights were out and everyone was gone, as I expected. I would have just picked up the car and headed home, but I hadn't been able to phone Eli, so I went on up to the office. There were a couple of notes on my desk from Yaneth and one from Mike. One of the notes told me that Eli had phoned. The other two notes didn't need immediate attention, just a heads up on a couple of clients. Eli's call had been at 4:45. I suspected by now he would either be home or on his way, but I tried his office number anyway. He picked up on the fifth ring.

"Eli here!"

"Hi Eli, I just came back to the office after meeting with a client at the Dorado. Yaneth left a note that you had called."

"I was on my way out, when the phone rang. It took me a few seconds to get the door open and make it to the phone. Glad you caught me. I was able to talk to Allen and he confirmed that the trip is a go. Do you have enough flexibility that we could add a half day more onto the trip if need be?"

"Which end?"

"What do you mean?"

"I mean; do you want to add a half a day at the beginning, or at the end?"

"Oh, return Thursday afternoon instead of Thursday morning. Allen just wants a little more flexibility in case some of our meetings take longer. We may need a little more time in any one of the stops. You know that is the reason we can't do this kind of trip on commercial airline schedules."

"Yeh, sure I know that. I always plan on some flexibility. As you well know, frequently the weather dictates when we come or go. I just wanted to know whether we were leaving earlier, or coming back later, but sure, I can plan on coming back later."

"Great! Now all I have to worry about is scheduling the meetings with our people and clients."

"I am really looking forward to being with you and Allen."

"Allen said he was looking forward to seeing you too. By the way there might be one passenger more, in addition to Allen and myself. I don't know who it is, so no need to ask. Allen just asked if there would be room for another person. I told him that I was sure there would be, since your plane holds six. After I told him there would be room, I got to thinking that I better run it by you. I remember you hauled three others and me in your plane last year, but that was a shorter trip. Anyway, is it okay if he brings an additional person?"

"Sure. The plane can handle pilot plus five, if need be. We aren't going into any short runways, so the plane can handle it just fine. Just let me know."

"Good. I don't have any idea who Allen wants to bring along. It might even be his new wife. 'Ahh'! I just thought of that. If that is the case, I hope he tells me in advance. If his wife comes, Amparo would want to plan something with you and Linda. Anyway, I'll fill you in as soon as I know what's up. Have a nice evening Orv."

"You too, Eli. Good night."

It was after 6 p.m. when I left the office. I arrived home just in time for dinner. Monday was our family night at home. It was the one night a week when none of us planned on being anywhere else, or with anyone but each other. The general rule was that it was just family. Linda and I didn't normally invite guests and neither did our children. We held family council, one of us (adults and children alike) led a scripture based lesson, we sang, and the rest of the evening was dedicated to fun. We played board games, cooked a desert together, and sometimes went to a movie, a theatrical performance, or a circus or similar event when offered. We just played table games that Monday. The children were in their bedrooms by 9:30 p.m. and Linda and I had some quiet time until 11:00 p.m. She was always interested in what I was doing and I enjoyed hearing about what she and the children had been up to.

CHAPTER 6
TUESDAY, AUGUST 5

On Tuesday morning I went straight from home to the airport. Since Jorge Alfaro ran in some of the same flying circles as me, I had an idea that the airport might be a source of some information that could be helpful on his case. I needed to go to the airport anyway to oversee the installation of new Cleveland Brakes on my plane. I wanted to make sure the job was completed by Friday morning, since I had promised to fly the family for an overnight stay in Flores, near the Tikal Mayan ruins in the extreme Northern province of Petén. We didn't all fit in our plane, so Mike was going to fly some of the children with him in another plane. He had some work to do for a client in the Petén and we were able to fit his work in with the family trip.

I owned a 1969 Cessna Turbo 337 Skymaster. The Skymaster is the most efficiently configured light twin-engine aircraft on the market. Many pilots familiar with them call them Push-Pulls because instead of having the engines on the wings, the engines are located front and rear on the fuselage. This centerline thrust configuration affords several advantages over the standard side by side.

For one, they create less drag. In a few words this means, the engines use less of their power to pull themselves through the air and have more power available to pull and push the aircraft through the air. Wing mounted motors, which are standard on other aircraft, do not provide symmetrical thrust. Generally, whichever engine is upwind will provide more thrust. Also if you lose power in one of the wing-mounted engines, the plane literally has to fly somewhat sideways with the un-powered wing following the powered wing. You lose fifty percent of your power, but in addition you lose another twenty-five to thirty percent of your airfoil efficiency through drag and loss of lift. On the Skymaster, the engines are in line, one behind the other, and thus they provide symmetrical thrust in all scenarios. Also, if you lose the power in an engine, you merely fly straight ahead, much like you would in a single engine aircraft with only a loss of power, but no substantial loss of airfoil efficiency.

Another important advantage of the Skymaster over standard twins is balanced loading. Balanced loading of standard twins is always critical and challenging. Balanced loading of the Skymaster is easy. With engines on both ends of the fuselage, it is nearly impossible to get away from the Center of Gravity. The turbo Skymaster flies comfortably at fifteen thousand feet with a useful load of over 1,600 pounds. If it has a luggage pod underneath, like mine, it can carry six adults and two hundred pounds of luggage over five hundred miles distance, at a respectable 185 to 190 MPH.

I was an oddball for flying a Skymaster. It never caught on with the civilian pilots, probably because of its looks. Some pilots thought it didn't have the sleek look of standard twin-engine aircraft. Most civilian pilots couldn't get beyond its looks to evaluate its efficiency. The only thing that kept the model alive was sales to the U.S. Department of Defense. In the military, it was designated as an O-2. They placed two pylons under each wing, one for a 40-caliber machine gun, and the other for rockets, flares, or cluster bombs and used them for reconnaissance and rescue flying. They proved to be extremely reliable and sturdy, being agile like a single engine aircraft, but capable of higher speeds and payloads. Once the Vietnam War was over, the civilian market was insufficient to sustain manufacturing, so Cessna quit making them in 1980. Reims of France purchased the manufacturing and marketing rights from Cessna and continued to build them for a couple of decades, mainly for military use in several countries. Used or new, they remained popular with some of the small air forces in Africa, Asia, and Latin America. They were a mainstay for several of Latin America's dictators, including Somoza's Air National Guard in Nicaragua. The few of us that continued to fly them, swore by them.

Ralph Younger serviced my plane. He was a top notch FAA-A&P mechanic from Arkansas. In the late sixties, Ralph was a member of the U.S. Army, based in Panama. In 1968 he spent a month in Guatemala repairing an army Twin Otter aircraft that blew an engine during takeoff after a stop in Guatemala. During his first week in Guatemala he met Gabriela at a birthday party and dated her during the remainder of his stay in Guatemala. A few weeks after he returned to his base in

Panama, Gabriela discovered that she was on a death list along with several other university students, some of whom had been assassinated and others unaccounted for. On her way to exile in Spain she stopped to visit Ralph in Panama. Ralph had experienced some pretty challenging assignments during his stint with the armed forces, but nothing had prepared him to resist the charm of a Gabriela. Within those few short days he found himself committed to a lifetime contract. They married and after he completed his time with the Army and the political climate was safe for Gabriela in Guatemala, they moved back, and had remained there ever since.

Ralph kept three fully certified mechanics, a couple sheet metal and fabric specialists and three or four assistant mechanics busy servicing Guatemalan and U.S. registered aircraft. He also owned and flew a Skymaster and kept plenty of spare parts on hand from a half dozen 0-2 airframes and engines he had. After looking over the progress on the brake installation Ralph and I walked back to his office. He assured me that my plane would be ready on Thursday afternoon. We sat in his office for a few minutes just talking shop and about our families and summer vacations.

While out in the shop, I was glad to see that one of the Alfaro planes, a four seat Cessna Turbo 210, was there for service. They also owned a Piper Navajo. Having just walked by their plane in the shop, gave me an opening to casually inquire about them. Ralph told me that their chief pilot, Saul Gámez was still working for them and that they had just fired their junior pilot. He was a young smart pompous ass by the name of Ortiz. Neither of us could remember his first name. According to Ralph, Saul had discovered him making unauthorized flights and fudging on his expense account. I found it interesting to hear that Raul had handled the actual firing just outside of Ralph's shop in late June and that both Raul and the pilot were pretty agitated. I couldn't get much more information from Ralph without it looking like an inquiry, so I wished him good day and left.

I drove on down to the MAG hangar to say hi to the owner, Brenda García. Brenda operated a small airfreight business and had several aircraft under leasing contract from owners that did limited flying of their aircraft and liked an arrangement whereby their planes could earn a little income instead sitting idol in the hangar. Most all machinery lasts longer if it is used regularly and receives regular maintenance, but it is especially true for planes and boats. Brenda rented the planes to executives that needed to fly, but didn't own aircraft. She earned a small percentage above what the owners received. She would rent them with a pilot, or the renter could provide their own pilot, with her making sure the pilots were qualified to fly.

Brenda and I were good friends. I had rented planes through her on a regular basis many years before while we lived in Honduras. With limited resources after leaving UltraChem and moving to Honduras, we placed other priorities ahead of owning a plane. I rented a plane on occasion in Honduras and discovered Brenda's plane rental business very useful in Guatemala. I would fly a commercial flight to Guatemala and then use one of her planes for any travel in Guatemala, or El Salvador. That day I wanted to reserve one of two 206's that Brenda leased. One had a standard aspirated engine and the other had a Turbo boosted engine.

Alba and Minor were in the front office as I entered. After greeting them, I inquired about Brenda.

Alba addressed me as 'Captain Orville'. In Latin America, anyone that pilots a plane is called Captain. She told me that Brenda was on the phone in her office and that I could go on in.

I gave a knock on Brenda's office door and went on in, as instructed by Alba. As I had been told, Brenda was on the phone. She mouthed a hello, as she listened on the phone and pointed to a chair in front of her desk. I sat and welcomed the cool of her air-conditioned office. The only problem was the smoke, which you could cut with a knife. Brenda was a chain smoker.

Brenda said bye to her caller and hung up. She came around the desk for a mutual hug and kiss on the cheek.

"Hi Brenda. How's business and how are you and your family doing?"

"Everyone is doing well and the business is growing little by little, Don Orville. You haven't been to see me for a while. I see you are fine. How are Linda and the children?"

"Everyone is fine. We just arrived a few days ago from summer vacation, so we are still in the process of settling back in to life in the tropics."

After we filled each other in on our work and families, I asked her if the TG-DYR, a Turbo Cessna 206 owned by Clark Rogers of Rogers'

Tours, would be available for Friday and Saturday. She picked up the phone and rang Alba and asked about the 206. She hung up with a "Gracias" and turned again to me.

"You may have it Don Orville. Is your Skymaster in service?"

"No..., well yes it is, but it will be done in time for me to use it. The problem is that I want to take the whole family to the Petén and we all won't fit in any one aircraft. I need the 206 for Mike to fly part of my family. Is Mike current with you for flying the 206, or do I need to have him come by?"

"No, no, that won't be necessary. Mike Cunningham has been flying several of our aircraft. Until you mentioned him now, I had forgotten that he works for you. We know him well. He is an excellent pilot. He seems to be a very dependable person; I would think that you are good for each other. You are fortunate to have him as an employee, and he is fortunate to have you as a boss."

I knew that Ortiz had worked a while for Brenda, so after making firm arrangements for the 206 and exchanging a few other cordialities, I broached the subject with her. She knew the Alfaros had fired him and she expressed that she felt a little awkward that she had recommended him. She said she had also caught him in a few tricks, but just figured him for immature and thought he had changed.

Over the years, she had provided employment for quite a few young pilots that were building hours until they got a break with bigger planes, or permanent employment, or both. Brenda was a talker, so she gave me a lot of details on Ortiz's background. She always did a background check on her pilots before she contracted them and she learned a good bit more while he worked for her. He came from a good middle class family, but he had given his parents a rough road to hoe. Brenda had heard that they had pulled him out of a couple financial quagmires and she was withholding part of his income to pay off some debts, some of which were not with very reputable people. Apparently Ortiz liked to live above his means. He had just finished paying off the debts she was deducting for when he got the opportunity to work for the Alfaros. Brenda was like a second mother to a lot of her young pilots and she thought she had been instrumental in helping this one make a turn around, which apparently he hadn't. If he came back, she would probably admonish him and give him another chance. She was such a tender one and saw the good in everyone.

Brenda didn't ask about why I was inquiring and I didn't offer. We chatted a few more minutes, mainly about changes in administrators at the Civil Aeronautics office, and then I said good-bye and went on my way.

After a quick lunch, I arrived at the office around one thirty. Yaneth was on the phone when I got to the office. I waved and went on back to my office.

Yaneth switched the phone ring from her desk to my office and the four of us started there. Although it was three weeks away, I confirmed with Yaneth that I would be traveling the 26th through the 28th with Eli and two others from UltraChem to Puerto Barrios, Belize and Honduras. I asked Yaneth to check my schedule to see if I would be able to use all of that Thursday with UltraChem and I let her return to her desk to work on my planning calendar.

The rest of the afternoon was spent with Roberto and Mike. First I filled them in on my meeting with the Alfaros and set a few things in motion towards getting more information regarding the Alfaros' problem. I assigned Mike to do some research regarding persons that might have a grudge against any of them. We went over Raul Alfaro's itinerary and routes so we could analyze specific points where Roberto and Mike could station themselves to observe without being observed. During that discussion we determined that we needed a third person to be able to give adequate surveillance, especially in the evenings. We decided to have Roberto contact a couple of his friends that we occasionally used, to see if one of them was available to help with this job.

Finally we all three laid out our August calendars to determine blank spots which we could commit to fieldwork on the Alfaro case. We determined that one or the other of us would be able to spend three to four hours a day for the rest of that week and then starting the following week, a total of ten to fourteen man hours a day with the additional contracted help. We finished 4:50 p.m. I gathered up my things and headed home.

As I pulled the car through the gates to the garage, I noticed all of our children in the front lawn, jumping on the tramp and playing with the dogs. It was just them. There weren't any of their friends with them. I parked the car, left my stuff in it, locked it and went straight from the garage to the front lawn. I played with the two younger girls and the dog, and then joined the others at the tramp. I even took a turn on the tramp. I could do back flips, but it always scared the crap out of me, because I usually ended up near the rear edge of the tramp, close to going off the end. I never was able to complete a forward flip. So, I mainly just jumped and clowned. It seemed to please the children that their old dad could even jump on a tramp. We played and talked until suppertime. Linda was surprised when I came walking in with the children; she had been unaware that I had gotten home.

After dinner and a little time with the family in the living room, I left the house around 8:30 p.m. and drove to within three blocks of Raul Alfaro's residence in Zone 11. I left the car and stationed myself one and a half blocks down the street from his house. I had just found a niche in the wall shaded by a huge bougainvillea bush when Raul and his two body guards arrived from the opposite direction, one in his car and one following on a motorcycle. The one on the motorcycle opened the gate and entered while the other remained outside in the car with Raul. The first guard exited the house within ten minutes and then Raul and the guard in the car drove in and shut the gate. After another five minutes, the motorcycle guard came out the small walkway gate, looked up my way then the opposite direction and then got on his motorcycle and left the same way he had come. It was 9:30 p.m. I stayed put and watched two other neighbors arrive and pull into their garages via automatic garage door openers. At 10:00 p.m. I gave up and went home.

CHAPTER 7
WEDNESDAY, AUGUST 6

I arrived at the office just as Yaneth was getting there at ten till eight. I had a meeting scheduled with Bank of America at 9:00 that morning. I worked on my notes for that meeting until 8:45. I would still arrive ten minutes before the meeting was scheduled, since we were meeting at the Bank of America office on the bottom floor of the Etisa Building.

The meeting was of a routine nature with security personnel. We could have covered the agenda in one-hour max, but part of it was social interaction between security personnel from different agencies, so we finished the meeting at five after eleven.

I went back up to the office and asked Yaneth if there were any calls. There weren't, so I decided to run my Audi over to rotate the tires. The place I did my brakes and tires was just two blocks over by McDonalds. I ran the car over and talked with Alfonso, the manager. We decided he should check the brakes while he was at it. He said he would have it done by one if there were no brake repairs and two if there were. On my walk back to the office, I saw a blouse I thought Linda would like in the window of a boutique on Seventh Avenue across from McDonalds. I bought it and was back at the office just before noon.

I wanted to review some things that had come up in the Bank of America meeting with Yaneth and she had a few things she wanted to cover with me, so we decided to do a work lunch at Los Cebollines. Linda had taught me to be generous with my tips and Yaneth and I were regulars at Cebollines, so everyone treated us with a high degree of cordiality. They had four party rooms and there was almost always one or more that were not being used during the lunch hour. If a party room was available, the manager always invited us to use one, rather than eat in the public dining area. That day we took the room. I always passed on the little green onions and the guacamole they served with all their lunches, but I liked everything else. The Mexican sirloin steaks were not as tender as a good steak in the states, but they always tasted good. I had good teeth, so given a choice; I would always take flavor over tenderness. I ordered the 'Típico' with refried beans, 'plátanos', and fried tortilla chips. I put plenty of their special hot sauce on the beans. Their hot sauce had a good flavor and was plenty spicy. I had learned to go light with the sauce until I determined how spicy it was. The chilies that made up the spicy part of the sauce varied considerably in how hot they were. I discovered that little jewel of information the hard way. After eating a medium hot sauce the first time I ate at Cebollines, I put plenty of hot sauce on my second visit. After one mouthful, it felt like my teeth were burning.

Yaneth was always on a diet, so she nibbled on a salad and mainly talked while I ate and listened. She had the status on our bank accounts and a few credit card accounts to go over. That reminded me that I was still carrying the $20,000 check from Hugo Salinas. I took that out of my Day-Timer and handed it to her for deposit. We were able to cover all of our business over lunch.

I spent the afternoon at the office planning and evaluating some of the research done by Mike and Roberto. They provided me material for two of our regular consultant clients and some info on the Alfaros. The rest of the day went pretty quiet with a few phone calls and dictation of some correspondence to Yaneth. I was able to do some planning while watching the afternoon flights through my balcony door. The wind was from the North, so I was watching takeoffs on Runway 01 when Eli called.

Yaneth rang the intercom and told me Eli was on the line.

"Hi Eli."

"Hi, how is my gringo friend doing?"

"I can't complain. I have been busier than I thought I would be, after having been gone on vacations. It feels like I have been back a couple of weeks instead of a few days. What's up?"

"Allen told me who might accompany him. It's Joe Levi. He is still not sure he can make it. He may have to travel to the Philippines. Even though it is not a sure thing, Allen wanted to give us a heads up. He knows that it will add another dimension to the security issue having Joe along."

I thought, 'He wasn't kidding about that, with Joe being the Vice President of UltraChem's International Operations.'

I said, "Thanks for letting me know. I will put a little extra thought into every aspect of the trip that depends on me."

Eli said, "Orville, I want you to be our backup on security for each leg."

"Eli, I think you are aware, but I must remind you, that I am licensed to carry my weapon only in Guatemala and Honduras. I don't think security is much of an issue in Belize, but you need to know that I can't carry there."

"Thanks for reminding me, but I agree with you. Belize should not be a worry as to security. Anyway, as soon as I have a firm itinerary, I will fill you in and we can work out the details together. Have a nice evening."

"Same to you Eli."

At 2:30 I walked over to the shop to pick up my Audi. The brakes could have gone another five thousand, but Alfonso went ahead and put new linings on. He knew I preferred safe over sorry. I went back to the office and continued working for the rest of the afternoon.

* * * * * * * *

LANDIVAR

At 5:30 I left the office and drove through the carry out window at 'Pollo Campero' fried chicken and drove up to Landivar University. Landivar was founded around 30 years before by some Jesuit Priests in the mountains on the Eastern edge of Guatemala City. It was at the top of Zone 15, beyond the American School. They built several massive concrete buildings in the middle of a rolling campus that overlooked the City. Each building housed several different areas of study, so they were not named or known for the subjects offered in them. They were merely identified with letters of the alphabet.

I was concerned about when and how to show the university-parking pass that Mike had gotten for me. I had been told that Raul Alfaro used a large parking lot by M Building, beyond the East Gate. I drove through the main entrance North Gate without anyone stopping me, so I figured that perhaps the pass was required for the parking lots. I followed the traffic on through the campus and arrived at the parking lot around 6:15 p.m. It was starting to get dark.

The attendants stationed at the entrance to the parking lot didn't ask for my pass. They were holding the gate up and I just drove on through with the rest of the traffic. The pass was overkill. I decided not to tell Mike. I hated to discourage his efforts and I had no idea how much work he had gone to in getting the pass.

M Building was on the Southern extreme of a complex of five buildings. They were all rectangular, three story, flat roofed buildings, some joined by covered passageways. I didn't really have a plan. I was just looking for a vantage point from where I could observe the parking lot and the street leading to it. I found a parking place five rows in. I parked facing the entrance to the parking lot, which meant I was also facing M building and another connected building close by on its right.

I reached into the back seat and grabbed my old accordion leather briefcase with a shoulder strap. I figured a person would more likely look out of place on a campus without a book bag or a briefcase. I walked through the ground floor of M building into the ground floor of the next building, which I found was called 'J Building'.

I walked on through to the East side of J Building, which had a small parking lot next to it, probably reserved for professors. They had blocked off an area next to the building on the parking lot side with an eight-foot high fence enclosed with metal roofing placed horizontally. The fencing extended out about ten yards from the building, about half of that extending into the parking lot. I walked out to the corner of the fence and saw that it extended about the same distance along the front of the building. It had a contractors sign on that side of the fence, which identified it as a project area.

I looked around and saw there was no one in sight. The gate to the area had a simple metal latch, which I easily slipped. That side of the building was dark. I took my flashlight out of the briefcase and flicked it on for a moment. The materials lying around indicated that they were probably doing some maintenance on the roof. The scaffolding was immediately opposite the gate.

I tightened the shoulder strap on the briefcase securing it up under my arm and started climbing the scaffolding. The ladders had been removed, but I was able to move up the angled brace between each tier.

As I got near the top, I realized that the scaffolding did not reach quite to the top of the building. The last brace of the scaffolding was about four feet shy of the top of the cornice around the top. By standing on the top brace I could barely reach over the concrete edge enough to scale onto the rooftop. As I stretched my one leg over the edge, I realized that it would probably be the last time I used those pants as they gave out in the crotch. Oh well, I was hot enough from the climb that the extra air down there was welcome and I wasn't planning on being part of any fashion show that evening.

Once on top, I looked around and confirmed that indeed they were in the middle of repairing and sealing the roof. They were concentrating the material on top of the J Building and moving the material by way of bridges from the roof of J Building to the roofs of the adjacent buildings. After getting my wind, I crossed over the bridge to M Building and walked over to the front side of the building remaining well back from the edge so that my silhouette would not be visible from below or from any of the other buildings. As I had hoped, I was granted a good view of the parking lot. I found an old crate over by a roof vent. I carried it over to my vantage point to sit on, and pulled the fried chicken out of my briefcase. After the climb I was wishing I had brought something to drink. I only had enough saliva to eat two of the three pieces of chicken. I pulled the binoculars out of the case. A little bit of grease from the chicken had leaked on the lens cap, but there was none on the lens. I merely wiped it off on the inside of the right leg of my pants. That was about all they were good for at that point anyway. The lights around the parking lot and sidewalks were adequate for use of the binoculars. There were a few blind spots, but I could see most of the parking area and surrounding walkways.

I had been observing the parking lot for around fifteen minutes when Raul's motorcycle guard arrived, followed by Raul and the other guard in a tan Opel two door coupe, four minutes later. They both walked Raul to the edge of the parking lot and remained there while Raul continued on up the walk into the M Building. Raul's guards then walked over and began conversing with a university guard at the secondary entrance. After a few minutes one of Raul's guards walked over to a vendor's stand, where he bought a couple of cigarettes from the young woman operating the stand. He stuck one in his jacket pocket and asked the vendor for a match and lit the other. The other guard joined him and mooched the cigarette he had put in his pocket and a light from his cigarette. They began flirting and joking with the vendor. I kept scanning between them, the exits to M Building and the parking lot.

After fifteen minutes, Raul came out of M Building with two other young men who accompanied him up to the third floor between M and J Buildings. They disappeared into the third floor corridor of J Building in the direction of L Building, where he disappeared, probably into a classroom. A half hour later, Raul's guards tired of chatting with the vendor in between her attention to other customers, and moved on up the driveway out of view. It was 8:30 p.m. By then I was just scanning the area in general and the parking lot. I searched the perimeter of the parking lot to see if I might discover where Roberto was stationed, if he was out there, but it was too dark and I knew he would be in one of the shadows if he were there. I really didn't know what I was looking for. Often it was like that. I seldom knew what if anything was going to turn up, I just observed.

At a quarter to nine I noticed some movement around the Opel. Two guys in typical jackets that had been sitting in the back of a pickup, two lanes over, were now beside the Opel. One of them dropped to the ground beside the car, while the other watched. It was time to go. I slipped the binoculars in the case, snapped it shut, and ran in a crouch over to the back of the building. I waited for a couple of people to pass, and then when it was clear, I quickly crossed the bridge back over to J Building. It was complicated getting to the scaffold by hanging over the edge of the cornice and feeling for the braces. I pushed off of the cornice to drop onto the wooden platform at the top of the scaffold, the board broke and I fell to the next level, landing on my right leg and falling over on my right side onto the briefcase. Somewhere in that process half of the board that broke and fell with me, smacked me up side the head. I got erect again and began scrambling down the outside frame of the scaffolding. I hit the ground in a run, which turned into a limping fast walk after about ten paces.

I held myself to a less noticeable fast walk as I left the construction area and went around the outside of M Building through the lawn that joined the parking lot. I looked up the street towards where Raul's guards had gone, but they were nowhere in sight. I moved quickly towards Raul's car in the parking lot. I had my Mauser in hand by the time I saw the Opel and the sentry. I shouted for him to put his hands in sight and stay put. He didn't do either. He dropped quickly out of sight. I was thirty yards away when this happened and I began moving cautiously towards the Opel. By the time I reached the Opel, they were not there. I heard the pickup start and again tried to run, this time towards the pickup. I found I could not run. My right hip was not working like it was supposed to. Before I got anywhere near, they were on their way out of the parking lot and I saw that Roberto was running alongside their exit route two lanes over. Neither of us was close enough to get a tag number, or determine more than the fact that they were driving a dark blue Datsun 1200 with no tailgate and only one taillight, as they left through the East Gate.

Roberto caught up with me as I walked back to the Opel. By then I had extracted the flashlight from the briefcase. Roberto shined his light on me and let out a "Hay Diablos"–Oh hell. I looked so bad; he assumed that the two of them had thrashed me. My pants no longer exhibited only the crotch problem; they looked more like a long kilt than pants. Both legs were ripped down the inseam. The one side of my face was soiled and bleeding where the board had smacked me and in general, I was not my normal lilting self, in appearance, nor movement.

I assured him that I was not broken beyond mending as we began looking over and around the Opel. We noticed a set of pliers on the ground beside the passenger door. Roberto could stoop easier than me, so he lay on the ground alongside the Opel and began searching the underside. He quickly discovered a little accessory that had not been installed by the manufacturer. He checked it over thoroughly and determined that it had not yet been connected and could be safely handled. I stooped beside him to illuminate the area while he used the set of pliers we had found and a screwdriver on his pocketknife to remove the bomb. Epoxy and screws held it in place. The epoxy had not set yet. Except for the wires dangling off to one side, it was a pretty neat little package. I had arrived just before they made the electrical connections.

Roberto had parked three blocks away. We walked back to my car and drove together to his car. We decided that he should take the bomb with him and get some of his explosives expert friends involved in our problem. We should know by tomorrow noon, just what it was and what it was intended to do. It was a strange package in that it was rather small. Bombs can be designed for all kinds of different effects. Also, their placement and intended time of detonation can be just as critical as their design.

I arrived home a little after 9:30 p.m., the broken hero. I could hear Susan playing the baby Grand as I came up the steps from the garage. There was no one in the front hall as I went into the master bedroom. I was glad to see that none of the children were in our bedroom. Only Linda was there, reading in bed. Apparently the children were reading in the living room or in their rooms. Linda jumped out of bed with a gasp as I limped through the bedroom towards the bathroom. I heard her lock the bedroom door as she followed me into the bathroom.

She whimpered around me as though it hurt her more than me. I assured her that I was not as bad as I looked. I discovered I had lost a perfectly good pen and the pants and shirt went directly into the trash. I took a shower to get the dirt and blood off, then we settled down beside each other in the giant tub, with her sponging and cooing over me as I related my expedition. In spite of her empathy, Linda could not resist laughing uncontrollably at my experience with the scaffold.

Once out of the tub and dry, our inventory of me showed a large bruise on my hip, a reddish bruise on my rib cage, and a three inch bruise mixed with scratches on my cheek. The rest of me definitely looked better naked and washed than with my torn and tattered clothing.

After bathing and a little bit of antiseptic on the scratches, we retired to bed. I limped in to the bed as Linda put up the medications and turned out the lights. I was more, or less finding a comfortable position, when she slid over to my side of the bed, rose up and kissed me on the nose. I was about to ask what that was about when she said, "Happy Birthday Dear. I hope you can sleep okay!"

I answered, "Sure enough, it is the sixth of August. With tonight's events, I can truly say that I barely survived another year."

I wasn't up to anything, but for holding one another, and that was the best medicine for both of us at the end of a long and challenging day.

CHAPTER 8
THURSDAY, AUGUST 7

In some ways it didn't seem possible that we had been back in Guatemala nearly a week and in others ways, so much had happened that I felt like I had lived a month during that week.

I didn't think I could do it, but I jogged a kilometer and a half that morning. I wasn't even going to try to jog; period, but Linda had literally pulled me out of bed. The anti-inflammatory that she had given me the night before must have helped. I was going to give it up at the kilometer mark, but there was something that prodded me on as I saw Linda jogging out in front of me. I was sore, but by the end, my hip was working pretty well. I walked back to the house with a near normal stride. Linda was in the driveway doing her routine of stretches and bends, like she could go on all day. I saluted her as I went by to go in for my shower.

I always liked to shave first, and then take my shower. I danced the razor carefully around the bruise and scratches on my cheek. I heard Linda come in the door as I was adjusting the water in the shower. We had two showerheads in our oversized sunken tub. Sometimes we would shower together and the two heads came in handy, but when I showered alone, I found it too complicated to lather with water coming from two directions. I was lathered and defenseless when Linda appeared in the shower door to ask if I wanted company. She wasn't kidding! My surprised hesitation was taken as yes, and she jumped in and explained that my arriving home scraped and worn the night before had been unfair to her and that I would have to pay my dues that morning. Her words were powerful, but in the end her body language was what convinced me. She was a very demanding woman and before I knew it, I saw things her way. Just when I was feeling a little beat as a man, she always knew just what to do to pull me out of my shell and make me feel whole again.

Afterward, she applied some of her makeup to cover the bruise and scratches on my face. I was looking in the mirror and intermittingly at her while she applied the makeup. I was fascinated by both images, to see the scratches and bruises disappear as she worked on my face and to watch her changes in expressions as she did her thing. Near the end while she was doing the final touchup, I found myself staring at her beautiful face, and then I remembered the blouse I had bought for her at the boutique on Wednesday. As soon as we finished I went down to the car to retrieve the blouse from the trunk of the car while she went to see about some breakfast for us.

With no school, the kids were sleeping in, so we had a quiet breakfast together. Linda had talked to Amparo and confirmed the barbecue for Saturday the sixteenth. She also shared her plans for the day, which included a service project for one of the orphanages. She had recruited the four older girls to accompany her. On our recent trip from the U.S. we had brought used clothing that she had picked up at Deseret Industries in Utah and new shoes she had gotten at a store close out in Indiana. She had packed approximately one hundred fifty pounds in our allowed luggage plus an additional one hundred pounds of excess baggage. They were taking half of that to an orphanage that week and they would distribute the other half to another orphanage the following week. They never just dropped off the clothes. The girls would have the orphans try them on and do a lot of 'oohing' and 'ahing' and then they would spend a few hours helping with anything they felt needed done, including kitchen and bathroom cleaning. I loved to feel Linda's enthusiasm, as she would tell me about her projects.

After eating and our little visit, I gave her the blouse. She was so happy; you would have thought I had given her a diamond. She was always so appreciative of every little gift.

I arrived at the office around 8:30 a.m. I could tell that my arrival interrupted Roberto's filling in Yaneth and Mike about the night before. As I walked into the outer office, all three looked up as though I had returned from the dead.

Roberto exclaimed, "Wow, I didn't expect to see you until maybe this afternoon! You don't look anything like I left you last night. Did you not break anything?"

"You are so easily deceived, Roberto. I was just acting hurt last night. As all of you can see, I am in perfect condition, so if any of you thought you were just going to have a soft day with me out of the office, you were mistaken. We have lots of work to do."

As the four of us entered my office, Yaneth reached up and lightly touched my cheek, at which I flinched.

She said, "Sorry! You almost fooled me. I bet that hurts."

I smiled and answered, "That's okay. It doesn't hurt much. It's just that you surprised me."

We looked at our original plans for the day and began changing priorities and making modifications to our plans as influenced by the new events of last night. Roberto had already delivered the explosive device to his experts in the military. He had explained the location where we had discovered the device and he was supposed to meet with them at noon for a preliminary report. I told him that I would be joining him for that meeting.

We decided that we needed not one, but two of Roberto's friends to help us with surveillance and we needed them then, not the next week. Roberto and I shared the view that I should recommend that the Alfaros replace their present body guards with guards of a higher degree of professionalism from *Wackenhut* or one of the Israeli companies. His regular guards may have been okay for surveillance at the factory, but they were not sufficiently qualified to provide protection for members of his family.

It was determined that Yaneth would handle the banking that day, so that Mike could be free to track down some information at Landivar and also to follow up on some leads in his investigation of some of Alfaro's competitors. I also asked him to determine if any of the houses close to Raul's house in Zone 12 were vacant. I was not sure how we might use that information, but I wanted to know anyway. While I was on the subject of Raul's neighborhood, I thought of Raul's neighbors and asked Mike to also get me a list of Raul's neighbors, with a background on each one, including how long they had lived there.

Yaneth reminded me that I had a meeting with Jorge Alfaro at 4:30 that afternoon. I reminded her that I would need some extra cash for my trip to Tikal the next day. We determined that Roberto would locate his two friends to help us with the surveillance, if possible before noon. He and I would meet with his explosives experts at noon at the military compound off Reforma Avenue in Zone 10.

All three of them scattered to their assignments, while I made notes of the things I needed to cover in the meeting with the Alfaros at 4:30 that afternoon. I finished with my office work at a little before ten, picked up some additional information I had requested from Yaneth and headed out to the Aurora Airport to check on my plane.

The brakes were done. Ralph's chief mechanic had also discovered a small hydraulic leak in the left main gear door servo. It was an O-ring that had gotten pinched or worn. They had replaced it and just lowered the plane off of the jacks after testing the landing gear. It was ready to go. I phoned the Aero Club to file a local flight plan to the San Raymundo practice area. I hadn't flown the plane for six weeks. We pushed the plane out of the hangar and while one of Ralph's men cleaned the windows, I did a 360 ° exterior check. I was getting ready to invite Ralph to join me on the test flight, when another customer walked up to inquire about his plane. I said hi to the man whom I recognized, but couldn't remember who he was or what he did. I told Ralph that I would be back in a little while and got in the plane.

I buckled up, put on my headset, adjusted my seat and then pulled out the checklist card. I went through the preflight checklist, item by item and then laid the checklist in the co-pilot's seat. The next item on the checklist, starting the engines, required two hands. The two continental 210 horsepower engines on the Skymaster were much easier to start than the larger continental engine my previous single engine Cessna had.

I always started the rear engine first, because it was hard to hear what was happening with it if the front engine was running. I never used the primer. I pushed the mixture to full rich for both engines. Then I advanced the throttle for the rear engine with my right hand while turning on the aux pump for the rear engine with my left hand. I did that only long enough to bring the fuel pressure up into the green arc on the gage, then turned it off. Next I pulled the throttle back to 1/4 with my right hand and hit the rear engine starter with my left. With two cranks of the starter, the rear engine came to life. I immediately looked at the oil pressure gauge to make sure the needle came swiftly into the green and then pulled back on the throttle to idle the engine at 1,000 RPM. I repeated the same procedure for the front engine. Once I determined that all the gages were normal for the engines, I flipped on the electrical switches one by one, set my instruments and then I turned on the beacon and navigation lights.

Next, I tuned in the radios and selected the ATIS 126.5 frequency to hear the weather and runway conditions of the hour. Information Uniform told me that the wind was ten degrees –meaning from 10 degrees, at 12 knots, the runway in use was zero one, and the altimeter setting was three-zero-two-one –30.21. I made note, checked the time, 10:20, and then switched to the ground control 121.9 frequency, buttoned the mike and began talking.

"Aurora Ground Control, this is November-two-six-three-two-sierra (N2632S), by Younger hangar on Echo –East side of the airport. We have information uniform, request taxi instructions."

Ground Control came on sort of scratchy because I was in between some hangars: "November two six three two sierra, we do not have your flight plan. When and where did you file?"

I answered: "Three-two-sierra, filed for San Raymundo with Aero Club at 16:05 Zulu –16:05 Greenwich time which was 10:05 a.m., local time."

Ground: "Three-two-sierra, I'll look for flight plan. Taxi approved to Foxtrot intersection, hold short of active runway. Caution with mowing operations on East Side of runway."

I turned on my taxi lights and started taxiing out towards the runway. On the way out to the runway, I continued to check some of the instruments that would only respond with movement and I tested the new brakes at each intersection. They squealed a little more than the old brakes, but they stopped me pretty sudden. I determined that I could apply a little less pressure than with the old brakes.

As I was approaching the holding point at the Foxtrot crossing, ground control called: "Three-two-sierra, I have your flight plan to San Raymundo area. Cleared to cross the active and taxi to position one. At position one, contact tower on one-one-eight point one –118.1 frequency."

"Three-two-sierra, roger, crossing the active."

I crossed the runway and turned left towards position one at the southern extreme of Runway 01. There was only one aircraft ahead of me and he taxied onto the runway as I pulled into the run-up area. I switched the radio to the Tower frequency and then with the checklist in my lap, I performed the run-up and preflight check. For the first flight in six weeks, I was a little more observant of each item on the checklist. I did some of them twice. I looked out to my right and saw the landing lights of an aircraft on final. I checked the time, 10:40 a.m. and then I buttoned the mike and told the tower that I was ready for sequencing for takeoff. They told me to hold short for traffic, as I knew they would. I waited for a DC-9 to land. The tower cleared me to position my aircraft onto the runway and to hold for takeoff clearance. I did so. Once the DC-9 was off of the runway, the tower cleared me for takeoff.

With the brakes held tight I took the Manifold pressure to 31 inches and the RPM to 2800 on both engines. I gave a quick look over all the instruments and then released the brake. With just me in the plane, the Skymaster jumped out of the gate with a surge. Within 800 feet I was off the runway. As soon as I was in a positive climb I tucked the landing gear, which rapidly increased my rate of climb. By the time I passed the tower I was already 250 feet above the runway. Those turbos really showed their stuff at an airport elevation of 5,000 feet.

While climbing to 7,000 feet, I headed on out to the San Raymundo practice area, which was about 20 miles Northwest of the city. I kept the plane between 7,000 and 7,800 feet, which was approximately 1,000 feet above terrain and between 1,200 and 2,200 feet below instrument approach traffic. I took the plane through its paces and it took me through mine. I verified my instruments to make sure everything was clicking the way it should. I did a couple of turns to see how my gyrocompass and HSI were working with the magnetic compass. I verified the turn and bank coordinator and the artificial horizon instruments. Then I practiced some turns to headings, climbing turns, descending turns, steep turns and engine out and stalls. I was a little rusty at the start. Six weeks of not flying my aircraft was too long, but by the end of the session I was back in the saddle.

After being away from my Skymaster for a while, I was always amazed at its stability compared to other aircraft. I had rented planes a couple of times during the summer while on vacation. Linda and I had flown from Indiana to her alma mater in Berea, Kentucky and from there to my alma mater in Bloomington, Indiana, and we did a couple of other short trips, plus I had taken some of the relatives up for a spin, but none of the aircraft I rented were anything as nice as our Skymaster.

At 11:30 a.m., I was satisfied with the plane and myself. I radioed the tower and they cleared me for a left downwind to runway zero-one. I reported downwind, and then left base, and then the turn in on final approach. The tower told me the wind was out of twenty degrees at ten knots and cleared me to land. The Skymaster can be landed with power like a standard twin or without power like a single engine. I generally landed with power when I had passengers, because I could more easily silk it in. Alone that day I decided to bring it in intentionally a little high to float it down with the engines idling. Then I did the other thing one can do with a Skymaster that is not safe to do with standard twin-engine aircraft, I pushed the rudder in one direction and turned the ailerons in the opposite direction. This is called a slip and is a quick way to lose excess altitude. I straightened it out and flared ten feet above the numbers. I missed the moment just a little and did a light bounce, and then I hit the brakes. The tires yelp a little and I had to let up on the brakes. I thought, *Yep, those Cleveland brakes make a difference.* I turned in on the first exit to the taxiway on the right. I couldn't have made the first exit with the old brakes.

I switched to ground control and got clearance to taxi back to Younger's hangar. Once I shut down the engines, Ralph came out of the shop to meet me as I exited the plane. He was glad to see my thumb up. He looked over the brakes on both sides and then we walked back to his office. The Skymaster was mechanically set to go for the next day. I asked him to have his men wash the plane, have it fueled and ready to go for an early morning departure.

I headed out of the East airport gate at 11:45 and arrived at the Military compound five minutes before our meeting. I could see that Roberto hadn't arrived yet. I slipped the Mauser out of the holster and laid it in the seat. I started to take off the holster but determined that it was totally unobtrusive and left it. I reached under the dash to the left of the steering wheel column and pulled a small lever, which popped open, a steel door in the place where the Audi factory would normally install a radio. The little trap door was covered with a standard Audi plate for those that didn't order a radio from the factory. There I had installed a steel box with a holster that was a perfect fit for the pistol. Unless someone found the little release lever, they would need a wrecking bar to gain access to the gun. As to music and news, my Panasonic Radio and Tape deck were in the Glove compartment, which made it less tempting for thieves.

Roberto showed up right at noon and parked next to me. We walked to the gate of the Military compound. He handed his gun to the guard just inside the gate and we waited for the guard to hand him a receipt. Roberto carried an Israeli 9 MM.

A sergeant accompanied us to the laboratory. In spite of our being dressed as civilians, several soldiers saluted us as we crossed the courtyard, probably just in case we were someone. We saluted back and continued. We climbed three stairs onto a pillared verandah on the front of the main building and continued to the end of the building, where we descended the veranda and took a sidewalk to the back of the building. You would have thought Roberto was a long lost friend as we stepped through the door into the laboratory. All four men in the Laboratory turned and greeted him. Two came over to give him an 'abrazo' and then he presented me to them and each of them to me. They were all G-2 Military Intelligence personnel. I can't remember their names except for the head technician who was dressed as a civilian and presented as Lieutenant Malvo. They all gave me a hardy 'bienvenido' and then Lieutenant Malvo led us over to where they had dismantled the device we had found on the underside of the Opel.

As it turned out, it really wasn't a bomb, in the pure sense of the word. It was not intended to explode. It was more sophisticated than that. It contained four 7.62 mm firing chambers with short barrels. For clarification let us say that the top of the device was the part that was placed against the underside of the automobile and the front was towards the front of the automobile. Looking from the top towards the front of the device, two firing chambers pointed off to the right horizontally at about a thirty-degree angle. Then there were two chambers on the topside angle slightly towards the rear of the device. I had never seen anything like it. The lieutenant said the same thing as he started explaining how it was intended to work.

Each of the two horizontal chambers contained an explosive tipped AK-47 shell. The two chambers on the top of the device each contained a steel jacketed shell of the same caliber. Although the design of the device was sophisticated, the operation was quite simple. There was an electrical timer, which would operate off of the vehicle's 12-volt current, once the vehicle was started. The timer was set to operate for ten minutes before releasing current to a magnetic coil. The coil would then shove a plunger against two steel arms that would in turn release the firing pins onto the four shells.

The technician then asked us about where we had found the device. I had, and I am pretty sure Roberto had, figured by then how it was intended to work. We explained to the technician that we had found it under the floor on the passenger side of the vehicle. The wiring that came out of the side was to the inside, which meant that the two horizontal chambers with the explosive tipped shells faced to the front and the two angled chambers on top were aimed to the rear and up.

Roberto and I began explaining our conclusion at the same time. I yielded and he took the lead. Roberto explained that the explosive bullets aimed at the front were designed to destroy the right front tire. They would have been effective even with reinforced, so called "bullet proof tires". The explosive bullets were designed to cause a violent blowout, which would have immediately immobilized the vehicle. Roberto then explained that the steel jacketed bullets aimed to the rear and up were designed to pass through the floorboard into the lower extremities and perhaps as far as the abdomen of whomever was sitting in the passenger seat, in this case, the bodyguard. Sophisticated, but simple!!

The lieutenant took some pictures before his aid reassembled the device. Then he took some more pictures of it assembled. He then handed it to Roberto in a small box, minus the AK-47 shells. We were just getting ready to leave, when a tall man entered the lab, saluting and saying an accented "hola" –hi to everyone. Everyone in the lab called out a 'hi' to *Don* Jan as he walked over to extend his hand to Lieutenant Malvo. Malvo presented the two of us to Jan Karn... something. I didn't get the last name. It sounded German or Austrian, as did his accent. He spoke Spanish well, but with a strong accent. Malvo didn't tell anyone what the others did, or what we were there for, but I could tell that Jan was well known and highly regarded in the lab.

The lieutenant asked our forgiveness for not escorting us to the gate. We told him that it would be unnecessary. We thanked the Lieutenant, then said our goodbye and shook hands with he and Jan. The lieutenant was about to give instructions to one of his assistants, when all three of them asked the Lieutenant if it would be okay for them to go eat lunch. Malvo said it would be fine, but for one of them to escort us to the gate. One of his assistants then escorted us out to the gate, where he explained to the guard that we were authorized to leave with the package un-inspected. We shook hands with the assistant, and then turned in the tag for Roberto's gun. The guard handed him his gun, saluted, and we exited.

It was one o'clock. I told Roberto that I was meeting the family for lunch at the Club, but that I wanted to meet with him and Mike at the hotel, thirty minutes before my meeting with the Alfaros. I took the device with me, and we each headed our separate ways.

I arrived at the club at one-fifteen and walked all over looking for Linda and the children. They were obviously not there. It was a big club, but you couldn't hide nine people, especially my rowdy troop. Just as I had decided to head to the inside dining room, I heard my younger children running and shouting through the corridor that led from the rear parking area. I stood tight against the wall and jumped out at them just as they came around the corner into the club area. They were so absorbed in their chatter that my scare was completely effective. Edna threw a floaty at me and Margaret dropped her ball and came over and pounded me a good one on the hip for scaring them. "Ouch!" I was laughing too hard to think to turn my sore hip away from her. Edna's and Margaret's aggression turned into hugs and daddy this and daddy that. Asher and Daniel were vying for me to go immediately to the racket ball court so that they could put another notch on their racket handles. The older girls walked by in a dignified manner that indicated that they were not part of our rowdy group. The only thing that gave them away was that they said, "Hi Dad! " as they passed.

Finally, Linda brought up the rear and pinned me against the wall for a kiss. Her upper lip was perspiring and several locks of hair were damp and fallen to the front. I gathered that she had experienced a busy morning. We boys headed to our locker room and the girls headed to theirs to change into bathing suits. While in the locker room, I convinced the boys that I was not up to playing that day and that there would have been no glory in trouncing me. Upon leaving the locker room, they headed on to the ball court and I turned to the pool. The girls weren't out yet. I dived in and started laps. I was doing one lap with a scissors kick and then the next with a frog kick. I had done three laps when Susan, Valerie and Stacy joined me. Somewhere around the fifth or sixth lap, my hip began feeling pretty limber, so I completed twelve laps. I turned it into a fast pace during the last lap and a half and I was breathing heavy by the time I pulled myself out of the pool.

We had lunch at the tables around the pool. Linda and I sat together and ordered. The others sat around at other tables and ordered as they arrived. I told Linda that the plane was ready and that from my side we should be all set for an early departure Friday morning. I told her about my test flight and an overview of my work in the morning. She told me that her morning went well with the girls. She said that she needed to make a quick trip back to the orphanage in the afternoon, because they had taken too many shoes for girls and not enough for boys. They had finished at the orphanage a little later than planned, and then when she arrived home to pick up the younger ones, Asher and Daniel had to be tracked down. They were visiting at a neighbor's house without having told anyone. Sounded familiar. The last item she had to report was that the air conditioning was not working in the van. The mystery of her perspiring lip was solved!

CHAPTER 9
LANDIVAR IN DAYLIGHT

I had planned on staying a little longer with Linda and the children, but I decided to leave them at the poolside at 2:30 and walk back to my office parking lot. I had been mulling over the timer attached to the device and I wanted to check out the significance of the 10 minutes it was set for. I retrieved my Audi and headed up to Landivar.

My office parking lot exited onto Thirteenth Street. I turned right onto Seventh Avenue with the thought of crossing over to Reforma Avenue, which ran parallel with Seventh. There was a sizable backup of traffic from the Plazuela España to Reforma, so I decided to remain in Zone Nine on Seventh until the Tower at the intersection of Seventh Avenue and Second Street. The Tower was a 500-foot replica of the Eiffel Tower. The traffic flowed pretty smoothly on Seventh and from there I turned onto Second Street to the East which changed into Vista Hermosa Boulevard once it crossed La Reforma Avenue into Zone Ten. I took the Boulevard until I arrived at the turnoff at the Channel Seven T.V. Station in Zone Fifteen, and from there to the Guatemalan American School and Landivar University, which was in Zone Sixteen. After Channel Seven the street narrowed to a two-lane, winding strip of asphalt.

On the left was a baseball diamond and there were houses bordering on the right for only a couple of blocks. After that it turned into grass and brush on both sides for the distance of a mile. The street descended alongside a steep hillside on the right down into a narrow grassy valley. Anywhere along that part of the route would have been ideal for a kidnapping or assassination. On the opposite end of the valley the street made a sharp turn to the right where it started a steep ascent up past the Guatemalan American School and then a more gradual ascent to the main gates of Landivar. From there the street paralleled the next valley on the left and the Landivar campus on the right with sharp ninety degree turns as it descended into the next valley.

I entered the Landivar University Main Gate. That time there was a guard that stepped out to look at my pass. I was glad I had left it in the glove compartment. He told me that I should display it while on campus. I put it on the left side of the dashboard as I started back up and drove to the parking lot in front of M building. The attendant waved me on into the parking lot. I entered and drove over to an empty slot close to where I estimated that Raul's car was parked the night before. I pulled into the slot, which had me facing M Building. I sat for a moment, studying the buildings and surroundings in the daylight. I looked up at the roof of M building to picture more or less where I was located the night before. There were workers on the rooftop. It appeared that they were scraping and chipping on the flat roof.

I decided to exit the car to get my bearings a little better. I walked on through the M building to the East exit of J Building as I had done the night before. There was a dump truck parked alongside the project fence and workers were throwing old roofing material over the fence into the dump truck. I returned to the parking lot, but instead of going back through the buildings, I cut across the lawn at the end of M building, as I had done the night before. As I looked at the parking lot from that angle, I got a better feel for where the Datsun 1200 was probably parked the night before.

I walked out two lanes beyond where my Audi was parked to where I estimated the Datsun 1200 had been. Only a few of the parking spaces were occupied that time of day. I walked around the area looking on the ground. I got down on my hands and knees and studied the ground under three cars that I thought were pretty certain to be within the area where the Datsun was parked. The sun was bright, so it was on a second look in the shadows under the third car that I discovered some little pieces of plastic that didn't fit in with the surroundings. I had to lie down on my stomach with my head and right shoulder under the car to reach them. They were small little plastic strips of something that I couldn't make out in the dark of the underside of the car. I had just picked up all the little pieces and was getting ready to push back out from under the car, when someone tapped my foot and instructed me to back out slowly. I stuffed the little pieces in my shirt pocket as I pushed myself out from under the car.

He apparently was back by my feet, alongside the car, but if he had been near my head, I still would not have been able to see any detail. The sunlight was blinding after adjusting to the dark under the car. Once I was out from under the car, he walked out adjacent to my body. The voice belonging to military boots and kaki pants said, "Stay down, do as I tell you and make each move slowly. First I want you to move farther from the vehicle, then spread your legs and place your hands behind your head."

I didn't answer. I just obeyed.

He did it by the book. He ran his hands down the insides and outsides of my legs, then he asked me to rotate onto my left side so that he could check my front. After that he stepped back three steps, then invited me to stand facing the car with my hands spread on the car and my legs spread. He remained a respectable distance from me while he moved from behind me to my left side, and then did the same to my right side. He was polite, smooth and efficient.

Then he said, "Your wallet is in your left rear pocket. I want you to lower your left hand, remove your wallet from your pocket and toss it to the rear. Do not drop it or throw it too close to you. Be sure it gets close to me."

I complied. I heard the metal of his carbine touch something as he bent to pick up my wallet, then silence.

"Now I want you to empty your left pocket and place the items on the top of the car, then turn your pocket wrong side out."

I did that and then it was the same for the right front pocket. He told me I could return the items to my pockets. Upon doing so, he told me I could turn around, facing him. As I turned, he tossed me my wallet. I removed one of my calling cards from my wallet and held it out to him. He said I could keep it, since he had already taken one. He looked sort of relaxed with his weight on one leg, but I could see that the look was deceiving and he held his carbine in ready position. He was young, probably mid to late twenties, black hair, and indigenous-Caucasian mix, not large physically, but well put together, maybe a runner, or swimmer.

"I saw you park your Audi, walk up to the buildings and come back and start searching the ground and looking under these cars. I know you are not a student, or faculty member. Would you mind telling me who you are, and what you are doing here?"

"Hi! My name is Orville Fletcher. I work as a security consultant. I was here last night and lost a favorite pen, and I was walking the places I had been in hopes of finding it. I saw something shiny under this car, but it was merely a piece of gum wrapper. I can see how my behavior would look somewhat bizarre and I should have spoken to security before starting a search. I hope you will forgive me for causing you any stress."

"Sorry I put you through the rigors just now, but we have had a few scary incidents on and around the campus, and you didn't fit the profile of our normal traffic. I will keep an eye out for your pen. What kind was it?"

"Black with gold trimmed, Parker. Had my initial and last name."

"I'll tell my coworkers to keep an eye out. Have a good day?"

"You know my name, may I ask yours?"

"Guzman, Silas Guzman."

I reached out and we shook hands.

"I could use a man of your training Silas. If you would be interested, give me a call at the number on my calling card. If I am not in, you can set up an appointment with my secretary. Her name is Yaneth."

"Are you serious."

"Of course I am."

"I may call you."

He turned back towards the guardhouse and I walked to my Audi, knocking a little dust off my shirt and pants on the way. I had an idea of what I had retrieved from under the car and now had in my shirt pocket, but I didn't want to hang around any longer in the parking lot, I couldn't inspect it while driving on the winding road back to the boulevard and I didn't have time to look for a pullover. I pushed the buttons on my Casio Watch to get into the stopwatch mode and then I started the timer as I started the engine. I backed out of the parking slot and drove out of the parking lot and left the campus through the East gate. Once at the bottom of the hill below the East Gate, I had to wait for two cars on the main street to pass the exit, before making a sharp left turn onto it. That street paralleled the Campus going back towards the Main Gate.

It was the same narrow road where Raul's first incident occurred. There were three dogleg turns on the way up the hill. I figured that the first attempt on Raul occurred in one of these three sharp curves. I decided to drive at a moderate speed back to Vista Hermosa Boulevard, although on that portion of the road it would have been impossible to drive anything more than moderate speed. I passed the Landivar Main Gate at the three-minute mark. I passed the Guatemalan American School in a little over four minutes. One minute later I reached the base of the hill and started along the valley floor. At six minutes and fifty seconds I reached the other end of the valley and started up the grade towards Channel Seven. At seven minutes and forty seconds I was where the houses start and I reached the intersection of Vista Hermosa Boulevard at eight minutes and thirty seconds. I turned west onto the Boulevard and made the ten-minute mark approximately where the second attempt on Raul occurred.

I pressed the button on my Casio to switch to time mode and noted that it was 3:30, time to head back. I pulled into the Etisa parking lot fifteen minutes before I was supposed to meet Roberto and Mike at the hotel. When I pulled into the parking lot, I noticed that Roberto's car and Mike's motorcycle were there. I retrieved my briefcase containing my notes and the device from the trunk and headed to the office. Mike and Roberto exited the elevator that I was getting ready to board. I signaled them and they turned back into the elevator as I got on. There were two others on board, so we just rode in silence up to the fifth floor. The other riders continued on up. As we stepped into the office, I said that we might as well hold our meeting there in my office. Yaneth was on the phone with someone. I signaled for her to put them on hold for a second. Once they were on hold, I told her to come on into my office once she had finished with the call.

As I sat down at my desk, I removed my day-timer from my shirt pocket, and then dug out the parts I had retrieved from under the car. There were three short pieces of insulation, approximately one inch long. They were of the same colors and gauges as the wiring that extended from the device. I knew they were from the device. They had waited until arriving in the parking lot to strip the wires. I doubted that the pieces of insulation would be any help in solving the puzzle, but finding them was another confirmation that the night before hadn't been a dream, as if the bruises I carried were unconvincing. The little pieces of insulation were just catching Roberto's attention when Yaneth walked in. I told Roberto that I would explain later.

I started out the meeting by asking each of them to report on their assignments.

Yaneth was first with, "Hugo Salinas called requesting that you meet him for lunch at the *Club Guatemala* on Thursday the twenty-first, or Friday the twenty-second."

"Set it up for Friday, the 22nd."

She told me of a few other calls, two of which I needed to phone back on. Mike suggested what to do on one of the calls I would be returning. With nothing else to report, she handed me the cash I had requested that morning.

I looked to Mike and he told me that he was able to obtain the information I had requested from Landivar. He had started checking into Alfaro's competitors. He had a partial list and expected to complete it along with a description of the interrelationships, by next Monday afternoon. He had a realtor friend looking into recent move-ins and vacant properties close to Raul's house. The same realtor would acquire a list of Raul's neighbor's. He couldn't do much more since he was going to help ferry the family to Tikal.

Roberto had been able to contract his two friends to help with the surveillance. Alberto would start a twelve-hour shift that day at 6 p.m., ending the next morning at 6 a.m. José would relieve Alberto at 6 a.m. and end at 6 p.m. and so forth. Roberto said that they were looking for a third man for the seventh day, but until we got him, they would cover the seven days a week. Getting a third man just for a day is not so easy, since most guard shifts go from 7:00 to 7:00, but we needed 6:00 to 6:00 to cover Raul's schedule. Anyway, we had the two in place starting that day. Roberto told me that they each had their own motorcycle. That was something I hadn't thought of, but very necessary with as mobile as Raul was. Roberto had a picture of each to show the Alfaros.

I told them about my time measuring trip up to Landivar. Roberto commented that I could be headed to a wrong conclusion with the times I had marked. We didn't have any more time to discuss it, since it was 4:15. I informed Roberto that I wanted him to be in the meeting with the Alfaros. I gathered up the three pieces of insulation and stuck them in a used envelope, which I placed in my briefcase. I snapped the briefcase shut and carried it as Roberto and I headed over to the hotel. As we exited the elevator, we noticed that it had rained, but was not raining then. We decide to walk to the hotel. The air had cooled during the half hour that we were in our meeting and even though it wasn't raining, we got a little wet from the dripping trees, and had to jump the water next to the curbs at the two intersections we crossed. I thought: 'Maybe walking wasn't such a good idea after all.'

We were shaking water out of our hair and I was drying my briefcase with a handkerchief as we entered the hotel lobby five minutes before our scheduled time. The Alfaros were waiting on a bench in front of the staircase leading from the lobby up to the second floor convention rooms. I presented Roberto as we stepped to the elevators. There were three elevators and I laughed as I read a sign taped to the middle elevator doors. The others looked at me to see what I was laughing at, but I was the only one that understood enough English to find humor in the translation, 'Out of Work', instead of 'Out of Order'. We took one of the operating elevators up to the fifth floor suite that Yaneth had reserved.

Jorge was a *get to it* businessman, so we didn't have to go through much formality. We sat down on the love seat and two wing back chairs and started the meeting. Jorge started the meeting by handing me a check in the amount of $5,000 made out to the corporation. He said that he decided to bring it to the meeting instead of sending it to the office. I thanked him and said that was just fine. I explained that I didn't have any receipts with me. He said not to worry, we could give him one later. I handed the check to Roberto to give to Yaneth, since I did not plan to go to the office on Friday.

I then asked Raul if he had observed anything since our meeting on Monday. He stated that everything seemed pretty normal. He mentioned that he had seen me exiting the parking area at Landivar that afternoon. I confessed that I was so involved in what I was doing that I had not noticed him. He had gone to do some research at the Landivar Library, knowing that he would not be able to make it just before his classes, due to the meeting we were holding.

I then asked him, "When you were traveling with one guard, where did he normally sit?"

Raul answered, "In the right hand passenger seat. Why do you ask that?"

"There are a couple of reasons, but first let me ask, "Has the guard always sat in that position?"

Raul answered, "At first they always sat behind me, which was fine if I had a friend, or family members with me, but if it was just me, I preferred they sit in front. When they sit behind me, I feel like a taxi driver."

I explained, "Now to answer part of your question. The other part of the answer will be obvious in a moment. Generally speaking an expert bodyguard when working alone, will place himself behind the driver for several reasons. One, he has more freedom of action with his gun and can better control movement in all four directions, front, back, and both sides. If bodyguards are in pairs, then the best arrangement is one behind the driver they are protecting and one to his side in the front passenger seat. Well-trained bodyguards, never mess with anything but guarding. They don't carry groceries, or school bags, or do anything that might compromise their effectiveness in protecting their person. They should be strong enough to tell an employer, that he should not be requesting such compromising services."

I pulled the device out of my briefcase and placed it on the coffee table. Then I remembered the little pieces of insulation and emptied them from the envelope. As I laid them by the loose wire ends, it was obvious that they had been stripped from those wires. I then told them what had happened the night before, while Raul was in his class. They sat in silent awe as I related the incident. I didn't think the part about my falling on the scaffold would add any relevance to our discussion and it surely wouldn't enhance my image, so I left that out. After I finished the part that I knew, Roberto added that he had followed Raul home last night and hadn't observed anything or anyone suspicious.

I hadn't said anything about where his guards were during the episode I had related, but Raul asked. I related that part to him and told him and Jorge that his guards were another matter we needed to discuss. I then let Roberto explain how the device was intended to operate.

He started by explaining, "Upon detonation the device would kill or at least incapacitate the guard. Simultaneously it would destroy the right front tire and force Raul to stop the vehicle immediately. At the place where it was intended to detonate, you would have been in heavy traffic and driving between thirty and forty kilometers per hour. A less skilled driver may have gone off the road, but I suspect that Raul would have been able to make a controlled stop. Nevertheless, if the car had left the roadway, it would have done so at no more than twenty kilometers per hour, which in the area it was intended to happen would have left the car upright and Raul merely shaken and vulnerable. The perpetrators could have easily controlled the situation. I suppose they would have had one or two of their men dressed as National Policemen to keep the traffic moving while a couple of their men, quickly moved Raul to one of their vehicles. End of the capture part of the operation!"

Finally, Roberto explained that he figured the device was intended to detonate somewhere in the valley between the Guatemalan American School and the ascent to the Boulevard. I interrupted him at that point to remind him that I had driven the route that afternoon, specifically for the purpose of timing it, and that the ten-minute mark I had detected was a good ways down Vista Hermosa Boulevard.

Roberto explained that he had followed Raul home for the past three nights and although he hadn't timed it, he was pretty sure that the ten minute mark would fall somewhere in the Valley. At my puzzled look, he clarified that I had driven the route during the afternoon, not after the evening classes, when all the students were exiting.

Obviously, I hadn't thought of that. I shared my thought that the open valley had seemed like the best place to perpetrate a kidnapping, but was puzzled by the fact that the timer was set for more time than it had taken me to drive it.

Raul asked, "If they wanted to be specific about the location why would they use a timed device, rather than one with a remote control, with which they could control the precise location?"

I started to explain my thoughts, but yielded to Roberto, who was more versed on the subject.

Roberto began explaining: "There are several reasons to use the device we are looking at rather than a remote control device. First of all, remote control devices are not as dependable as a timing device. Even those frequencies supposedly reserved for military use, are widely used throughout the country. It is also complicated to set up antennae that would transmit and receive to or from a device on the underside of a moving vehicle. Frequencies can vary with such factors as distance, humidity, or even bouncing off of other objects or electrical devices, such as a car radio, tape deck, or a garage door opener. The device may have gone off as you (pointing to Raul) were leaving the parking lot, or when you were turning off your alarm, or maybe never. A transmitter-receiver would have to be larger than this device and would be harder to install. Even my friends in G-2 were impressed with the simplicity of the design and sophistication of this device."

Jorge was in deep thought and perspiring. He said, "Who would want my son so badly to go to that much trouble? We are obviously not dealing with amateurs. These are determined people. I haven't felt this threatened since the Sandinistas were out to get me."

He then asked three questions in succession: "Can you guys handle this? Should I be in line over at the U.S. Embassy soliciting visas for my family? What is your game plan?"

I answered: "I think so, maybe, and we have a few ideas."

Jorge gave me a puzzled look, since he wasn't sure what I was answering.

I clarified: "I think we can handle the situation. As to whether you should get your family out of the country; that is a very personal decision that only you and your family can make. If I assure you that everything is under control and tell you to keep them here and something happens, I would feel responsible. I am not willing to make that kind of call. I will tell you that sending your family abroad may not solve the problem. Although the U.S. is much safer than here, determined enemies have been known to successfully carry out operations in the U.S. You may remember the assassination of the former Chilean Ambassador, Orlando Letelier, in D.C. The lack of prevalent danger in the U.S. also produces a lack of prevention and protection. Also you would be faced with the decision as to when, if ever, it would be safe to return to Central America. As to your last question, we do have a plan and we intend to be flexible enough to constantly improve on our plan."

Jorge, who had been on the edge of the chair, scooted back and said, "Let's hear it!"

I asked, "Did you work up a list of enemies?"

Jorge pulled his attaché up on his lap, opened it and handed me a sheet of paper and said, "The names above the line are potential enemies that I can think of, and the few below the line are names that my wife and children came up with. I need to clarify, that we don't feel that any of these people could possibly be motivated to harm us in the way we are seeing here. Frankly I can't imagine anyone that would perpetrate what you are describing and if you had shown me this device before the attempt last week on Raul, I would have figured you were the problem."

I laid the papers on the table where Roberto could read them along with me. As I read down the list of names, I recognized a few, some of them prominent citizens of the community. I looked up and told Jorge and Raul that our next step would be for them to write a brief description of their interaction with each of the names they had listed and I asked them how soon they would be able to get us that additional information.

Jorge said that they could have it by the afternoon of the following day. I suggested that they continue searching their minds for other potential enemies going back as far as four or five years.

Next I explained that there were five of us working directly on their problem and a few others helping with research and analysis. I suggested that they get bodyguards that were more professional. I told them that in addition to the guards' failure to watch Raul and his car at Landivar, that we had observed numerous other in-attentions to detail. I described a couple of the problems, such as the motorcycle guard driving off as soon as Raul was inside, rather than remaining posted outside on Tuesday evening. I told them that whether they decided to stay, or go, as long as they were in Guatemala, they needed better guards.

Jorge and Raul expressed surprise at how much we knew about Raul and his guards' movements and particularly how unaware they were that we had been that close without any of them or their guards noticing.

Jorge then asked if we had any solutions for improving the bodyguard situation. Roberto handed him a sheet with the phone numbers and contact persons at *Wackenhut, SIS* and *Ebano*. Roberto said he had talked to all three of the contacts and that Jorge merely needed to mention Roberto's name.

I suggested that Jorge consider a 24 hour guard service for himself, Raul, his wife and daughters and one to remain at home, whether they were there, or not. I told him that it might be less expensive and less traumatic for his wife and daughters to spend a few weeks in the U.S., if they had someone to stay with. He answered that they did have relatives in Florida, Texas and California.

Raul interjected that it was six o'clock and he had an exam at seven and couldn't afford to miss it.

Jorge thought our ideas about guards and his wife and daughters traveling to the states were good, and thanked us for all we were doing and stated that he definitely felt better with us on the case. I told him that I would be in the Petén from Friday through Saturday evening, but that he should feel free to contact Roberto for anything that he felt we could do. I confirmed that he had my home phone number.

That was all there was to talk about at the moment. We gathered our things, shut off the lights and descended together to the lobby. While in the elevator, Roberto suggested that just he accompany Raul to Landivar. Both Raul and Jorge thought it was a good idea. We continued on down in the elevator to the basement parking. As we walked over to where Raul had his BMW parked, his guards sauntered over from where they were visiting with the parking attendant near the exit ramp. While Roberto checked under Raul's car with his flashlight Jorge told Raul's guards that they could take off for the night. Raul and Roberto left and Jorge insisted on dropping me off at the Etisa Building parking.

I thought, 'Great! I get to be home in time for dinner with the family tonight. I will surprise them. I had told Linda not to plan on me, since I did not know how long the meeting with the Alfaro's would last. 'We'll have some fun together and a good nights rest before the flight to the Petén tomorrow.' I was suddenly hungry and wondered what Linda had prepared for dinner. I probably should have phoned home before leaving the hotel. 'Naw', better to surprise them! If I am lucky, they will all be at the table and I can make it in the garage and up the stairs without them hearing. It's worth a try.

CHAPTER 10
FRIDAY, AUGUST 8
TIKAL

We had a relaxing evening at home on Thursday. After dinner, the boys took turns playing games on the MacIntosh and the younger girls played checkers while the rest of us read books in the living room with Susan and Lynne entertaining us on the piano and flute, respectively. For a while the two of them practiced for a special musical number they were giving at church on Sunday, then Lynne read with the rest of us while Susan kept playing great classical music. Several of us drifted off to the bedrooms around 9:30. At 10:30 when I went out to secure the house and turn on the alarm, I discovered several of the children taking turns on the computer. I closed that down and shooed all of the children to bed, reminding them that I would not listen to any tired whiners when we were traveling the next day.

I awoke at 5:30 on Friday morning and went over some of Yaneth's notes and signed some checks she had placed in a manila envelope. I then spent a half hour studying the flight charts and making my flight plan.

I finished up in the den at 6:30 a.m., took a shower, was out of the house and headed over to the airport by 7:00 a.m., which was only five minutes from the house. Ralph's hangar wasn't open for service until 8:00 a.m., but his guard was supposed to be on duty. I banged and yelled at the hangar door for about five minutes, wondering how the guard could be so deaf. While I was in the middle of a bang, the guard silently rode up behind me on his bike and scared the crap out of me by merely saying "hola". It caused a few seconds delay for me to return his greeting.

He reached through an opening in the small door and unlocked a padlock. Once we got in the small door, we pulled the pins on the big sliding doors and the two of us pushed them open. As requested, the

Skymaster was in front, facing out. We hooked up the tow bar. Then he pulled and steered with the tow bar, while I pushed on the wing strut to move the plane out onto the apron in front of the hangar. The guard cleaned the windshield while I did a 360-degree check out of the plane. I noticed the right main tire a little low on air, so I asked him to check all three tires and fill them to the required pressure. He did that while I completed the inside check and set the instruments.

I left the Skymaster ready for flight at 7:25 a.m. and headed over to MAG to see if Mike was there yet. He was. He had just finished checking out the Stationair. The Stationair 206 carried six seats, just like my Skymaster. It is a single engine aircraft and only 200 pounds shy of carrying as much as the twin engine Skymaster, but this one did not have a luggage pod. Since there was going to be eleven of us, we had one more seat than we needed, so we decided to remove one of the rear seats to allow space for a cooler and some baggage. We took the right rear seat out which is next to the door and would make it easier for us to load. We finished by 7:40 a.m. and Mike accepted my invitation to have breakfast with us. He followed me home in his pickup so that we would have enough room for the family and the luggage.

The family was already at the breakfast table when we entered. The food was spinning on the lazy susan and the forks and china were clanging. After a couple of attempts at getting their attention, Linda had to physically take hold of two of the younger children that were sitting next to her to move them over a space so that Mike could sit by us. Mike and his wife only had one son. I could tell that he was a little taken by the feeding frenzy, so I explained that he better get some food on his plate before it all disappeared. We were still eating and chatting as some of the children finished and started leaving the table. I told the children to gather their things and place them at the entrance to the living room and to report there in fifteen minutes. At 7:30 a.m. we all met in the living room, except Susan, who operated on a slower clock than the rest of us. We finally got her to join us for family prayer and then we loaded the car and the pickup.

We drove both vehicles to MAG. The Stationair cruised twenty MPH slower than my Skymaster, so we figured to get him ready to go first. Susan, Valerie and the boys would fly with Mike, on this leg. They took the large cooler, a couple of small bags and some fishing gear that fit better in the Stationair than in our Skymaster. The rest of us headed over to Younger's hanger to load up the Skymaster with the remaining luggage. We loaded the luggage in the pod and were getting in the plane when Ralph Younger stepped over to wish us well. I noticed that the sky was beautiful as we taxied out to the runway. We were taxiing to the run-up area at the end of the runway when Linda pointed out that Mike was on his ground roll for take off in the Stationair. We waved to the kids in his plane as they waved to us. Five minutes later we were playing catch up with them as we flew out to the north. It was 8:55 a.m. local time.

I held the Skymaster under 9,000 feet until we passed Rabinal VOR station, twenty-six miles north of Guatemala City. From Rabinal, I was cleared to 11,500 feet. I switched over to an agreed frequency to talk to Mike. He said that he was over Cobán, which was twenty-five miles to the north of my position. Although normal cruise for the Skymaster was a little faster than his Stationair, the climb speed was about the same. Now that we were both at cruise altitude, I would start to gain a little on him. There were a few clouds around the peaks, but the rest was crystal clear. Seeing the clear skies gave me an idea.

I said, "Hey Mike, it is such a clear day over the mountains, what about us flying a little East of course and see if we can get a view of Lanquín and Semuc?"

Mike answered, "I was just thinking the same. It looks pretty clear from here to the North East. I will head that way and tell you what it's looking like as I get closer to Lanquín."

"Roger, that."

It felt good to be flying with a full aircraft across these mountains on a beautiful day. Flying in Central America is especially rewarding due to the rugged terrain and lack of roads. A straight flight in our type of aircraft to Flores, Petén took from one hour to one hour and fifteen minutes. If we would have made the trip in a vehicle, it would have taken us two days on treacherous winding roads and the wear and tear on the vehicle would have been like six months of driving in the U.S., not to mention what it would have done to our bodies.

We crossed to the East of Chixoy Reservoir, then over Cobán. At that point we were leaving the high central mountains and over-flying lower mountains with narrow valleys. Guatemala is a country of beautiful contrasts. The Southern third consists of coastal plains with swift rivers that flow from the mountains and end on black sand beaches. The central third consists of high volcanic mountains with several active volcanoes along the chain of fire. On the north, the mountains descend onto an uplifted shelf of limestone that continues all the way north to the Mexican beaches on the Yucatan Peninsula. This northern area is pocked with sinkholes and numerous caverns.

Mike radioed to say he was about five miles from Lanquín and that the whole area was clear. He said that he was going to make a couple of circles over Semuc Champey. I told him that I intended to do the same with my group.

We had been to Lanquín and Semuc Champey a couple of times in four-wheel drive vehicles. On our last trip we had gotten stuck in the mud twice and suffered three flat tires, but it was a fun trip. The main attraction at Lanquín was a cavern, which had a sizable stream flowing out of its mouth. Within a hundred yards after exiting the cavern, the stream cascades over a water fall into a crystal clear pool, thirty feet below. My children had a ball jumping and diving into the pool of water. I took the dare for one dive. The undercurrent pulls you down and spits you out on the other side of the pool. It gave me enough of a thrill that I couldn't muster the courage for a second jump. Linda was the smart one. She walked down a path to get to the pool.

Semuc Champey is located only twelve miles beyond Lanquín, but it takes over an hour in vehicle. It is worth the trip. I believe that Semuc Champey was formed eons ago when the Cahabón River found an exposed entrance to a cavern under the limestone shelf. Most of the river disappears and flows under the shelf. About five percent flows slowly on top, forming numerous shallow pools, some of them heated by volcanic gases. The part of the river that flows under the shelf and the part that flows on top, join in a rush about seven hundred yards downstream. The area is in the midst of high mountain rain forests with a great variety of flora and fauna, including the rare quetzal bird. Even on busy holidays there were usually no more than fifty people in the pools and surrounding 600 acres of parkland. It was one of those trips that only the hardy tourists made.

Six minutes after Mike reported leaving the area I descended to 6,000 feet and began circling over Semuc Champey. The whole scene was beautiful from overhead. The pools were totally transparent. The difference in depth and temperature of each pool caused them to take on various shades of green and blue. The different shades and colors were barely noticeable when we had visited the pools on the ground, but they were very impressive from above. My girls were all "oohing" and "aahing". Lynne exclaimed, "This is beautiful, Dad." as though I had painted it for the family.

I passed Mike about midway between Chinajá and Sayaxche. We waggled our wings at each other. Just South of La Libertad we encountered a solid layer of stratocumulus clouds. The tower in Flores informed us that they were under the same solid layer, so I decided to practice my Instrument Flight skills. I requested an IFR clearance from the Tower. They radioed back in couple of minutes with the clearance. At Flores we descended on instruments in a VOR approach and broke out of the clouds at one thousand feet above terrain. I reported the runway in sight and we landed. I followed the flagman's directions to the East end of the ramp and noticed that it was 10:15 .am. when I shut down the engines.

I saw the Stationair on final approach as we were exiting the Skymaster. By the time we had unloaded the luggage, Mike was pulling in beside our plane. I told the ramp attendant that we would not need fuel, but could use a luggage cart. Both aircraft had enough fuel to make a couple round trips and we were only making one. Linda and the children walked on into the terminal, while Mike and I unloaded the luggage from the Stationair. By the time we had secured the planes, the ramp attendant was back with a four-wheeled cart, much bigger than we needed for our luggage.

Once we were in the terminal, I asked the attendant to wait a moment with the luggage, while Mike and I went into the Civil Aviation Office to close our flight plans. The procedure was simple. They required pilots to personally inform them of their point of departure, and how long and where they would be staying. The formalities would only take a couple of minutes, but they always liked to visit, so it took closer to 10 minutes. The family was impatiently milling around the terminal when we came out of the Aviation Office. I took Linda's hand and said, "let's go!" and it was as though I had released a spring. The four youngest nearly trampled us getting through the door ahead of us. Forget about any of them holding the door. If I hadn't already expected it, the returning door would have hit us.

As we stepped up to the curb, a white Mitsubishi Van pulled up in front of us with the driver shouting Tikal out the passenger window.

I leaned in the Window and asked how much he would charge to be ours exclusively from then until 2 P.M. the next day. He asked where we would be going. I told him that we would go to Tikal that day and come back to the Cabaña Hotel for the night and then back to Tikal the next day and return to the hotel and then the airport, with a probable side trip to Santa Elena somewhere in between those points. He thought for a moment, then held up three fingers, –which I knew meant three hundred Quetzals. I suggested two hundred fifty. He said two hundred eighty. I walked around to his side of the car. By then Daniel and Asher were stuck to me like glue. They knew what my next step would be and that was the part they liked best.

I pulled out a 25-cent coin and showed the driver both sides. Then I told him to call it. He smiled and said if he won he would get three hundred. I said no! If he won he got two hundred eighty and if I won I would pay two hundred fifty. He said, "okay". I flipped the coin into the air. He called heads while it was still in the air. I grabbed it with my right hand and slapped it onto the back of my left hand and I raised my hand for us both to see that it had fallen tails. He exhaled, "¡Púchica, que suerte!" –Wow what luck.

I walked back around to the passenger side with Daniel and Asher ahead of me declaring to the rest of the family, "Dad won, like always." I didn't always win, but for some reason I won a lot in their presence, so they thought that I had some kind of magic with coins.

We loaded the luggage in the back, Mike tipped the attendant and we all climbed in. On the way to the hotel to leave off the luggage, the driver asked for an advance payment of a hundred Quetzals so that he could put gas in the car. He didn't have the attendant fill the tank or put in a hundred Quetzal's worth. He asked for fifty Quetzals worth. When the attendant returned fifty Quetzals in change to the driver, he pocketed it. The drivers never had gas in their cars and always had to get an advance at the beginning of a run. It seemed as though the idea of transporting tourists was something that occurred to them at the last moment, not something that was their daily calling.

Our hotel was close to the airport and consisted of a series of thatch roofed, wooden cabins on stilts out over Lake Petén Itza. The cabins were joined by plank walkways to a larger similarly styled building, also on stilts, that housed the restaurant, lobby and offices. Linda and the children remained in the van, while Mike and I walked into the lobby.

I asked the bellman to bring our luggage from the car while I checked us in. Mike went out with him to make sure he left the smaller coolers in the van. On my way out of the lobby I met the bellman on the way in with our luggage. I told him to just leave it in one of our rooms and I reached for my wallet to get him a tip. He told me that my friend had already tipped him.

As I walked up to the van Mike was saying goodbye to the family. While I accompanied the family to Tikal, he was going to be meeting in Santa Elena with PPL Oil Company's Peten manager and his head of security. Mike had opened that account for us just six months before. He had cultivated some mutual acquaintances and was able to set up a meeting for both of us with the company president and his security head. It was in that meeting that I was awed at how much knowledge Mike had about the petroleum industry and the peculiar security risks the petroleum industry faced. I went into the meeting prepared to lead the discussion and ended up listening and learning.

Mike pretty well ran that account for us. I had an open invitation to their security meetings, but unless there was some special need for me, I usually deferred to Mike. He was the man they counted on.

I asked Mike if we could drop him off anywhere. He said he had time to freshen up in the hotel before our client picked him up for their meeting.

The rest of the family was loaded in the van, anxious for us to get on our way. The boys were in the front seat talking the driver's leg off, so I got in the back and sat next to Linda. We ate our lunch from the coolers on the way to Tikal and pulled through the park gate at noon and parked over by the Jaguar Hotel on the far side of the parking area. During the 70's there was a runway that ended right in front of the hotel. I landed and took off right there in front of the ruins numerous times. During that period, the Guatemalan government actually kept a contingent of customs and immigration officials at the site. I thought it was nice, being able to fly directly from the neighboring countries to the ruins, but in 1982, the conservationists convinced the Guatemalan government to close the runway. The conservationists pulled some powerful allies under their umbrella of protecting the forests. They brought in the archaeologists, and the mayors of Santa Elena and Flores to help their case.

The archaeologists' argument was that the vibrations and exhaust gases from the aircraft were harmful to the ancient edifications. The communities of Flores and Santa Elena thought it was a good idea, because it would mean the tourists had to come through their airport, stay at their hotels, eat at their restaurants and travel in their taxis. I think the conservationists and archaeologists had a flimsy case, since vehicle traffic is probably more harmful to the ruins than aircraft, but in the end the economies of Santa Elena and Flores were the factors that swayed the undecided.

The old runway in front of the ruins became host to a very nice stand of five-year-old Ceiba trees. Even though it was convenient to fly in at the ruins, I liked the idea of planting the trees. It seemed a hopeless cause though, since we would never catch up with the number of trees that were stolen by poachers, or destroyed by the ancient practice of slash and burn throughout the Mayan kingdom

The walk down the jungle path to the Gran Plaza at Tikal was as pleasant as I had remembered it. The path was a little muddy in places and the growth of underbrush along the sides was very dense during the wet season, which included August. I liked to hear the animals move on the ground and through the trees. The howler monkeys were particularly impressive with their growl-grunt that sounded like that of a large predator. It was 12:30 p.m. and there weren't many people in the plaza. Perhaps most of the tourists were back at the Jaguar Hotel Restaurant having lunch. The children scattered around the plaza to explore the main buildings and stalae. Lynne, Susan and Valerie walked over to the Central Acropolis on the South side of the Gran Plaza. Linda and I walked over to the base of the Temple of Masks, where we sat down on the bottom step, looking towards the Gran Jaguar Temple.

The steps up the Gran Jaguar were temporarily closed for restoration. We wouldn't have climbed the stairs if they had been open. Linda went up them the first time we came to Tikal in 1979, but she had never wanted to since. On that occasion, she just kept climbing until she reached the top. She didn't notice how steep the steps were, or how high she had climbed until she reached the top. She turned to look out over the Gran Plaza and became so frightened she quickly sat down and crawled to the center of the top platform. I didn't even know where she had gone, until I heard her scream, "Orville, help me!" When I located where the scream was coming from, I climbed the temple and helped her slowly descend backwards using her hands and feet to secure each step. She had never had the desire to climb another pyramid.

While the children explored the area, we just absorbed the tranquility of such a sacred place. The ancient culture that inhabited that area was indeed very learned and organized. Each time we visited that and other similar sites, we marveled at how they could build structures that were still standing centuries after they had left them, in spite of the ravages of time, climate and natural disasters. We had learned a little, but could learn a lot more from such people.

From the Gran Plaza we went to the Jaguar Priest Temple, the Bat Palace and then to Temple IV, which was the highest of all in the Tikal group. Linda watched Margaret and Edna explore the adjoining N Complex while the rest of us climbed Temple IV. It was quite a challenge, because on some parts, it was like rock climbing. There were select hand and foot holds, so we had to climb with caution. Temple IV stood nearly a hundred feet above the jungle and afforded a beautiful view of Tikal, which itself is on a promontory above the surrounding area. Although the sky was overcast, the visibility was great. We could see ten or fifteen miles of jungle in all directions. I told everyone to be careful and then laid down and shut my eyes for a while. I was feeling like a nap and it also helped keep me from being nervous as the children ran around on top and stood near the edge to look over. From the time I started raising a family I became convinced that survival to adulthood is all a miracle.

We made it down without any mishaps. As we came around to where Linda and the younger girls were waiting, we saw that they were feeding a tepiezcuinte, which is related to the possum, albeit a larger, hairier version. They had purchased some miniature bananas from a vendor, and were giving them a half at a time to the animal. The boys talked Margaret and Edna each out of their last banana like they were going to feed the tepiezcuinte, and then they popped the bananas in their own mouths. It brought such a loud protest from the girls that it scared the animal away, which made them even angrier.

Linda looked at her watch and said aloud to the group, "It is now 4:15. Your father and I are walking a direct route back to the parking lot. The rest of you can explore other areas and meet us at the van by a quarter after five. Stay on the paths and in no less than pairs."

We walked leisurely back to the parking lot. I loved my children, but I cherished my alone time with Linda. We are able to talk through a few decisions on our way back to the van. We got back early enough that we decided to go on into the Jaguar Hotel for a soft drink. We were able to continue our conversation while we drank in the cool shade of the dining area. Everyone was back at the van more or less at the time we had agreed. Daniel and Asher had found a stream somewhere, because they arrived streaked with mud. The drive back to Flores was relaxing and we pulled up to our hotel at just after dark.

We agreed to meet in the dining room within a half hour as we all headed for the showers. With eight children, orders and agreements were merely a stated objective. The hotel only served breakfast and dinner. The tourists that visited the region did not hang around the hotels during the day. They were there to visit the ruins, period. For lunch, the hotel kitchen served sandwiches, chips and drinks, which they also packaged in a box for those who wanted to take a picnic to the ruins.

The bathrooms only had showers. Few people wanted to sit in a tub in the tropics. The beds in the cabins were standard double beds. Our cabin had two beds. Mike and the boys shared a cabin with two beds and the girls all shared a cabin with three beds. The cabins and the dining area were furnished with plain but comfortable wooden furniture. Upholstery was not practical in that humid climate. The dining area adjoined a lounge area where people congregated to visit, play table games and read. There were no TV's anywhere in the hotel. It was all open with no doors or air conditioning, just overhead fans that were numerous and turning at full speed. The concept was to cool the guests and to ward off the mosquitoes.

It was 7:15 p.m. when about three fourths of us entered the dining area. There was a group of eight or ten at several tables pushed together and three couples already seated at individual tables. A good number of the guests turned as we entered and most everyone greeted us with a "Buenas Tardes", as would be customary in this setting. We returned the greeting as we followed the waiter to two long tables that would seat six each. Mike joined us just as we were being seated.

"Hello Fletchers! Did you enjoy the ruins?"

Everyone shouted a 'hi' to Mike.

Linda answered: "We had a great day at the ruins. The weather was fantastic and the ruins were beautiful as always. Too bad you were too busy to be with us."

"Yeah, I would have enjoyed that. I am glad I finished in time to spend the evening with you guys. I am anxious to see who I can beat at dominoes or checkers after the meal."

That brought a few challenges from the children. Lynne moved to another seat so that Mike could sit next to me.

I asked: "How was your meeting with the petroleum people?"

"After lunch, the manager invited me to accompany him and his security chief to their asphalt production facility in La Libertad. The visit to their plant made me aware of some particular security concerns here in the Peten that I need to discuss with you next week. We can probably expand our services to this client, but I need your advise on how much we can commit to and I need help in crunching the numbers on the costs of providing the additional service I have in mind."

"Are they pleased with our services so far?"

"Oh yes, they are and they are very interested in exploring other areas in which we may be able help them."

"Good. I can tell that you have established a great rapport with this client. We'll discuss your ideas with Roberto and Yaneth on Monday."

As the menus arrived, the rest of the children straggled in, except Susan, who operated at her own pace and hurry was not part of her vocabulary. The menu afforded a choice of two appetizers, two different fish meals and two different meat meals and 'flan' or cake for desert. For appetizers, Linda ordered the avocado salad and I ordered the "Ceviche", so we could share. About half of the family ordered either the typical meat filet plate or the sirloin tips; the rest of us went for either the broiled or pan-fried "White Fish".

The "White Fish" is native only to the Lake Petén Itza. I don't know if anyone has bothered giving it a scientific name since it is not found any place else in the world. At some ancient time in history after Lake Petén Itza was formed and isolated from the rest of the water world, the "White Fish" became as unique as the ecosystem it grew in. The lake where this fish has flourished is definitely a unique natural lake. It is approximately twenty miles long and three miles wide at it's widest. A large gentle watershed of forested hills feeds it with no major streams flowing into it, nor any streams draining it. The water drains through a hidden underground aquifer somewhere near the western shore that resurfaces about ten miles to the west of the lake as a pretty sizable stream.

White Fish is delicious with a light flesh that tastes very similar to trout, or fresh water bass. I wondered if it would still be around during my children's lifetime, but I doubted that it would survive for my grandchildren to taste. The problem was not in the consumption of the fish, but in the pollution of the water and reduction of its food chain due to a destruction of the watershed. Every year the water draining into the lake was more contaminated and less nourishing for any animal that inhabited the lake. The Petén province, along with the northern portions of two adjoining provinces, at one time made up one of the largest most flourishing jungles in the western hemisphere. It was a sponge for the smog and smoke produced by the industrial and consumer societies of Mexico and the U.S. Each year thousands of acres of jungle were cut by illegal loggers or burned by farmers. For every mile of road built into the area, ten square miles of jungle were destroyed. I realized that if something weren't done to reverse the trend, the whole northern part of Guatemala would become a barren landscape. Sadly, the same was happening in numerous other parts of the world. Most of Mexico's forest had disappeared by 1950. Only a few isolated pockets of forest have been preserved.

Thinking of the bleak future of our planet made me extra hungry for that disappearing fish variety. I was glad to see the waiter finish up taking our order. Susan arrived just after he went to the kitchen to place the order for the rest of us. We enjoyed a delicious relaxing meal, except for fighting off a couple of hardy mosquitoes that had found refuge from the fans under our table.

After dinner some of the girls went to the cabins to read, others along with Mike stayed in the lounge area for some table games. Margaret, Asher, Daniel and myself decided to try our luck at fishing in the lake.

We could have fished in front of the lounge or our cabins, but the boys thought the best spot would be off the pier that jutted into the lake on the outer edge of the circle of buildings. We begged some raw strips of chicken and beef from the kitchen, dowsed ourselves with mosquito repellant and grabbed the fishing gear from our cabins on the way to the pier.

The hotel had four spotlights projecting out over the surface of the water so that we could see our floaters if we didn't cast the lines too far out. Fifteen to twenty feet away from the pier seemed to have an abundance of hungry fish at about five feet depth. Mostly we ended up just feeding the fish, but we snagged several around six inches and smaller, which was plenty exciting for the children. Asher caught a twelve to fourteen inch white fish that weighed a little over a pound. It wasn't easy to convince him that it would not be good to eat by the time we arrived back in Guatemala City. The fish was just barely alive enough to swim away by the time I convinced him. We were still fishing at 9:30 when we heard an increasing roar out over the lake. It took me a few seconds to realize what it was and by the time we had-cranked in the lines, the rain had reached us. We ran towards the thatch covering of the walkways under some heavy drops, which turned into a deluge just as we reached shelter. Daniel volunteered to run back out to the end of the pier to empty the can of bait into the water. He was looking for an excuse to get wet, but I convinced him that there was plenty of fish right alongside and under our walkway.

As we headed to our cabins we noticed Mike and several of the girls, coming from the lounge area towards us. We were all ready for a good nights rest. Linda was in bed reading when I walked in.

She glanced up from her book and asked, "How was the fishing?

"Fine, the children had fun and we got to visit some. Asher caught a nice one about a foot long. It almost died before I could convince him to put it back in the lake. Margaret was into the fishing as much as the boys. How about the rest of you?"

"I only lasted through one game of checkers and then I came back to the room to read. That walking around the ruins wore me out. I have seen Tikal so many times now; I am beginning to lose some interest. I think only the older children understand what the ruins represent. The younger ones merely treat them as another place to romp and climb, which by the way, makes me nervous to watch them."

"I feel the same. It is hard to relax when the boys are hanging over the edge of something, or seeing if they can out-climb the tree animals. The only way I could relax on top of Temple IV was to take a nap."

"You took a nap on top of Temple IV! Orville, I can't believe that! The children were standing right next to the edge yelling over to the girls and me. Daniel and Asher were actually swinging out on some kind of bar or stake. I convinced the girls that we would be more comfortable over under the trees where you found us. I was thinking that if the boys could not see us; perhaps they would stop showing off for us. I assumed you were right there watching and supervising them. If you are going to go off alone with the children, especially on something like that temple, you have to keep them under control, you can't just let them....."

"Well I don't want to kill their fun and I remember how I used to climb everything there was to climb and most of the time my parents weren't even around. The truth is, I took a nap because it makes me nervous, just like it does you!"

"Well no one is climbing any of those temples tomorrow. In your over concern about not killing their fun, some of them are going to kill themselves, or at least, end up brain dead! Honey, you have to be more conscious of the dangers. Just because they don't put up warning signs like they do in the U.S., doesn't mean it is safe."

I knew she was right. I didn't have any more answers, but I didn't feel like admitting that yet. I went on into the bathroom to wash the fishing gear and hopefully let her cool down.

As I came out of the bathroom from washing the gear, she was standing outside the bathroom.

She threw her arms around my neck and said, "I am sorry I spoke the way I did."

"No, you were right. I should have taken better care of the children and kept them under control. That really was risky up on top of that Temple IV. What say we go somewhere other than Tikal tomorrow?"

"Like, what do you have in mind?"

"I was thinking maybe we could fly down to Sayaxche. There are two ancient ruins nearby and neither has any high temples, or we could take a quiet boat ride to Lake Petexbatún. That whole area along the river is really nice this time of year. What do you think?"

"Sounds good to me. Let's see how the rest of the family feels about your idea. You may have to juice up your description a little bit to convince the kids."

By the end of our conversation, we were sitting on the edge of the bed, brushing the dust off of our feet. Linda climbed into my arms as we lay down on the bed. I didn't discover if she had anything in mind, because I think I fell asleep within thirty seconds of when my head hit the pillow.

CHAPTER 11

SATURDAY, AUGUST 9

SAYAXCHE

I could never remember when I fell asleep and I slept like the dead, unless there was a sound or a feel of something unusual, *like then!*

I was falling off of Temple IV. I kept falling. No, I was in the plane! The motor was coughing and sputtering with a weird roughness to it, and I was going down! Then the motor was giving a high-pitched sound I had never heard it make before!

I awoke with a jerk and realized it was a dream, but strangely, I could still hear the motor. I sat up in bed and tried to understand the sound and then it hit me, it was a boat motor. Whew, I was not going down in the plane! Yeah, I was in a hotel on Lake Petén Itza. The boat must have started there by the cabins. I could tell that it was headed away, out into the lake, as the pitch increased and the sound diminished.

Linda mumbled, "Is everything okay?"

"Everything is fine dear, just a dream. Go back to sleep."

She did, as I eased out of bed.

I glanced towards the shaded window and saw that there was daylight. I checked my watch; it was 6 a.m. I got up, showered and dressed and left the room at 6:30. Linda was still asleep. I had to step softly on the walkway around the cabins so as not to disturb anyone. As I passed the room where Mike and the boys stayed, Mike cracked their door. He stepped out to join me. He liked the mornings too. We didn't say anything; we just signaled a 'howdy' wave with the hand. Once we got out of range of the cabins, Mike asked what I planned to do. I told him we were thinking we might go to see some of the sites around Sayaxche instead of returning to Tikal and asked him what he thought about the idea. He said he had only flown over Sayaxche, but had never landed, or driven there, and that it sounded interesting to him.

I told him that I had landed on the grass strip at Sayaxche several times in the Stationair he was now flying, but I had never done it in the Skymaster. I explained that it had been years since I had landed there, and suggested that we mosey over to the airport to see if anyone knew what condition the Sayaxche runway was in. There was nothing moving on the road at that hour, so we jogged the mile to the airport.

In the terminal we talked to the attendant in the flight planning office. He told us that he didn't know anything about the runway, but that he knew a couple of pilots that flew regularly into Sayaxche. He gave us the name of a pilot that we might find in a stall at the other end of the terminal. When we got to the stall, a young woman pointed to a pilot out on the ramp loading a Cessna 185. He was bent over with just his legs out of the plane when we walked up behind him and said hi rather loudly, so that he would know that he had company. The pilot finished adjusting a box in place before rising up and turning to return our greeting.

We each presented ourselves and I asked him, "Where you headed today?"

"I am taking some parts and parcels over to the oil company in El Naranjo."

I pointed to our aircraft and said, "We are thinking of flying into Sayaxche today in that Stationair and the Skymaster, and wondered if you have flown in there recently. I have landed a couple of times with the Stationair, but it was a while back."

"Yeah, just last week I took a couple of fellows that were headed to the Ceibal Ruins. What's your landing distance on that Skymaster?"

"About the same as a Stationair, but it's a lot heavier than a Stationair, so it wouldn't work too well on a soft field."

"You should be okay. The field is all drained well, except for the last 200 feet of the East end. One of the neighbors left some hogs on the field and they shoved enough dirt around to stop up the ditch on that end. The town council made him remove his animals, but they haven't fixed the ditch. I might take a couple of men with shovels and do it myself, if they don't get to it before the October rains."

"We sure appreciate the info. We are pretty full of people, but if you need to send any package to Sayaxche or the Capital, we would be happy to take it for you?"

"Naw, I don't need to send anything, but thanks for the offer. You said you been at Sayaxche before, so you probably already know that you need to be careful about the animals and people. I always make a low pass over the runway, before I set down."

"We'll do that. Thanks for the advice and have a good day."

When we left the airport, a car headed our way stopped and the driver leaned over and offered a ride. We took him up on the offer.

At breakfast we told the children that we were thinking of changing our agenda and visiting some of the sites near Sayaxche rather than going back to Tikal. I told them about a couple of archaeological sites near Sayaxche, Dos Pilas and El Ceibal. Then I told them a little about Lake Petexbatún. We took a vote. Eight voted for Sayaxche and the other three said they would go anywhere we took them.

In addition to our breakfast, we had the kitchen staff prepare us a dozen lunches. As we left the dining room, I noticed our van driver waiting in front of the hotel. While the family headed to the cabins to pack, I walked out to the Van.

I said, "Jorge, we are flying out this morning, instead of going back to Tikal."

"Oh, señor. I hope you have not a problem. (Sic.) Do some of you have illness?"

"No Jorge, we are all fine. We just decided to go see some sites in Sayaxche."

"Sayaxche good place, you like. I take you to Sayaxche for the same fare as Tikal!"

"Thanks Jorge, but it is on the way to the Capital. It is better for us to fly there."

"Very expensive to hire plane, cost less to ride with me."

"We have our own plane, Jorge. That is how we came to Flores yesterday."

"Oh, I think you come on commercial flight. I did not know you have plane. You get around very well in your own plane, right?"

"Yes we do, Jorge, but do not worry, I will pay you as agreed."

"That not necessary, sir. You should only pay yesterday and the ride to airport today."

"That is very kind of you Jorge. Let me settle up with the hotel and get the family packed. We will be out in a few minutes"

Everything went smoothly in getting the family out of the hotel and to the airport. After deducting the Q100 advance I had given the driver for fuel the day before, I paid him the remaining Q150 of the Q250 we had agreed to on Friday. He again insisted that I was paying him too much. I insisted that it was fair, since we had agreed to the two days. He thanked me profusely, and gave me a small card with his name stamped on it.

I was glad we were flying, instead of driving to Sayaxche. By vehicle it took a little over an hour, whereas in the planes it would take us only fifteen minutes.

Most of the communities in the Petén remained dependent on airplanes and the rivers for transportation. During the past fifty years the government had been able to build a few roads between major communities, but many of them were impassable in parts during the rainy season. The drive from the Capital to Flores was at least two days of grueling road during the dry season. In the wet season it would take several days. The only roads in the Petén that were kept passable during the wet season were between Flores and Tikal, Flores and Melchor de Mencos on the border with Belize, Flores and Poptun, and Flores and Sayaxche, which didn't actually reach Sayaxche, but to the Passion River in front of Sayaxche. From there one had to board a ferry over to Sayaxche.

I worked in the Sayaxche and Flores area several times in the early eighties, while I was living in Honduras. Most of the time I flew in, but there were a couple of occasions that I took the road to Flores and even beyond to Melchor de Mencos and Poptun. I was working on a freebee for the Guatemalan Government and an Archaeologist by the name of Arthur Denton that was working the Dos Pilas dig with a group from Vanderbilt. I had met Denton in the Hotel Camino Real at a lecture he was giving. In a conversation after the lecture, we discovered some common acquaintances from Indiana University. We hit it off and had dinner together several nights. On one of those occasions he commented that he and his hieroglyph expert had discovered that some key pieces had been recently removed from some steps on one of the palaces they were excavating in Dos Pilas. I was between jobs, so I offered to attempt to track the whereabouts of the missing pieces for expenses only. It took me a month, but I was able to track the pieces to the Mayor of one of the neighboring towns and a former Military base commander at Fray Bartolomé de las Casas. I didn't actually participate in the retrieval, just the locating. I never knew what if anything happened to the perpetrators. I just knew that the pieces were returned to the Dos Pilas site and Denton was forever grateful.

Linda stayed with the children in the terminal, while Mike and I filed our flight plan and then had a porter cart the luggage out to the planes. We figured it would be simpler loading and checking out the planes without the children running around. Once the luggage was secure and the planes ready to fly, I went in to escort the family through security. We had them buckled in their seats by 9:15 a.m. I started and communicated with the tower first. We had decided that I would takeoff and land first, since I was more familiar with the landing strip.

The Flores tower used one controller and one frequency to handle ground and air traffic, so I buttoned the mike and said: "Flores tower, this is November two six three two sierra, do you read me."

"We read you November two six three two sierra, go ahead."

"Three two sierra flying to Sayaxche today, request clearance and taxi instructions."

"Three two sierra, wind one three zero degrees at six knots, runway one zero in use, altimeter setting two nine nine six. Taxi to run-up area, hold short of runway."

I set the altimeter according to his instructions and said, "Three two sierra, roger. Taxi to run-up area, hold short of runway one zero."

As I was adding power and starting to roll, Mike came on his radio to tell them that he was headed to the same place as three two sierra and had copied the tower information they had given me. The tower controller cleared him to follow me to the run-up area.

While doing my run-up, I was listening to transmissions between the tower and an incoming aircraft. I buttoned my mike and said, Flores tower three two sierra ready for takeoff."

The tower came back with, "Hold short of active runway three two sierra, Fokker on three mile final."

"Three two sierra holding short."

I had anticipated before he told me that he was going to instruct me to hold short. The Fokker touched down, using about one half of the long runway. He made a u-turn on the runway and started to taxi back to the terminal.

The tower controller said, "Three two sierra, cleared to position and hold until Fokker exits runway."

"Three two sierra roger, cleared to position and hold pending exit of Fokker."

As soon as the Fokker left the runway, the tower cleared me for takeoff and a right turnout on course to Sayaxche. We were on our way.

It was 9:45 a.m. when we arrived over the grass runway at Sayaxche. The runway ran East and West. The municipality never bothered to mow it. They merely allowed the neighbors to pasture their sheep, goats and cattle. It was not too hard to scatter the animals, but the people were another matter. I lined up for a low pass over the runway. I usually did this at full speed for fun. One could not fully appreciate the speed of a plane unless you were doing it near the ground. The only time it was legal, and safe, to fly low was over a runway, so I took full advantage of the opportunity.

I was doing 180 mph as I straightened the Skymaster on final for a low pass from West to East. As we flew fifteen feet over the runway, the animals scattered to the sides along with their herders. The girls were squealing with laughter as I pulled up abruptly at the end of the runway. I made a wide turn and came back for one more pass about fifty feet above the runway, from East to West and slower, so as to visually check the runway conditions. I saw a few reflective glints off of the standing water near the East end, as reported by the pilot in Flores. By the time I made a wide circle West of the runway for landing, Mike radioed that he was holding to the North until I landed. I made my approach and sat it in smoothly as though I had been flying every day the previous week. My girls were duly impressed as we taxied off near the East end of the runway.

I turned the Skymaster so we were facing somewhat back towards the West where I could observe Mike's approach and then I shut down the engines, but left the Master switch and radios on. I radioed Mike to tell him that we were clear of the runway and that the runway was in okay condition. I saw his landing lights on final and kept watching as he brought the Stationair down towards the runway. He set it down smoothly, then the unexpected happened as a bike-rider rode out on the runway 500 feet in front of him. I pressed the button on the microphone to warn Mike, but before I could speak he reacted to the emergency. I heard the Stationair engine cough and then accelerate to full power and watched as the plane seemed to suspend itself, undecided whether to stay on the ground or take to the air. They were quickly overtaking the bike rider who was totally unaware of what was happening. The rider finally heard the roar of the plane behind him and looked over his shoulder. He immediately fell down to his right as the Stationair skimmed over him grabbing for air. I could see Mikes face as he pulled back on the control, climbing the plane on the border of a stall, ten feet above the ground, fifteen, twenty and then he veered left away from the center of the runway towards us, and roared directly over our Skymaster.

The door was on Linda's side. I reached across, unlatched the door and quickly climbed out over her. I ran out to the middle of the runway to look back and see where the Stationair had gone, hoping it hadn't caught any trees. I could see him through a break in the trees climbing safely, probably around 200 feet above ground. I noticed that the only break in the trees on our end of the runway was right behind the Skymaster. I ran over to locate the bike rider. I was wondering if he had been struck by the landing gear. He wasn't a he, but a she, and she was only shaken and scratched. She was sitting up sort of dazed. I walked her and her bike off of the runway, over to the Skymaster. The family was out of the plane by the time I got back.

I reached in the Skymaster, took the microphone and radioed Mike: "Mike, do you read me? Is everyone okay on board Mike?"

"We are a little shaken, but okay. Is the boy on the bike okay?"

"The boy is a girl and she too is a little shaken, but okay. You can land it now if you want. The runway is clear, but I will stay on the radio just in case. There are a few people standing along the sides to see if you have any more stunts to show. I suggest you fool them and just make a normal landing on this go around."

I saw the Stationair turn from base onto final approach with the landing lights shining right at us. He brought it in smooth, just like the previous landing, except he got to keep it on the ground that time. He taxied over next to the Skymaster and shut it down. I clicked off the master switch on the Skymaster and walked over as the kids were getting out of the Stationair.

Daniel exclaimed, "Wow dad, did you see that? Uncle Mike does a lower fly over than you give us. I like flying with him. He really knows how to do it."

The older children that had been in the Stationair apparently understood what had happened, as they were a little pale and starry eyed.

Mike crawled out and walked over to the girl with the bike and asked about her well-being. The girl was embarrassed by his expression of concern for her. She kept saying she was sorry, that "never do two planes land, only one." We offered to have a doctor check her, but she bravely insisted that she was fine and that none of the abrasions hurt her.

We asked her if she knew who we could contract to watch our planes while we were gone for a few hours. She answered us as she turned away from us that she would be back with a guard in a minute. Mike and I looked at each other sort of puzzled as the girl rode back across the runway in the direction she had come from.

Mike said, "Do you think she understood what we were asking?"

"Maybe our accent is heavier than we thought, or maybe she bumped her head when she fell. Who knows! Let's lock up the planes and start the family walking to the town center, then we can find someone to watch the planes."

We decided to only take the two small coolers with sandwiches prepared by the hotel kitchen and a bag of bananas. As we finished securing the planes, the girl returned with her father. She presented him to us and we presented all of us to them. She explained that she and her father would guard our planes.

After we made arrangements with the girl and her father, we started walking the fifteen blocks to the dock on the Passion River. Mike was subdued and pensive as we walked away from the airport, and I realized that he was reflecting about what he had just been through with the landing. I had experienced similar situations. I noticed his hands were shaking a little when he had reached down to pick up one of the coolers. He and I were each carrying a cooler walking along a few paces behind the family.

As we walked through the gate, Mike said, "Hey Orville, I am sorry about that...."

"Sorry about what? You just saved yourself and four of my children with some of the best flying I have ever seen. I don't trust many pilots with my children, but you just confirmed why I trust you! There was no way either of us could know that the girl was going to ride onto the runway. I honestly don't know if I would have been able to make the quick calculation that you did, to take off in time to miss the biker and find the only space between the treetops big enough to fit the Stationair through. I had no idea what was happening when I saw you turn the plane toward us instead of continuing straight ahead. It wasn't until I exited the Skymaster and looked up where you had gone that I realized why you had veered in our direction. I don't know how many lives you have, but I believe that you just used one of yours and one of mine in the process!"

We stopped, looked at each other, and grabbed a solid handshake and a shoulder squeeze, then we quickened our step a little to catch up with the group. As we caught up with the family, Linda asked, "What are you two smiling about."

I answered, "Oh, we probably smile like that when we are talking over boy stuff. You know how it is with you girls! Before we get to the dock, let me tell you what our options are and we can take a vote. We can go to the Ceibal Ruins, which are about an hour up river and another half hour walk from the landing. They have two plazas that are for show and the rest is mainly forest, or we can go down river for forty five minutes, plus an hour walk to Dos Pilas, which is being worked pretty heavily now by a group from Vanderbilt, or we could take the boat up the Chacrio tributary to Lake Petexbatún and just cruise around the lake and marsh area. What do you and the children want to do?"

Most of the children were listening while I explained the options to Linda. Some of the younger ones asked if they would be able to explore the lakeshore. Some of the older ones said that riding in a boat sounded relaxing. None of them seemed interested in walking through any more ruins, so the vote went for the cruise to Petexbatún. By the time we finished the discussion, we had reached the town center, which really was not in the center. The town spread away from the river. All the business and government offices were within a few blocks of the river and the housing population spread out from there.

Linda and the girls entered the open market to buy some fruit, while Mike, the boys and myself walked over to some boatmen to negotiate the trip to the lake. We hired Carlos and his longboat that would seat fifteen plus Carlos. It was a dugout made from a single large mahogany tree trunk and was painted a bright aqua. It had a mermaid painted in black on the bow with the name 'Yolanda' painted in red underneath.

There was a different name fading through from underneath, 'Yolanda', probably a previous flame.

By 11:00 a.m., we were all loaded in the boat and headed down the river. The twenty horse Evinrude outboard struggled to move our heavy dugout and it was on the slow side, but that's the way we wanted it anyway. We saw a couple of crocodiles sunning themselves along the riverbank; one was seven or eight feet long. It only took a half hour to the turnoff up the Chacrio tributary. Here the water was totally smooth. You couldn't notice any flow. The banks were covered with grass and lined with trees, mainly a weeping branched tree similar to the willows of North America. The branches drooped down to touch the water. In some narrow parts of the stream the top branches of the trees on one side of the stream touched the top branches of the trees on the opposite side. There were monkeys chattering at us, and swinging through the trees in our direction of travel. Some of them kept up with the boat for a short distance, but soon we were slicing through the water with only the sound of the small motor.

We tracked up the narrow, winding stream for a half an hour, and then suddenly the trees and the stream's boundaries ended in a broad, shallow marshland. There were isolated patches of grass and small trees in the shallows for a kilometer in either direction. Our boatman maneuvered expertly around the little islets until we exited into Lake Petexbatún.

We fished in the lake, picnicked on the shore, explored the forest and in general had a fun and relaxing day. Around four a rain cloud came over the forest and with little warning started drenching the area. Our boatman saved the day by pulling a large vinyl plastic sheet out of the boat that provided cover for all of us. The rain lasted only fifteen or twenty minutes and we decided that it was time to leave after it passed.

We were back at the runway by five. I asked the guards to ride their bikes down the length of the runway and clear it for our takeoff while we loaded the planes. They were back in few minutes and told us that all was clear. I paid them and all of us thanked them and bid them good by and good luck. The wind was calm so we were able to pull directly out onto the runway and takeoff to the West. I again allowed Mike and his group to takeoff first, since his stationair was a little slower. Once we had attained sufficient altitude to receive a radio signal, we informed the Flores tower of our take off, destination, type of aircraft, number of persons in each aircraft, fuel on board, and estimated time in route. We filed for and received clearance for an instrument flight plan into Guatemala City, which was required since we would be arriving after dark. The Civil Aviation Controller assigned 14,000 feet altitude for Mike in the Stationair and 15,000 feet for me in the Skymaster.

The cloud cover turned pretty solid until we reached the mountains, then became broken and scattered. The visibility above the clouds was excellent. We passed the Stationair around Coban, just at the edge of dark. From there we flew over a solid layer of clouds that remained two to three thousand feet below us. Above the clouds, the moon and the stars shined in a transparent sky. There was a sensation of floating on a sea, with our strobe lights flashing onto the cloud layer immediately below us, and the clear night skies above us.

As we neared Salamá and Rabinal, several mountain peaks stabbed majestically through the cloud layer. Soon after we passed the mountain peaks we encountered a large break in the clouds, which expanded over Guatemala City, providing a spectacular view of the city lights, sparkling like pearls in the clear air after a rain. There were wisps of mist floating in some sectors, which added to the beauty. Further to the South, the cloud layer continued and the peaks of 'Agua' and 'Fuego' Volcanoes, at elevations of nearly fourteen thousand feet, protruded through like islands in a sea.

The conditions were right, so I decided to cancel instrument flight and requested to land under visual conditions. The tower Okayed the request and authorized our descent to land. We spiraled down over the Northwestern sector of the city. It took four wide spirals to reach the downwind approach altitude of six thousand five hundred feet. Five minutes after we started our descent, Mike made the same request and was able to follow us. I made it in clean, but the tower had Mike circle and extend his downwind leg in order to allow a Copa Airlines flight to land on instruments.

By the time we got the planes unloaded and hangared, it was 7:30 p.m. Mike followed us home and we offered to feed him, but he understandably wanted to get home to his family. We sent him on his way with a thanks and a good night.

Linda hadn't left any instructions with the maids, but on their own they had decided to have some vegetable beef soup waiting for us. We were tired, but hungrier than tired, so we fell on the soup like hungry animals. The trip was fun, but it was good to be back home. After being in the heat of the Petén, we found it somewhat chilly at the 5,000 feet elevation of Guatemala City, so I built a fire in the fireplace. Linda always loved a fire. Susan played the piano, while the rest of the children played table games and read in front of the fire, a calm ending to a weekend adventure. I left them to their relaxation in the living room and headed to the den.

CHAPTER 12
The Dash

The phone was busy on the first three attempts, but I finally got through to Gloria, Roberto's wife. She told me that Roberto had been calling to see if she had heard from me. She had just hung up with Roberto when my call went through. I asked her if there was anything particular that he wanted to talk to me about, or if she knew where he was, but she said she didn't know anything. I don't know why I asked her. I already knew that Roberto didn't tell Gloria anything about his work, other than his day went fine. She said that she would tell Roberto that I was back in the city if he called again.

I piddled around with some files on the computer and went over the list of names of possible enemies that the Alfaros had provided. I wasn't really doing anything productive on the computer or the paperwork scattered on my desk. Mainly I was mulling over the different branches of the Alfaro problem, trying to figure an angle and trying to anticipate the next move, or moves. That was the stage that was most frustrating to me. Until we identified the enemy or enemies, we had no way of anticipating how, when or where they might launch their next move. Right then the only thing I could see that kept us on a near even footing, was that they probably knew as little about my team and me as we knew about them. Tending to look on the more positive side, I always hoped that we would get to know everything about them before they knew anything about us. The pie in the sky almost never happened and I would adjust as one or the other of my flanks became exposed.

The phone startled me out of my thoughts. I quickly glanced at my watch and noticed it was 9:30 p.m. as I picked up on the second ring.

"Hello! Oh, hi Roberto. Where are you and how is it going?"

"I am outside the Dash discotheque in Zone ten. I have been here for thirty minutes and this is the second discotheque tonight. There was a brawl as we were leaving the last place in Zone four. It had nothing to do with Raul, but had his bodyguard and me hustling. It would have been a prime opportunity for the other side to grab him or harm him. I am still sweating thinking about our exposure. I tried to talk him out of going into Zone four, but Raul wants to just keep on living his life as though everything is hunky-dory and nobody is out to get him. I only have an hour and a half more to follow him if he heads home by 11:00 p.m., like he promised his dad."

"Where in Zone ten is Dash?"

"It is on the right just before the Geminis Building on First Avenue. Why? Are you coming?"

"Yea, I think I'll cruise over and have a look around."

"Sure, boss. Gotcha!"

We both knew through previous arrangement, that if we saw or ran into one another, we would not acknowledge prior acquaintance in any way.

I hung up, shut down the computer and arranged the loose papers on my desk, before leaving the den. Linda had left the fire and retired to the bedroom. I stopped by the bedroom to get my shooter and to tell Linda not to wait up for me. As I was leaving the bedroom I decided to return for a good night kiss and my jacket. After spending a few days in the sweltering heat of the Peten I was particularly aware of the nighttime chill of Guatemala City at five thousand feet elevation.

I decided to drive the Citroen. The Audi had a bigger engine than the Citroen by nearly 1,000 cc, but the Citroen was pure silk to drive. It made up for the smaller engine with superb gear synchronization, and road hugging like a racer. I bought it for Linda, but I liked to use it whenever I could. As I slid into the car, I put the gun and the extra ammo clip in the glove compartment. I wasn't sure yet if I would be carrying it, since I was undecided as to whether I would enter the club. If I entered the club, I would draw more attention by having to turn the gun in at security.

As I pulled out of the cross circle to head back towards the hotel district, I noticed that Las Americas Avenue was void of traffic, so I took the opportunity to blow a little carbon out of the Citroen engine. I held it at a steady 3,300 rpm on the last stretch just before the Obelisque Plaza and went through the circle onto Reforma Avenue at just under 60 mph. The car didn't even rock in the turn. I slowed it down with the gears in time to turn off of Reforma onto 14th street.

I ended up parking three blocks from the Dash, in the parking lot of the Hotel Camino Real. Since I was a couple of blocks from the Dash, I decided to slip the Mauser into its ankle holster and put the extra ammo clip in my jacket pocket. As I exited the car and stepped clear of hotel buildings, the wind out of the north kicked up a little debris on me. It was gusting ten to fifteen miles an hour and I would have been cold without the jacket. Instead of walking directly towards Dash, I turned right on 14th Street to Second Avenue, which ran one block East of and behind the discotheque. I walked two blocks to Twelfth Street and as I turned left towards the Dash, I saw the metallic blue Datsun pickup. I quickly melded into the wall and a tree on my left.

The tree actually grew right next to the wall, leaning out slightly from about chest height. I had a limited field of vision between the wall and the tree and there was a small branch hanging low that intermittently blocked my vision as the wind moved it. I could see the pickup and the street, but only a portion of the sidewalk to the left of the pickup. The pickup was midway in the block. I concentrated on it. I wondered if it was the same one that I had seen leaving the Landivar University parking lot the previous week. If not it could have passed for a look alike.

There were several trees lining both sides of the street. I had driven along these streets for years, but I had never noticed how many trees there were until then. I concentrated my vision in the vicinity of the pickup. After about a minute of watching, I saw a hand with a cigarette move out from behind a tree adjacent to the pickup. I wondered if he was alone. The cigarette appeared and disappeared a couple more times, then he stepped out from behind the tree, and looked up and down the street as he flicked his cigarette butt across the pickup into the middle of the street.

I pasted myself tighter against the wall. I was sure he couldn't see me, but wondered if he had sensed me. My field of vision was a little less than before with my change of position, but I could still see him and the pickup. He stepped over by the pickup and dropped something through the passenger window of the pickup. He was definitely related to the pickup. Next he stepped on my side of the tree and unzipped his pants and urinated against the wall. I gave another studied look on both sides of the street.

Feeling more confident, I pulled myself from the wall to gain a better view of the street. I could not detect anyone else that seemed related to the Datsun, or the man behind the tree. In fact, there was no one else anywhere in view. My intended quarry and I had the street all to ourselves. He zipped up, looked around, lit another cigarette and returned to his position on the opposite side of the tree. His buddies were probably around the corner in or near the Dash Club.

His hand with the cigarette appeared again. I surmised that the cigarette remained in his right hand, which would mean that his back was against the tree and he was facing the other way. I unsnapped the strap and extracted the Mauser from its holster. I gave another glance up the street, then left my tree behind and started walking towards him. It was no wonder that there wasn't anyone walking on this street. The sidewalk was broken and littered and the trees blocked most of the light from the only one streetlight in the middle of the block. I had to concentrate to avoid tripping or making noise. Fortunately I was walking into the wind, which I figured would carry any small sound I made away from him.

As I approached the pickup, I could see it was missing a tailgate and I was certain it was the one from the previous week. I quietly stationed myself on the opposite side of his tree, which was much bigger than it seemed from afar. I could smell his fresh urine mingled with that of numerous others that had used the same spot. I slipped the Mauser into my jacket pocket and waited less than thirty seconds for his hand with the cigarette to appear. In one smooth motion I placed my right foot firmly beyond the tree trunk and grabbed his wrist with my right hand, continuing momentum with a downward motion jerk. As his head came out from behind the tree, I completed the motion by grabbing his neck with my left hand, thrusting him out from behind the tree and down. My plan was to control him by acquiring a hold around his neck with my left arm, while levering his right arm up his back.

I never got that far. I had more leverage than I had anticipated and I caught him so off balance that he crashed to his knees, striking his head against the back corner of the pickup cab. I continued to hold onto his arm as I placed my knee in the small of his back. I had so much adrenaline pumping that it took me several seconds to realize that he was unconscious.

I looked around and determined that no one had witnessed the action. I felt his hip pockets and removed his wallet from his left hip pocket. I rolled him over and searched his front pockets where I found a handkerchief, a pocketknife, a comb and a set of car keys. That was all he had in his pants. The only thing in his jacket was an envelope with some papers. Finally I removed a 9 mm shooter from his shoulder holster.

I stuffed everything except the comb and handkerchief into my pockets. I didn't want to spend any more time than necessary out in the open, but I decided to have a look in and around the pickup. The guy's head was blocking the door, so I grabbed his legs and drug them around parallel to the pickup bed and then I drug him a little towards the rear of the truck, to where his head lay clear of the door.

I flicked on my penlight and first looked into the pickup bed. The only things there were some empty beer bottles and some used paper cups. I stepped to the back of the pickup and erased any doubt that it was the pickup used for the Landivar episode. Besides the make and color, it was missing a taillight. It didn't have a license plate in the rear either. I walked back to the right door of the pickup. The item the guy had dropped into the passenger seat was a wool cap. I shined my penlight into rest of the interior. The glove compartment didn't have a lid on it and contained a snout nosed set of pliers, a regular plier and couple of screwdrivers. Under the seat were a couple small rolls of insulated electrical wire. I borrowed the snout nosed pliers to cut a piece off each roll and put the pieces in my pocket.

The rest of my search netted a length of rope, jumper cables, an almost empty bottle of rum and a few coins. I drained the four or five ounces of rum on my still unconscious fellow and placed the bottle between his hand and his hip. Except for the pieces of wire, the snout nosed pliers and the rum bottle, I left everything the way I found it. The last thing I checked was the front license plate. It was so scuffed and the lighting so dim, that it was hard to read the numbers. I knelt close and traced each letter and number with my finger and wrote the numbers down on the back of my hand. Every few seconds I would glance up over the hood and around to see if anyone was coming my way.

As I stepped away from the pickup, I heard talking from up the sidewalk towards the club. I looked that way and saw two men walking towards me. As I reached into my pocket to put my hand on the Mauser, they both must have sensed something amiss and quickly crossed to the opposite side of the street. I could tell that they weren't part of that party. I waited until they were well down the block and then I walked in the same direction on my side of the street. They continued talking and turned to the left at the corner. I continued walking to the corner, listening but not turning back. I turned right at the corner. After a couple of steps beyond the corner, I stopped dead silent and just listened for a moment. Then I looked up and down the street. I was alone.

I stepped back to the corner of the building and looked up towards the pickup between the same tree and wall that I had used earlier. Three men were just coming around the corner in a fast trot. My guy was coming to and sitting up against the side of the pickup. He was holding the bottle with one hand and rubbing the top of his head with the other as his accomplices arrived at the pickup. In the midst of a lot of shouting one of the men jerked the bottle from his hand and the biggest of the three jerked him upright against the pickup.

I had seen enough action and decided that it was time for me to move on. There was still no one in sight on Second Avenue. I retraced the direction I had come from the parking lot. I didn't trot, I ran as fast as I could down Second Avenue towards Fourteenth Street. I slowed to a normal walk just as I reached the corner of Thirteenth Street. Once across Thirteenth, I resumed my run until the corner of Fourteenth. I walked across Fourteenth and then up the opposite side of the street to the Camino Real parking lot. There were a few people ahead of me, but they were walking away from me towards the Hotel.

Just before I arrived at the parking lot, a young couple came walking out of the lot. They too turned towards the hotel. As soon as I stepped into the lot, I trotted over to the Citroen, emptied my pockets and placed my booty in an empty box in the trunk. Before getting in the car, I stepped my left foot upon the doorsill, raised my pant leg and returned the Mauser to its holster.

I turned left out of the parking lot onto fourteenth and crossed to the other side of Reforma Avenue where I took the southbound lanes to the Obelisque and Liberation Avenue out to Zone Twelve. I arrived in the block of Raul's house just as he was pulling in his garage. I pulled to the curb and shut the Citroen down to wait for Roberto to exit. They didn't shut the garage doors. Both guards remained at the driveway entrance as Robert slowly backed his car out of the garage to where he was facing me. I flashed my lights twice. Roberto recognized the distinctive yellow lights of the Citroen and pulled on towards me. He stopped with his window abreast of mine and saluted.

"How long have you been here?"

"Oh, I just pulled up as you were pulling into the garage. How was the rest of your evening?"

"Fine! Thank God, no more thrills! I was glad Raul didn't decide to make any other stops. I am ready to hit the sack. I was watching for you at the Dash. What you been up to before showing up here?"

"I had a little fun with our adversary. I was real close to the backside of the Club, but I never made it around to the front.

"You were there, near the Dash?"

"Yeah. It's late, I'll tell you about it on Monday and we can look over some items I picked up."

"You got some things? Let me see 'em'!"

"Lets wait until Monday. I don't know about you, but I for one am too pooped to pop and I have had more than enough excitement for one day. I have witnessed a great pilot save a part of my family, I have cruised a jungle river, flown some challenging flying, and slipped into the enemy camp and got away clean. We can't make out much here in the dark and we are both too tired to go to the office. I have a lot to tell you and a few things to show you, but it can all wait until Monday. Go home and sleep, Roberto. I am going to do the same."

"I don't want you to forget any details about the preview you just gave me, but I can wait. Do you need me early Monday morning?"

"No! What do you have going?

"I want to have breakfast with a couple of my police buddies and see if they have anything on a couple of requests I made."

"That sounds fine to me. I'll use the early morning to get the electronics shop started adjusting my VOR's on the plane and meet you at the office around ten. Sound okay to you?"

"Sounds fine."

"Hey before we separate, I just thought of something. Pull over to the side a moment."

Once he pulled away from my door, I got out and opened the trunk to retrieve the shooter I had taken from the guy. He was out of his car and walking towards me by the time I shut my trunk lid. I handed him the gun and said: "Since you are meeting with your police buddies tomorrow, you need to drop this off with your contact in DECAM and have them run a trace on it. I took it off of one of their men tonight. We both know that it was not going to be registered to him, but it could have shed a little light on our problem if we could get some background on the gun. It may have belonged to a registered owner here in Guatemala at some time. Anyway let's see if they come up with anything."

"Now I am definitely curious as to what you have been up to tonight. I can't wait for you to relate the whole story to me."

"I just remembered one other thing. Do you have something to write on?"

He did and I dictated the license plate number off of the back of my hand.

"Have your buddies start a trace on that license number."

"Will do, mi amigo. Saludos a Linda. ¡Hasta mañana y Buenas Noches!"–Say 'hi' to Linda. Until tomorrow and good night!

"Lo mismo para Gloria. ¡Buenas Noches!"–The same for Gloria. Good night.

As Roberto pulled away, I started the Citroen and drove by Raul's home. There was only one dim light burning on the second floor. On the way home, I rolled down all of the car windows to ward off sleep. I coasted into the garage and shut down the Citroen. I retrieved my shooter from the glove compartment as I exited the car. I took a spare key from its garage hidey-hole and opened my Audi. I put my shooter in its slot under the dashboard, along with the ammo clip, and took the box with the loot from the guy and the pickup and placed it in the trunk of the Audi. I closed everything up put the key back in its hidey-hole and went through the garage entrance to the house. I made my way up the stairs and to our bedroom in the dark.

As I undressed by the bedside, Linda mumbled, *"Mmmffff Airthin* okay hon?"

"Everything is fine dear! Sleep tight!"

And we did!

CHAPTER 13
Monday, August 11

Linda and I woke up early enough to do our exercise routine and have a quiet breakfast alone. I made it to the office at a quarter 'til eight. Yaneth and Mike were there. I inquired about Roberto and it wasn't until after both of them indicated that they didn't know of his whereabouts, that I remembered he and I had agreed on Saturday that he would meet with some of his sources before coming in.

I invited Yaneth into my office first, so that she could bring me up to date on appointments and messages from clients and whomever. Yaneth reminded me that I had an appointment at 2:00 on Wednesday afternoon with the security committee at Super Cajas, S.A. There were a half a dozen phone calls on Friday, four that I should return, including Eli and Jorge Alfaro.

After going over the checks she needed signed and the deposits that had been made or sent out, Yaneth handed me a small bundle of opened mail. When she first started working for me, like most secretaries trained by Latinos, she assumed that all mail addressed to the boss was private. It took me a while to convince her that my life at the office was not private and, for efficiency, she should open all mail that came to the office. Thus, she could assign one of the men to handle anything that did not require my personal attention. One of the effective ways to lose a client is to have them wait for the top executive to get around to looking at a problem that could have been solved more efficiently had it been handed to someone available.

It only took a few minutes with Yaneth and as soon as she left, Mike walked in. Mike sat down and pulled out a sheath of papers from a manila envelope he carried.

"This is the list of possible enemies that Alfaro made up. I got a little bored at home yesterday, so I came in to the office and started going over the list. I saw where Roberto had checked some names and I am sure that he will have some comments on the ones he marked, but I know the background on a few that he didn't mark! Is this a good time to talk about it?"

"Yea that would be fine. I am anxious to start analyzing this case from that point of view. Shoot!"

"Well first there is Jaime Leiva."

"I recognize that name. Isn't he in the construction business?"

"Construction and a few others. He is a major shareholder and sits on the board of three banks. He also owns, or has controlling interest in the Prince Hotel. In addition he is a landowner in the Zacapa area and that is where he and Jorge have had a little friction. The story is that Jorge bought the adjoining property a few years ago and ordered a survey in order to fence an area between the two properties that did not have an existing fence. Up to that time Leiva, and his father before him, had grazed their cattle well into the adjoining property. Leiva and Alfaro had some pretty hard words after Leiva's men destroyed the fence or portions of it several times. Alfaro finally took it to court and got an injunction against Leiva. But as you know, in these countries, a court ruling is only a battle, not the war. Rumor is that Leiva used his banking connections to block loans for Alfaro's projects and has been a major influence in Alfaro still depending heavily on financing outside of Guatemala."

"How old is Leiva?"

"Mid fifties."

"How old is this land dispute?"

"Five or six years."

"Okay, who's next on your list?"

"Hey I have one more little ditty in the Leiva relationship! Leiva's son got into a shoving match with Raul back a couple of years ago. I understand that Raul tromped him pretty good."

"Yep that is interesting. Keep Leiva marked and lets find out a little more about him and specifically any other connections or encounters with Alfaro. It will be interesting to hear why Alfaro didn't put him on his list. Who else do you have?"

"Well, there is Alfonso Guerra. He is the husband of Alfaro's former secretary. I haven't been able to find out if Alfaro and the secretary had some kind of relationship beyond that of boss and secretary, or if Guerra was merely an overzealous protector of his wife. Anyway Guerra ended up openly accusing Alfaro. When Alfaro laughed at the accusation, it threw Guerra into a rage that ended with him threatening Alfaro. His wife never went back to secretarial labors with Alfaro after that incident. That took place three years ago and I don't know anymore than what I just related."

"Okay, dig on that one too! Next?"

"That's all I have for now. Other than follow up on these, is there anything special you want me to do?"

"No. What else is on your list?"

"I am not sure I mentioned it, but on our recent trip to the Peten, Alex Mendoza, the security head at PPL asked me to be on the lookout for a body guard for the plant manager. I found a man that fits the bill. Unless you need me for something more urgent, I thought I might fly him up in the Skylane tomorrow to meet with Alex and the plant manager. It's possible they will want me to spend tomorrow night and part of Wednesday to go over some of their security concerns."

"Are we billing for the use of the plane?

"Cost, plus 50 an hour. We are just billing straight time for me, no pilot time."

"Sounds good to me. PPL has turned into a good account. I wish we had a couple more like them in the Peten."

"Alex has mentioned introducing me to the manager of a logging company near one of their drilling sites. Maybe we will get to do that on this trip."

"Just keep in touch with Yaneth in case she has any questions and keep her posted on your whereabouts. Have a good trip."

After he left my office, I could hear he and Yaneth talking for a few minutes until I got submerged in the "pending review" folder that Yaneth had left on my desk for me. She had placed notes with background for each of the calls I needed to return. I made the phone calls. I was able to reach three of the four. The one I didn't get to talk to was not in and his secretary didn't know for sure when he would return. I told her my name and office phone number and informed her that I too would be out of the office for a few hours.

Then I turned to the folder that Yaneth had left on my desk for me to attend to. The main thing in the folder besides the notes was a batch of checks that needed signature. It wasn't until I signed the last check that I realized that somewhere in the middle of the signing I had quit reading what I was signing and was merely signing. I had gotten lost in reflection on the Alfaro case. Duh! When a manager quits reading what he is signing, he may as well give his staff a rubber stamp with his signature.

I pushed Alfaro out of my mind momentarily and leafed back into the stack of checks to where I last remembered reviewing the substance of the checks. I went over them one by one like a good boy and did my job of reviewing. I was so glad to come across a typo, which I would be able to point out to Yaneth, and thus maintain my image as a manager that manages. I wondered sometimes if she didn't seed the reports, or checks with an error, just to check on me. Hmmm, I decided that my detective mind had just jumped into overcharge!!!

I called Yaneth in, gave her some instructions regarding appointments and a couple tasks that had occurred to me as I met with Mike and while signing the checks. Then I handed her the folder with the report and the checks. I had the check with the typo on top, which I pointed out.

She gave me a smile. I couldn't tell if it was a sly smile, a 'good hunting smile', or simply, a 'let me correct it smile'. I merely told her to correct it then so that I could sign it before leaving to Younger Aviation.

As soon as she left, I dialed Eli's Office.

"Hi Eli! What have you been up to?"

"Hi Orv! I just got off the phone with Allen. He told me that the other possible passenger is Joe Levi. Joe still isn't one hundred percent sure, but he is trying and he thinks he is going to make it. It has been nearly three years since he has been here in Central America."

"Wow, I bet you are a little nervous at the possibility of the International Vice President coming."

"You're right, I always feel a little anticipation when my boss is coming, but when my boss' boss is coming I suffer a double dose of anxiety. I think everything is pretty good, but you know how it is, there are always a few areas that could be better. At least I only have a week and a half to worry about it. I should know by the middle of next week if he will be coming."

"Well is there anything you need from me today?"

"No I just wanted to let you know who is coming. By this coming Thursday I should have our meetings pretty firmed up and perhaps by

Friday we can discuss your part of the arrangements, you know the security in Belize, flight times and so forth."

"Give me until Monday on the flight times. By then I will have the flight times and the information as to who and what will be waiting for us at the airport in Belize. My flight permits are all in order. I keep all of my aviation material at home and plan to work up the flight plans early Saturday morning. You know me, I can't sleep in even when I could."

"Monday will be fine. Sounds like you have your end under control Orv. Amparo told me that she and Linda had talked and that we are on for the barbecue this coming Saturday."

"Yep, that is what Linda told me."

"Okay, I will call if there is any changes in our planned trip. Talk to you later Have a good day."

"Same to you Eli, goodbye"

After hanging up with Eli, I dialed Jorge Alfaro's direct number at his plant. He didn't answer. I dialed the switchboard number and a lilting voice said; "Perfiles de Acero, S.A., habla Silvia, con quien quiere habla*r*?"–This is Silvia, may I direct your call.

"Hola Silvia, Habla Orville Fletcher."–Hi Silvia, this is Orville Fletcher.

Silvia continued in broken English. *sic* "Don Orville, Don Jorge is out of office now. He in meeting outside of plant. He say if you call that you leave number so he is call you back."

I admire a person that continues to practice their English, even if they know I speak Spanish, so I continued in English. "I am just trying to set up a meeting with Don Jorge. I will be out of the office for the next hour and half. Do you know approximately when he will be back in the office, or at another phone where I can reach him."

"He not return to office until eleven thirty or twelve minus fifteen. He not have access to a phone until then." *sic*

"Then I will phone him around noon."

"I will give your message Meester Fletcher. *sic* Have good morning."

"Same to you Silvia."

It was 9:30 a.m. when I left the office and I knew I wouldn't make it back by 10:00 a.m., which was the time I had estimated be back to meet with Roberto. I thought, "That's okay, he can use the time to bring his reports up to date.' I reflected that he probably hated doing reports almost as much as I hated doing reports back when I had bosses. I was sure glad I had made it to boss, with a secretary to whom I could dictate my reports. Of course, I always had Linda as a fantastic boss and she didn't require reports.

Sixth Avenue wasn't the way to get to the airport that day. I never did find out what the problem was, but finally after fifteen minutes I was able to make a u-turn and get over to Reforma Avenue, then Las Americas down to the 18th Street entrance to the Airport.

Ralph was in his office talking on the phone to a client. He motioned me to sit in one of the chairs in front of his desk while he finished his conversation. I could tell from Ralph's end of the conversation that the client had made an emergency landing with engine trouble at a remote strip on the South Coast after having taken off from the coastal city of Retalhuleu. I didn't recognize the place he had landed. Ralph told him he would be sending a mechanic to size up the situation and then listened and wrote down instructions on where to meet the client. After he hung up, he signaled me with the thumb and forefinger to wait just a minute. He then stepped to the door from his office to the hanger and shouted for Alfredo.

He came back, shook my hand and then sat again in his chair. He asked about Linda and the Children and I did the same regarding Gabriela and their son. I was just getting ready to tell him what I needed done on the plane, when Alfredo appeared at the door. Ralph motioned him in and Alfredo and I shook hands and exchange cordialities. No one ever leaves out the warm "saludos" in Latin America. Ralph told him about the clients forced landing and suggested it sounded like a magneto, or ignition problem. He recommended that he take ten gallons of fuel, just in case. He told him that the client would pick him up where the Highway to Tiquisate intersects the Pan American Highway. He gave him some money and told him to have another mechanic drop him off at the "Rapidos del Sur" bus station. Only in Latin America could you get passengers to ride a bus line that promoted its main service as being the fastest. In advanced countries we look for transportation companies that tout safety as their 'forte'.

When Alfredo exited, Raymond again turned to me.

I told him, "My number one VOR appears to be off 4 or 5 degrees on some headings. Also the copilot seat doesn't roll smoothly and I need the oxygen bottle refilled."

"No problem Orville. We will get right on it. Unless we run into some problem or discover something else, we will have it ready by this afternoon. Are the logbooks in the plane?"

"No they are not. I have them in the trunk of the car. I meant to bring them in as I came in, but forgot. Here are the plane keys. Let me get the books."

I got up and went to the car, retrieved the logbooks, brought them in and handed them to him as I sat down. The phone was ringing as I came in. Someone else picked up. I kept the logbooks in a rectangular waterproof Tupperware container. He popped the lid and was browsing at the Airframe Log, when his secretary appeared at the door to tell him that 'Carlos somebody' wanted to talk to him. He started to tell the secretary that he would call back, but I stood and said I needed to leave anyway. We said our goodbyes and he was taking the call as I left his office.

I stopped at the secretary's desk and asked if she had a phone line available. She did and I phoned the office. Yaneth picked up on the second ring.

"Hi Yaneth. Is Roberto there?'

"No, he phoned just after you left. I told him that you wouldn't be here by 10:00., more likely 11:00. He said he had some other contacts to talk to and it will keep him tied up until close till noon. He is going to call me back in a few minutes to see if I have a better estimate of what time you will return to the office."

"Tell Roberto that I expect to arrive around noon. Tell him to plan on he and I having lunch together."

"Bye."

I thanked the secretary and left. I wanted to make another call, but didn't want to tie up one of their two lines. It was 10:30. I drove over to MAG. Brenda wasn't there. Her office girl, Alba, told me she would arrive in a few minutes and that, "tu –your Mike" was out back checking out the Skylane. I decided to see what Mike was up to, while waiting for Brenda, so I told Alba that I would be out in the Hangar with Mike.

Mike was standing by the engine cowling working on something with his back to me. I think I startled him a little when I hailed him from behind. He fumbled the oil dipstick he was extracting from the engine and it fell to the hangar floor. We both reached for it and just about knocked each other down in the process. The clown like episode got us both to laughing.

I backed off and let him retrieve the dipstick, then asked: "What are you up to? I thought you weren't leaving till tomorrow."

"If I were flying the Stationair, I probably wouldn't have come over this morning since I just flew it. But I haven't flown the Skylane for a while and I like to check out a rental plane and logs the day before I use it. Sometimes the pilot before has reported a problem that hasn't been taken care of and I always like to check it out and run the engine for a few minutes. If something isn't right, hopefully I can get it taken care of the day before I need to travel."

"Wow, I continue to learn from you Mike. Maybe I take a little too much for granted as a pilot."

"Your situation is different, you don't have to wonder what condition the plane is in when you are the only pilot using it and you know who performed the maintenance and when."

He stepped a little closer and continued in a lowered voice: I am not too convinced by Brenda's mechanic. He hits the bottle a little too frequent, and is not of the same caliber as the crew over at Ralph's shop, where you service your plane."

I heard a car pull up to the side of the Hangar and figured it could be Brenda, so I took leave of Mike and went back around towards the office. As I stepped around the corner of the Hangar, Brenda was helping her little boy descend from the back seat of the car. She was clutching some files and holding onto a briefcase with one arm and trying to help her toddler with the other, while she held a cigarette in her lips. I stepped up and relieved her of the briefcase and papers as she smiled up at me. She plucked the cigarette from her mouth and said, "¡Que tal! don Orville–How are you?"

I smiled back and said, "We are all doing fine, Brenda. I hope you and yours are all well."

"We doing well, too, thank you. My maid not come today *sic*, so I have to bring Robby."

She picked up Robby while I closed the car door and then I followed her into the outer office. She handed the toddler to Alba once inside the door and motioned me back to her office. I went on in her office and was looking at her family pictures on the wall, when she came in a couple of minutes later.

She was lighting a new cigarette from the previous one as she came through the door. We met halfway between the pictures and her desk for a wordless hug and peck on the cheek. She moved around to her side of the desk and invited me to sit as she sat down in her chair. I was glad that she hadn't closed the door and that my chair was close to the open door, since the smoke was pretty heavy in the office.

She asked, "You want I should turn on the air-conditioner?'

"No, I feel comfortable with the door open if you do."

"Yea, I am fine. Can I get you something to drink?"

"Thank you Brenda, a glass of water would be fine."

She picked up the phone and rang Alba and told her to bring her a coffee and me a glass of water. Then she turned to me and asked, "Is there something I can do for you, Don Orville, or did you just come by to visit?"

I smiled thinking she is an astute businesswoman and with a mind of order similar to mine. "You cut right to the chase, Brenda. I am trying to help Jorge Alfaro solve a little puzzle and I had a few more questions about your former pilot, Ortiz."

"Strange you should ask about him. Otto phoned me at home this morning to ask to come back to fly for me. I told him I would see if I need him. Do you think I should hire him back, Don Orville?"

"Brenda, who am I to tell you whom you should or shouldn't hire?'

"Well I have gotten to know you in these years and I know you try to be fair. I know what you do for to live *sic* and you asked me about him, which makes me think you know something I don't. Sometimes, I am too anxious to see the good in others, and I am not always good in measuring people."

"Truthfully, I don't know enough about Ortiz to tell you one way or the other. I suggest you base your decision on what you have learned through past experience. If he is a safe pilot and handles your planes well, hire him for that. Then use your past experience to establish clear parameters for your relationship. Perhaps his past problems were due only to immaturity and he is ready to be more responsible."

"You think practical like me, Don Orville."

"I tell you what! If I find out anything concrete, good or bad, about him, I will let you know. What I would like, if you do hire him back, would be for you to help me meet him and get a feel for him. You know, like when he is here, call me so I can just happen by!"

"Yes, I will do that, Don Orville. Right now I have no plane for him to fly, but I am working on that. You should allow me to lease your plane for rental? We would take good care of it and always have it available for your use."

"Brenda, if there is anyone I would consider making such an arrangement with, it would be you, and I may just do that sometime in the future, but not yet."

"I think I have told you everything I know about Otto."

"Okay, that is all I had, Brenda. Just let me know if you hire him back."

"I will do that, Don Orville."

We hugged and did the cheek thing and I said bye to Alba as I walked out through reception area. At least I got his first name, Otto.

CHAPTER 14
Progress and Piccadilly

I made it back to the office by 11:30 a.m. Roberto was manning the phones. He answered a call just as I walked in and appeared to be trying to get a word in edgewise to whoever was on the other end as I walked through the outer office area toward my office. I gave a "hi" wave as I walked by him. As I was entering my office, I heard him tell the person that he was not Yaneth, but that she would be back shortly, and he would be happy to give her the caller's message, and no he wouldn't forget. The phone started ringing as he was hanging up. I reached for my phone to take the call, but Roberto picked up on the reception phone before I could retrieve it.

I was looking through the mail when Roberto gave a knock on the doorframe and came in. I stood to take his outstretched hand and gestured toward a chair as I sat back in my own. As he sat down he started telling me.

"I got here at a quarter after and Yaneth asked me to cover the phone while she ran some errands. She said to the bank and I think someplace else. Answering the phone for a while reinforces my conviction that I am not cut out for office work. If I found out that I would be confined to office work for the rest of my life, I promise that I would shoot myself."

"I wouldn't think of keeping you in my office. Your attitude would probably show and we would lose most of our clients."

He looked a little embarrassed about his statement, but then he smiled as I asked: "How did your meetings go this morning?"

"First, I need to give you a message from Yaneth. She said that Jorge Alfaro has been trying to reach you, but that you would not be able to reach him between eleven-thirty and one. He said he would call back."

"It is eleven-forty. Let me phone his office, just in case."

I phoned and had the receptionist put me through to his secretary. Alfaro had left the office ten minutes before my call. She would tell him that I phoned. She said that he intended to continue trying to reach me and would likely call me before returning to the office. I asked if he would be at home and she answered no, that he was having lunch with two of his project engineers. Nothing else I could do, but wait for his call or wait until one o'clock to phone him.

I turned to Roberto. "So tell me about your meetings this morning."

"They went different than I thought they would. I may have received some enlightenment, but first tell me about Saturday night."

I was more in the mind of hearing what Roberto had to report about his visit to DECAM, which stands for Department of Control for Arms and Munitions, but I knew that his curious nature would drive him crazy if I put him off any longer about what I had been up to last Saturday evening. I related the story in detail while he sat mesmerized by it. He laughed heartily when I got to the part about pulling the guy from behind the tree and again when his buddies assumed he had gotten skunk drunk. I figured if we were lucky they would surmise that their cohort had been robbed by street thieves and not have a clue that we had gotten that close to them. At the end of the story, I turned around to my credenza to get the box of items I had taken from the suspect and the pickup on Saturday night and placed it on my desktop.

I asked, "Were you able to start a trace on the license number and the gun?"

"I finished meeting with my police contacts around 9:30. Right after that I stopped by the office that starts the trace on the License Plate Number. We don't know the model year, but I told them it was a blue Datsun 1,000 cc pickup. I will need to check back tomorrow or Wednesday to see if they have anything. If you want, I could rush it some by doing part of the legwork myself with the vehicle registrations in Customs.

As to the gun, I made it to DECAM around 10:45. If the gun was reported lost or stolen more than a month ago, they will have record of it and have to search their reports. That will take a week to ten days. If it was reported lost or stolen less than a month ago, then it is still being processed by the Public Ministry, where the police report is initially filed.

Remember how you had to receive authorization and register your firearm with DECAM. Anyone that loses, or has a registered firearm stolen are required to file a report with the police, but it has to be moved through several offices at police headquarters and finally ruled on by a judge. That document is then presented to DECAM for their processing. Only after all three steps are taken is the original gun owner protected, if a crime were committed with the gun. I had contacts in the police department, but not in DECAM. The police chief helped me with that one. He made a phone call and gave me the name of a major to see. I first went to DECAM and got that to rolling. Then I went back to the last office that processes a stolen gun report, on the slim chance that this gun was recently reported stolen and still waiting for signature and seal from a judge. I'll keep ....."

Roberto stopped in mid sentence when I looked beyond him to Yaneth, who had just stepped to the door. I thought I had heard someone come in the front door. Roberto also turned and we both said hi to Yaneth.

She returned our greeting and said, "Hi, I finished up some errands. I saw your notes about the calls you took Roberto. Thanks for covering."

She looked at me and asked, "Did you return Jorge Alfaro's call?"

"I tried, but was ten minutes too late. He won't be back in the office until one o'clock. I left word with his secretary, and she said he may try to phone me before then, but if not I would be able to reach him after one o'clock. I will hang around the office until he phones. If he hasn't phoned by twelve-thirty, I will have one of you pick me up something to eat here in the office."

Yaneth answered, "Just let me know if you want me to get you some food. Is there anything either of you need me to do?"

I answered, "Not just yet. Roberto and I are talking about the Alfaro case."

"Fine, I brought some food, so I will eat here in the office and cover the phones. I will be at my desk if you need me."

She left and I turned to Roberto, "You had just said something about checking with the last office, or some place at the Police department."

Roberto: "Yeah, I went by there just to start the procedure to see if the gun may have been reported stolen. I doubt it, but I will keep checking. We probably won't hear yea, or nay for a couple of weeks."

"So much for the pickup and the gun, let's see if there is anything else of value in this little box."

I pulled out the little snips of wire I had cut from the two rolls in the pickup. I laid them on my desk as I turned to open my briefcase on the credenza. I removed the explosive device and the envelope with the snippets of insulation and lay it all on my desk by the wire I had removed from the pickup. It was obvious to both of us that it all matched. My gut feeling of Saturday evening was confirmed. I had been in the enemy camp and gotten away, with evidence.

When I looked across at Roberto, he was wearing as big a smile as I was. We knew we were on the trail. We both knew that we were a long way from knowing enough to eliminate the risks to our client, but there was a warm feeling having gotten to the point of knowing that we were headed in the right direction and that we had done it without over-exposing our flanks. Finally we were at a point to establish some theories. Some of them would be long shots, but one of them would materialize into a resolution.

The beginning of an investigation consisted of following all feasible leads and accumulating information, without knowing how and if it would constitute a piece of the puzzle. In a successful investigation one arrives at a point where some new information relates to other pieces already obtained and points in a certain direction. In the past we had learned that it was wise to keep an open mind to other possibilities, but usually fruitful to go in the direction of the strong leads.

At that point in the Alfaro investigation there were a lot of loose ends, but at least we were relatively certain that we were headed in the right direction. Sometimes it appeared as luck, but problems were usually solved by hard work, intelligent analysis, and tenacious follow-up on every promising detail. I always thought of it being like electricity. When one flips a switch, the light may come on suddenly, but the current that let it happen was an accumulation and correct placement of energy.

The ring of the intercom brought us back to the here and now. It was Yaneth.

"Jorge Alfaro on line one."

"Thanks Yaneth."

I hit the line one button.

"Yes Don Jorge, how are you and the family?"

"We are okay, Orville. How about you and yours?"

"Linda and the kids are doing well. We had a good trip to the Peten this past weekend."

"Had you been there before?"

"I have been there numerous times and I go there on business a couple of times a year, but it had been a considerable time since I had taken the family for relaxation. Besides the ruins, we took a boat up the Passion River to Lake Petexbatún. Very beautiful."

"Lulu and I enjoy the Petén area. We have not gone there for some time. You bring back pleasant memories. I think we will return there sometime soon. I have never been to Lake Petexbatún. You will have to tell me more about it."

After the typical Latino exchange of a few sentences of warm welcome before getting down to business, I asked, "Are you returning my call, or did you have something you needed to discuss?"

"Just returning your call Don Orville."

"I phoned you because I think we have some developments that we would like to run by you. Could we meet later today, or tomorrow?"

"Impossible today, I have back to back meetings with clients and bankers. How about tomorrow around 4 p.m.?"

"Okay, shall we meet again at the hotel?"

"Sure. I'll be there at 4:00."

"Good, I will see you then."

While I was on the phone, Roberto had reached into the box and pulled out the suspect's wallet. He was laying the contents out on the desk when I hung up. There were a few Quetzal bills. There was a paper with a list of eight names and phone numbers and an unrelated series of numbers and dashes at the bottom of the page.

The last items were an expired Nicaraguan driver's license, four pictures, one of a dog, one of a young lady sitting on a porch wall, perhaps a sister or girlfriend, one of our suspect, in company of three others, all dressed in military boots and fatigues, and lastly another picture of our suspect with an AK-47 cradled across his arm posed in front of a shot-up military jeep with three very dead soldiers frozen in varied grotesque poses. Although the last picture was intended to imply that our hero had taken the jeep and its crew out single handed, it was obvious that the jeep and its crew had been stopped by considerably more firepower, than one man and an AK-47. The driver's license belonged to the guy I had taken it from. His name was Arnulfo Calixto Bermudez Nuñez.

I was making a couple of notes in my *Day-Timer* when the lights went out. The lights went out frequently for short periods during our years in Latin America. I don't know if they didn't have all the sophisticated switching mechanisms for the substations, or what, but it was a fact that the electrical current we took for granted in the U.S. was not as dependable in the developing countries. I looked at my watch. It was a quarter past twelve. I looked up at Roberto and said, "We can't analyze much here with the little bit of light coming through the windows. I am hungry, let's get some lunch."

"Sounds good to me."

"Does Piccadilly sound okay to you?"

As we walked out past Yaneth's desk, she was disconnecting the principal phone line from the switchboard and plugging it into the direct phone. The regular phone would work fine without electricity, but not the PBX. It meant only one line would work, but since everyone that understood the phone system and electricity in Guatemala knew to try every line before giving up, contact with the outside world would continue.

I told Yaneth where we were going and that we would be back as soon as we finished eating. With the electricity out, of course the elevators were not working. We walked down the four and a half flights of stairs to the street level in company of a handful of other pedestrians headed our way. We met three walking up. They were mumbling about their misfortune of arriving just when the electricity went out.

We exited the building and crossed Seventh Avenue to get to Piccadilly. Crossing any avenue on foot in Guatemala was a scary undertaking, but doing it with the noon traffic and no traffic light to protect one while crossing was nearly suicidal. Once across and heading into the restaurant I suddenly felt very hungry. I wondered if there might be a connection between the adrenaline rush of crossing the avenue and my sudden hunger. Perhaps the survival of something life threatening triggers a primal response in the body to seek celebration of survival through feasting. 'Wow, the unoccupied mind can detour onto some strange highways of contemplation!'

Of course there was no electricity in the restaurant either. Fortunately, no one in Latin America counted on electricity. The Piccadilly never did turn on many lights, even at night. There were three main things required for a restaurant to operate and none of the three depended on electricity. The water was supplied by city pressure; the stoves and ovens worked on gas and the cash registers had hand cranks just in case the electricity failed.

There weren't many in the restaurant so close to noon, so we were able to pick a table close to the door and windows. This meant we would be able see our food and one another almost as well as we would have with lights. Piccadilly served a wide variety of middle priced meals, so they drew a fairly heavy lunch crowd from the banks and offices in the area. The business lunch crowd was their market. They didn't do much business in the evenings. We ate many of our lunches there, at Cebollines Restaurant on the opposite corner, or at Pollo Campero one block North.

I decided to go for the large 'churrasquito' steak lunch which brought a couple of small pieces of tasty steak, that required nearly as much chewing as jerky, accompanied with a steamed potato with parsley and a small salad. Roberto ordered the meat shish kebab, which included green pepper, onion and tomato on the skewer and came with the same accompaniment. I brought Linda to Piccadilly a couple of times. I knew not to order the meat for her. She settled for the pastas. For her, no amount of good taste could compensate for a hard chew. Linda ate her meat at home, or in the finer steak houses.

The Piccadilly is a busy restaurant, so we didn't talk any business. We talked about our families and I told Roberto a little about our recent travel in the U.S. It took a little longer than usual for the food to come, probably a few challenges with the lights out. Just as we were finishing our meal, the electricity came on and stayed on after a couple of false starts. We made it back to the office at one-fifteen.

Yaneth had stepped away from her desk to wash her lunch containers in the dining room. She could hear the phones from anywhere in the offices. She was just coming out of the dining room when we stepped into the reception area.

She asked: "How was your lunch at Piccadilly?"

I answered, "Fine, fortunately they don't depend on electricity. How was your lunch?"

"It was okay. I am on a diet and the food isn't as tasty as I am used to. Azel says I look great, but the scales and the fit of my clothes say the opposite. When Azel says I look great, I think he may have ulterior motives, so I am trying exercise and a new diet, instead of new clothes. We'll see if it works!"

"Well hang in there, and Azel will be pleasantly surprised. Were there any calls while we were gone?"

"Linda called, and a Sergeant Gutierrez for Roberto. I told them both that you were out to lunch, and that I expected you to be back shortly. Linda said it was nothing urgent and Sergeant Gutierrez didn't leave a number. He said you already knew it and that he would call back if you didn't call him first."

Yaneth didn't offer to place either call, she knew that we preferred to do our own dialing. Once in a while I would have her track down someone, but generally I didn't like the idea of someone holding for me, nor using a secretary to do something that I could do just as easily myself. Mike and Roberto handled their calls the same way.

"Thanks Yaneth."

I started back to my office. Roberto said he wanted to phone Gutierrez and would be in, in a moment. That worked out fine. I headed to my bathroom to brush my teeth. I loved the taste of a Central American meal while eating it, but I didn't care to keep tasting the garlic and other spices for the rest of the day. Linda loved garlic, but she couldn't stand the smell of it after it was ingested. She had a super nose and could accurately determine which restaurant I had eaten at hours after I had eaten there.

I sat down and phoned home. Linda answered and asked how my morning had gone. I told her that I had worked in the office, about going to the airport and finally where we had eaten, so she wouldn't have to be guessing when I arrived home. I asked her if the electricity had gone out at home and she replied that it hadn't. Then she told me about her morning. She had taken Lynne and Susan shopping for some clothes. Susan would be joining Lynne at BYU in the fall. This would be her freshman year, a big transition from high school home study. She was pretty innocent, so we felt glad that she had an older sister already studying there.

Within thirty seconds of my hanging up, Robert showed up at my door, so I figured he had monitored his phone set until the line light went out, indicating I had finished my call. I motioned him on in. We went back to analyzing the items I had taken off the guy Saturday night.

The first item of interest to both of us was his driver's license. Upon closer inspection, we discovered that the driver's license had expired

July a year ago. We concluded that it was not likely we would be able to find out much about his current activities, but at least we had the name of one of our enemies. Deciding how we could use that little bit of information was another matter.

Roberto felt it unlikely that the police would have anything on the man, but we both felt that it wouldn't hurt to run a copy of the license through his contacts there. We also decided to give a copy to lieutenant Malvo at military intelligence. We decided to do the same with the pictures I had relieved the guy of. Not much likelihood that anything would connect, but at this stage, any enlightenment could move us along towards a solution.

We decided that Yaneth should make four copies of the driver's license and Roberto would take the photos over to the Kodak lab in Zone Eight for six copies. We figured the government offices would be closed by the time the copies were done at Kodak, so he would drop three copies off at our office. He would take the other three copies of the pictures and three copies of the driver's license so that he could use Tuesday morning to take one set each to Lieutenant Malvo in Military Intelligence and his contacts in the Public Ministry and the National Police. While he was at the National Police, he was going to inquire about the trace on the Datsun license plate.

It was a little after 2:00 p.m. when Roberto and I finished discussing the case and he left with the pictures. I spent forty-five minutes on what I call busy work, which means I wasn't really accomplishing much. I decided to hang it up around 3 p.m. It was a beautiful crisp afternoon and I wished I had someplace I needed to fly to, but I didn't, so I decided to head home. I couldn't remember what if anything Linda had told me that she and the children would be doing. I daydreamed my way down to the car, before thinking of calling home to see what was up, so I decided to just drive on home and find out first hand. I was in such an inert mood, that it didn't matter much what happened the rest of the day.

José the gardener was working on the plants outside the gate and saw me coming, so he nearly had the gates opened by the time I pulled up. The children and four or five of their friends were making tracks in the newly mowed lawn. A couple of them ran alongside the car as I pulled into the garage next to the Citroen. I locked my car rather than pull out the pistol. Instead of going up through the interior door,

I walked out through front and accepted some hugs from my children and some 'hi's' from their friends. I was knelt down talking with the two younger ones when Husky and Amy knocked me over with a playful bump. While I was down, Husky dropped a stick in front of my face. I took the cue and picked up the stick as I stood up. He was trying to concentrate on which way I might throw the stick, but was having a hard time doing so since Amy was harassing him. Finally he snarled a 'sit still to Amy', which had no effect. She continued to bounce around and bite on him, so I threw the stick anyway. They both went running off, Husky after the stick, Amy after him. Husky caught up with me before I made it to the front door, so I had to make one more throw before going in.

I could hear Linda laughing and talking in the kitchen, so I headed that way. She had her back to me and I winked at Miriam and Rosita so they wouldn't give me away. She was so caught up in her conversation with them that I was able to get my arms around her from the back before she knew what was happening. She startled a little, and then turned in my arms to face me. She was wearing the new blouse. She looked up and said: "Hi darling. What are you doing home at this hour?"

The maids, somewhat embarrassed by our behavior, turned back to their work as though we were not there.

"Just came home to see if you spent the day in bed while I am out slaving for the family."

"Ha, while I am taking care of our pack of monkeys and four or five of their friends, I suspect you are in your comfortable, quiet office, tilted back in your chair, feet upon your desk, and Yaneth serving you hot chocolate and donuts."

She left the maids to doing whatever they had been preparing for supper, while we sat in the living room to visit. She told me about her day and I told her about mine, especially about how we felt we had made a break through on the Alfaro case. Our visit lasted for an hour. I don't know where my doldrums had come from, but being with Linda pulled me out of them. We had chicken and noodles for supper. Valerie, our fifteen year old gave an excellent lesson on obedience for family home evening and I was ready for bed around 9:30 p.m. I fell asleep while Linda was reading.

CHAPTER 15
Tuesday, August 12

I woke up refreshed and was at my desk in the library by 5:30 a.m. I was able to sort through several angles on the Alfaro case and went down at 6:15 a.m. to check on Linda.

She was up and dressed for our morning run. We did our stretches and then ran side-by-side talking until we got winded enough that we couldn't talk and keep up the pace.

It was a beautiful clear morning. We were in an Indian summer, which they call 'Canícula' in Central America. It is a period in the rainy season when the heavy rains cease for about ten to fourteen days, usually in the middle of August. Instead of raining daily from two to six hours, we were having an hour of rain every three, or four days. The leaves and flowers were brilliant with the unclouded sunlight. Linda talked pretty continuous through our shower and dressing. She had a lot to report on, their shopping for clothes for the children, and their work at the orphanages and she had talked to Amparo, and everything was set for the barbecue on Saturday, and we were in charge of salad and desert, and we were going to take our croquet set, and…. I loved to converse with Linda. I just had to stay alert enough to show I was listening.

We had breakfast a little later than usual that morning. The children were up and ready to have breakfast with us, so it was a good thing we had been able to talk before breakfast.

I knew that Roberto was going to be out for most, if not all of the morning taking copies of the photos and license to his contacts in the police department and G-2, and I seldom got to spend any weekday mornings with the family, so I lingered around home until ten after nine.

The girls showed me the results of some of their most recent shopping. Then Daniel hauled me to the front lawn to show me what they called, "a couple of new tricks" they had learned on the tramp.

The older three weren't interested, but the three younger girls followed the boys and me out.

I had noticed they had moved a stepladder over by the tramp, and I innocently surmised that it might be for something other than jumping on the tramp. Before I understood what was happening, Daniel scampered up the ladder, jumped to the middle of the trampoline and bounced up into the tree on the far side. Asher was halfway up the ladder before I called a halt. I thought we had established the parameters previously, but they obviously had not understood. I again told them to only jump on the tramp, and not from any object to the tramp, nor from the tramp to any object.

As I walked back to the house, I heard Asher chewing out his brother for having told me about their trick.

I got to the office around 9:30 a.m. Yaneth reported that Jorge Alfaro had phoned twice and request that I phone him as soon as I got in.

I went on back to my office.

I dialed the factory and Silvia passed the call to Jorge's phone. After we had each said hi, I asked what he needed.

He said, "Don Orville, I was wondering if you might have time to meet with me earlier than we had scheduled."

"Sure. Tell me what time and we will notify the hotel."

"Actually I think it would be better for me in your office. I have to go by the Banco Inmobiliario across from your building around one thirty. I don't expect to take long at the bank. I could make it to your office around 2:00. Would that be a good time for you?"

"That would be perfect, Don Jorge."

"Tell me again, what is your office number and floor?"

"Fifth floor, five zero three, once you get off the elevator, turn towards the front of the building, then left down the hallway, which ends at our office."

"Good, I will see you then."

I took a few calls and placed some others, but spent most of the morning on preparing my part of the agenda for the Super Cajas meeting. I had been able to make notes throughout the preceding days, so I was able to have Yaneth type them. She also made copies of some handouts and together we put them in sorted piles, which we later placed in slotted colored folders, so that each participant could receive a packet.

We were working right up till noon when Roberto arrived from his errands. It made me realize that I had cut it a little tight by staying home that morning. The only thing remaining to do for the next days meeting was to print name labels for each folder. Yaneth could handle that without my help. I was anxious to hear Roberto's report on his morning.

We decided to have Yaneth get all three of us Pollo Campero chicken to eat while we worked in the office. I turned to Robert and told him to come on back to my office. He said he would gather some things from his office and come right in, which he did.

I had no more than sat down when Roberto came in and sat across from me. I looked over and told him that it was good that we had decided to stay in the office, that Alfaro was coming to meet with us at 2:00.

Roberto started off with, "You remember the German we met when we were over in Military Intelligence last week?"

"Yeah, I remember him. Jan something!"

"Well, as soon as I started showing Lieutenant Malvo the photos and the drivers license this morning, he picked up the phone and spoke with someone, and then the German showed up in two minutes. I can tell you one thing for sure. He has more than a casual relationship with our armed forces. I got a more formal introduction today. He is working with some of the top military leaders, but I never really found out in what capacity. I get the feeling that he knows more about us than we ever will about him. He was quite interested in the license and the photos. He asked about Señor Fletcher, and said he would like to have an opportunity to meet with you. He was trying to make it feel social, but it wasn't. I didn't want to take it any further until talking to you."

Yaneth peaked in the door to tell us our chicken had arrived and asked whether we should eat in the dining room. I answered affirmative and we followed and the great smelling fried chicken to the dining room. While we were setting glasses and plates on the table, I remembered to tell Yaneth that Jorge Alfaro had requested to meet at 2:00 in our office, so she needed to cancel the room at the Dorado. That was the only business thing mentioned during our lunch. We savored the chicken, fries, and flan and just visited. By the time we ate and cleaned the dining area we had a half hour before Jorge was to arrive.

As we were leaving the dinette, I reminded Yaneth to cancel the Dorado and said, "Roberto and I will be in my office, just tell me when Alfaro arrives, no matter whether it is before or after 2:00."

"Should I put Mr. Alfaro in the conference room?"

"No, we will meet in my office. Just let me know when he arrives and I will come out and receive him."

Roberto and I walked on back to my office where he spent the next twenty-five minutes tracing his accomplishments at the Police Department and G-2 that morning. He told me that he had gone first to the Police Department and had been able to get the trace report on the Datsun pickup. He informed me that it had not been reported stolen and was registered to a Guatemalan by the name of Vicente Juarez in San Miguel Petapa. From there he had gone to the Military G-2 office.

As soon as Roberto finished the words "G2 office", he exclaimed, "Oh, I forgot to mention earlier that the German had seen the police vehicle trace document in my open briefcase and he was very interested in the information, so I also left him a copy of the trace document."

He had just finished his report when Yaneth rang in to say that Alfaro had arrived. As I got up from my chair, I motioned Roberto to join me in greeting Jorge. He had never met Yaneth so I presented them to one another and then Roberto and I shook hands with him. Yaneth asked if we would like something to drink. He asked for a cup of coffee. Roberto and I each asked for a glass of water. Then we led Jorge back to my office. He looked around, apparently admiring our offices as we walked back. As they sat down, I moved on over behind my desk where I could make order of the things on my desk, including some notes I had made while Roberto and I had discussed the case.

I looked up and said to Jorge, "Well, are you just dropping by for a report, or do you have some information that may help us?"

"I am afraid it is more complicated than that. It appears that my family is unwilling to continue with the twenty-four, guard service that we set up, and I am back to plan A, to send them to their relatives in the U.S. I urgently need to discuss some ideas with you about what to do."

"What happened?"

"Insignificant stuff, nothing really, just tension from this whole mess plus I have been against the wall trying to keep up with projects in process and two new start-ups. The banks never come through with the money when they promise, but the companies that contract me don't plan on financial delays...."

"Hey, Jorge! If you are in a financial pinch, don't feel pressured by our billing. You can pay us once your money comes in."

"No it's not like that. The finances for projects are in the millions. The cost for your services has nothing to do with that. Sorry I got off the subject. What I meant to say is I am covered up trying to meet deadlines and that means I am not around to do my part in keeping the family calm and focused on this security matter. Your charges are reasonable and the security people you put me onto are much more professional. In fact I need to end the contract with the other company at my factory and transition to the security company you recommended for all of our security needs."

"Sorry to have interrupted, continue your explanation."

"Well, its been building for several days, but came to a head this morning when my wife and daughters cornered me complaining about the guards."

My heart dropped. I know some of the Latinos and figured one of guards had made a pass at his wife, or worse yet, at one of his daughters. I interjected, "Did one of the guards do, or say something inappropriate?"

"No nothing like that. Sorry for my muttering around with such confusing conversation. I am a little disoriented after having had to cancel an important meeting with a client this morning because of this security issue with my family. I better start at the beginning.

First it was Raul, complaining about having to take the guards with him everywhere he went. He was okay with the previous guards, but apparently you boys and the SIS guards cramp his style."

He looked over at Roberto and continued, "He told me how you had gotten in his way during some club hopping."

Roberto said, "I just felt he was at risk in one of the clubs we went to."

Jorge answered, "I had a pretty good idea what had happened even with Raul telling it from his standpoint. I know my boy and it is not easy to send him in any direction he does not want to go. Anyway, he has been grumbling generally about the controls, but then on Sunday night I caught his guard on the way out of the gate after he had accompanied Raul home rather late. I asked where they had gone and he expressed his concern because of the areas that Raul had been driving to. Upon further questioning, he told me that Raul had spent most of the evening at a low class bar in Gallito."

I interrupted to ask both he and Roberto, "Where is Gallito?"

Roberto answered, "It is just west of old town in Zone 3."

Jorge added, "It is a poor area that is full of tuffs and bad dealings and it is just a notch above La Limonada. It's a good place to get hurt, lose your money, maybe your car and maybe your life. I have warned Raul numerous times to stay away from those areas, so the SIS guard was well based in his concern."

I said, "Sorry again to interrupt your telling."

Jorge continued, "After the guard left, I was going to go on up to Raul's room and climb him about the matter, but decided it would be best to leave it until Monday morning, figuring I might accomplish more after I had calmed down. Well as it turned out, I didn't even see Raul yesterday. I ended up going to the factory before daylight and went to bed before he got home from classes in the evening.

I broached the subject with him this morning. When I started talking to him over breakfast, he became agitated about the guard reporting his every move. Basically he exploded about the controls and I exploded back, and then the women got involved with a petty incident my 18-year-old daughter had experienced on Saturday.

Apparently she decided to get something from the kitchen with only a towel around her and she became upset when she ran into one of the new guards that had carried in some vegetables for the maid. So she and her mother joined the animated conversation to add that they were unwilling to live under present conditions. Everyone is on edge.

The short of it is this, while I work through this security issue, the women have decided they are going to visit relatives in the U.S., and Raul was adamant that he would not have any more guards. After a rather long discussion, we narrowed it down to the fact that he does not want to have any of the professionals you recommended. He apparently has a good relationship with one of his former guards, I think his name is Alejandro, and he says that if I insist on him having a guard, he will only accept him. When I conceded for him to call his old guard back, he told me he had already done so. I didn't know what else to do. I have always been able to reason with my oldest son, Miguel, but when Raul makes up his mind, I can't budge him."

Jorge was finished talking, and neither Roberto, nor I, had anything to say for the space of fifteen or twenty seconds, while we just sat there contemplating all the ramifications of what Jorge had related.

Finally Roberto looked at Jorge and said, "So what's your plan?"

Jorge answered, "I don't have it all worked out. The first thing I did was to cancel everything I originally had on my agenda for the day. Then I looked over the women's passports to see if their U.S. visas are current. They are! My wife is talking to the relatives and checking with the travel agency to see when she and the girls can get a flight out. They have decided to make a vacation of it for now. They are going to start in Florida and will likely travel from there to Texas and California. I just came from withdrawing some dollars from the bank, so they have travel cash.

As to Raul, I don't know what else to do. I tried to reason with him, but he is angry, and refuses anything that might restrict his movements. I might try to get him to go work with Miguel for a while in El Salvador. There is a good bit of rivalry between them and he might not go for it. Besides Raul finally seems to be turned on to studying and I hate to pull him out of the university at mid year, sooo, I don't really know what to do about Raul. I thought maybe you guys might have some ideas."

Silence again while Roberto and I looked at the ceiling. Finally I said, "Okay, so basically Raul doesn't want a guard that may hold him back, and report on his movements. It would make it harder and won't be as effective, but I am thinking that we could follow him and protect him from a distance. He may, at some point, detect that he is being followed, but that could only be a problem if he tries to elude us. I doubt that he hates us. He probably just wants some breathing room."

Jorge asked, "You think that is possible? Can you carry out that kind of surveillance?"

"Well, like I said, it won't be as effective, and a lot harder than being right with him, but it is better than just giving up and letting happen what might happen. I do think it is good that he at least has an armed guard with him, even if it isn't someone of the caliber that we had hoped for."

Jorge answered, "Well let's do it then. I knew you guys would have some ideas. I convinced Raul to go to the factory and cover for me this morning, while I worked through getting the women set-up for their trip. He will leave the factory around four to go home and get ready for his classes. I am not sure what his Monday schedule is, but he should head to the university for classes around 6 p.m. Can you guys take over that quick?"

"One of us will be outside your home before 4:30 p.m. Are you going to keep a guard at home?"

"It wasn't easy, but I convinced the women to keep both guards with them until they leave and I insisted that we keep a guard at the house twenty-four seven. I think that our main exposure for now is Raul."

"Good."

"Okay, I am sure you guys have things to do, and I have to make a couple of other stops for the women, so I'll get out of your way."

"Jorge, I know that you have a lot to do, but can you stay just a few minutes more? As I said, I was about to call you and request a meeting."

"Sure! I forgot about everything except what was on my plate."

"We just have a few things to show and tell you about what we have been up to."

I briefly related the Saturday night incident outside the Dash Club and expressed that we felt we had made a break in the case and were onto some good leads. We showed him the Nicaraguan license and the pictures. He said that one of the men in the group picture looked familiar, but he couldn't recall where he might have known him. He had no recall of the face on the driver's license. We gave him a copy of the pictures and the license to mull over them later when he didn't have so much on his mind. We explained that we had already delivered copies to some police and military contacts.

It only took us ten minutes to finish up our meeting and Jorge was standing up to leave when I indicated for him to sit again.

I said, "Pardon me for extending and taking more of your time, but another angle just occurred to me. When will you next see Raul?"

"I don't expect to be home before he leaves for the University, so probably tonight or tomorrow morning. It depends on what time he gets home tonight and maybe what time I finish up what I have to do. Why, what are you thinking?"

"I am thinking that it might be better if Raul knew we were shadowing him. I am thinking that he is frustrated with the controls that were forced upon him, but perhaps deep down, he does not resent your trying to protect him. He may even feel a greater level of comfort if he knows we are there for him. I don't doubt that you know your own son better than I do, but if he does accept our shadowing at a distance, it would sure make us more effective. What do you think?"

"Hmm, it could backfire on us. He might attempt to elude you. On the other hand there is a chance he will discover you anyway and really resent my having not been open with him. He has worked a lot harder than his older brother to declare his independence. It's a toss up."

"I sure would feel a lot more comfortable if there was even a small degree of cooperation between the protected and the protectors. You call it."

"No matter for this afternoon. The earliest I will have an opportunity to talk to him will be this evening, or tomorrow morning. I am just going to have to feel this one out. He wasn't listening, or talking when we parted this morning."

"Okay. Thanks for your time Jorge."

"On the contrary, thanks for helping me work through this. I will let you know what, if anything, happens and I will tell you as soon as I know when the women will leave, and be one less concern."

Roberto remembered to give Jorge a set of the photos we had made copies of and suggested he and Raul look over them to see if they recognized any of the people in them.

I walked Jorge to the front door to say goodbye. Once he was through the door I turned to Yaneth and told her to transfer the PBX to my office and come on in.

As I entered the office, Roberto snapped out of some deep contemplation and as I crossed to my chair behind the desk he said, "So what's the plan boss?"

"I have asked Yaneth to join us, she is just switching over the PBX to here."

Having said that, Yaneth walked through the door and took the other seat in front of my desk.

Looking at Roberto, I said, "From the sound of it I don't think Jorge will get to show Raul the photos we gave him until maybe tomorrow.

In fact I got the distinct feeling that Jorge was not even headed to the factory this afternoon."

I turned to Yaneth, "As soon as we finish up here, get the messenger service to deliver a set of Photos to Alfaro's factory in Zone 12. Put Raul's name on it and mark it confidential. Enclose a note from me. The note should say, 'Raul: These photos may include one or more persons that have been pursuing you. Do you recognize any of them?' I don't need to sign it, just put my name at the end of the note. Then I need you to track down Mike. If you are able to get in touch with him while I am here, I want to talk to him. If not, tell him to plan on returning no later than Thursday morning. We need him here to be able to cover. He likely will not be able to fly out on Wednesday afternoon because of the rains in the Peten, but I want him here as early as possible Thursday morning. If I don't get to talk to him, find out where and with who he plans to be tomorrow. He should tell you every possible phone where I can reach him and he should phone here as soon as he changes from one place to another. I think that's all we have for you right now, Yaneth. Go get started."

As she left, I turned to Roberto. "Fortunately, it isn't 24-7, but close. Each day one of us has to make sure we are on the street outside the Alfaro home, well before Raul might leave the home and our days should end once he returns home. I will be the principle tonight and every other day from today. On those days you will take care of other business, but be the back up. You will be the principle every other day starting tomorrow, Wednesday and I will be the back up. I will have to review my schedule with Yaneth and see what appointments I have and determine if I need to reschedule. Perhaps Raul will realize that this isn't just another night on the town, and that he and his family are really at risk. The frustrating thing is that while we are in this dedicated protection mode, we can't be very effective in solving the case."

Roberto said, "Thanks! I was a little confused as to how you intended to handle this. Hearing your instructions to Yaneth and to me has given me a better picture. I also had a couple of things planned for tomorrow, but I will put them on hold."

"Good. If Mike gets back on Thursday, he should be able to give us a hand on running down some of the leads. One other idea! I am not too fond of them, but I think we could use four walkie-talkies for communication, one for you, one for me, one for Mike, and one for the office. Do you know if we can rent walkie-talkies on such short notice?"

"I can tell you for sure after a couple of phone calls, but I feel reasonably sure we can. What is your plan?"

"I was thinking just for emergency communication. Whoever is on Raul will be able to communicate with the others. The problem about walkie-talkies is that they are indiscrete, but perhaps you could obtain radios that have earphone receptacles and a couple sets of earphones. That way, the person that is on duty could choose to not answer if they are in a compromising situation. Find a service that doesn't have blind spots in the Capital, which is our most likely area of circulation. Probably a service with a repeater on this side of Agua Volcano would cover our needs pretty well. I can't think of anything else right now, so go see about the radios while I phone Linda to tell her I won't be home till late."

I phoned home, but Linda wasn't there. The maids told me she had left a half hour earlier with the three oldest girls, but they didn't have any idea where they had gone. I no more than hung up with the maids, when the phone rang. Yaneth had been able to track down Mike and had him on the line. I explained to Mike the turn of events and that we needed him back by Thursday morning to help cover. He said that would work out fine, since he had been able to schedule everything for Wednesday and he had already planned to return on Thursday morning. He reported that his flight and the meetings so far had gone well and that he had two promising meetings with two different companies scheduled for Wednesday, one in the morning and one in the afternoon. We wished each other well and hung up.

Yaneth appeared in the doorway to report that the messenger had already come by and picked up the envelope of photos for Raul. They expected to have them to the factory within half an hour and would phone her back to confirm delivery. She asked if there was anything else I needed her to do. I asked her to try to track down Linda before I left, but if I didn't get to talk to her before leaving to shadow Raul, she should tell Linda that I would not be in until late.

As she left, Roberto came in. He said he had located the four walkie-talkies, just three blocks away over at Motorola on Sixth Avenue. We would need to sign a contract and leave a deposit of five hundred Quetzales for each radio with its charger. They had three earphones that cost one hundred Quetzales each. I dialed Yaneth and told her that Roberto needed a check for two thousand three hundred Quetzales and he was going to tell her who to make the check out too. I handed the phone to Roberto. We decided for him to go on his motorcycle over to Motorola and pick them up. Yaneth came in with the check for my signature and I sent Roberto on his way.

Yaneth started to leave, but I called her back and signaled for her to sit down. I opened my Day-Timer to see what appointments were coming up. I only had Super Cajas on Wednesday afternoon. I looked up from my Day-Timer and said to Yaneth, "I will be shadowing Raul Alfaro tonight, Thursday, Saturday, and so forth every other day. Raul will be tomorrow, Friday, Sunday, etcetera. Are you aware of any meetings scheduled for me this week other than Cajas de Carton?"

"I believe that is the only one, but let me get my book to verify."

Within a minute she was back with her calendar block, reading it as she walked in.

She sat down and said, "Super Cajas on Wednesday at 2:00 is the only thing I show for you."

"Good. We won't have to do any rescheduling this week."

Yaneth said: "I have question. Are we going to keep the office open on Friday?"

"Why do you ask?"

"Well, Friday is the fifteenth which is the Guatemalan Patron Saint Day, so all the businesses except some stores will be closed."

"I don't keep very accurate track of the holidays. Whoever is following Raul will be working, but nobody needs to come to the office if it is a holiday."

"Since we are not going to be here on Friday, are we going to move payday up to Thursday the fourteenth?"

"Sounds logical to me."

"The next question: Since you are going to be out of the office on Thursday, should I do the payroll checks tomorrow for your signature?"

"Yep, that would be a good idea."

Yaneth left and I was deep in thought when she buzzed me to tell me Eli was on the line.

"Hi Eli, how are you and the family?"

"Fine, Amparo and I were thinking that since Friday is a holiday, perhaps we could do the Barbecue on Friday instead of Saturday. What do you think?"

"Sounds like a great idea, Eli. I hadn't realized that Friday was a holiday until just a few minutes ago. I am sure that Linda will not mind doing it Friday instead of Saturday. Have Amparo call her if she hasn't already, just in case I forget to tell Linda."

"So how are things going with you guys?"

"Linda and the children are doing fine. Linda and the two oldest have been shopping for clothes before they head off to university. I have gotten some breaks on a case I am working, but at the same time the surveillance has just become very demanding, so I am covered up with that right now. How about you, Amparo and the children?"

"Amparo and the children are fine. I have been pretty busy getting the trip arranged for my bosses. I am looking forward to some relaxation this weekend."

"Either I will get back with you tomorrow, or Linda will talk to Amparo, but I don't know of any plans for Friday and I know Linda is looking forward to getting together with you guys. We'll be in touch."

"Okay, talk to you later Orv. Have a nice evening."

I turned to some notes I had made about the meeting at Super Cajas the next day. I read what I had written over the past week and added a couple of new items to discuss. It was 3 p.m. and I was wondering how soon Raul would get back with the radios. It was getting close to the time for me to drive to the Alfaro home in Zone 12. Just as that thought went through my mind, I heard Roberto come in the front door. It had taken a while to test the radios and the batteries, but all four were in working order. They were different models, but set to the same frequency, so we were set.

We had Yaneth do a label with each of our names, so that we wouldn't get confused as to which radio was being used by whom, when we were together. I left to the Alfaro home at 3:45 cutting it a little tight. I was down the block from the home about twenty minutes before the garage door opened and Raul's guard stepped through to guide Raul out.

It wasn't easy to keep Raul's BMW in sight on the way to Landivar, but I managed. I went through a couple of pink traffic signals, but I made it unscathed. I parked as close to the exit as possible in the parking lot. I was able to exit my car and be over to the front side of the parking lot in time to watch Raul go in to M building for his classes. His guard headed on down to the vendor's stand where he had a smoke while visiting the young woman attending the stand.

I was looking down toward the vendor's stand when, Silas, the guard I had met the previous week, tapped me on the shoulder and said hi, but before he got to the 'hi', I took an overdose of adrenaline. He noticed and apologized for giving me a start. He seemed pleased to run into me again.

He told me he was now on night shift. He didn't ask, but I knew he was curious and since he already knew what my line of work was, I told him that I was there watching over a client. He showed how observant he had been by asking me if it was the student that came with the guard over by the vendor's stand. I answered in the affirmative. He told me that if I ever needed any help there on campus to let him know.

I asked him if he thought about my offer to work for my company. He answered that he really appreciated the offer and that he knew that he would enjoy working for me, but that the university had made special arrangements for him to work and study for his degree and that was why he had changed to the night shift. We shook hands as he left to continue his rounds. I thought, 'a good, intelligent man, with worthy ambitions.'

The evening passed uneventful. I reported to Roberto a couple of times on the radio just to test the system. I lost Raul on the way to his home, but got there just as he was pulling his car in the garage. I thought, 'so much for trailing, versus being with the person you are protecting.'

It had been a long day, with a couple of major ups and downs. I was bushed when I crawled into bed a little after 10:30 p.m. I was able to do so without waking Linda.

CHAPTER 16
Wednesday, August 13

I had some nightmares, but I could not remember what they were about, but the last one woke me up. After awakening with a start, I lay there thinking about the Alfaro case, mulling over the different angles until I was awake enough to get out of bed. I finally got out of bed a little after 5:00 a.m. I washed my face and headed for the library desk to organize my thoughts. After staring out the window at the sunrise and scratching out a few notes on vague angles on the Alfaro case that occurred to me, I finally was able to apply a little thought to the agenda with Super Cajas.

Super Cajas was one of our older accounts. They were one of the first customers I established in Guatemala when I was still living in Honduras and handling all of the accounts without any associates. The owner of the company was a Palestinian by the name of Hussein Mubarak, a really pleasant family man. He was a practicing Muslim and a very astute businessman. His brother in law, Jasín (pronounced Hasseen) Zimeri, owner of a large textile in Rio Hondo, Honduras referred me to him. I had been working for Zimeri about eight months, when he asked if I could provide similar services in Guatemala. I answered that to date I didn't have any clients in Guatemala, but that I was pretty familiar with the country, and would like to expand there. He put me in touch with Mubarak.

Initially I was contracted as a consultant to do a study of the security risks for Mubarak and his top managers. They were impressed, in their words, "by my thorough and insightful" analysis of the risks particular to Guatemala and their specific exposures to those risks. After completing the study they contracted me as a permanent consultant. They were not a very large company, but they were a great start for me in Guatemala. They had directly referred over a dozen clients over the years and I never did make a count to determine how many referrals were sent by their referrals.

Perhaps it was because he was my first client in Guatemala, or just such a pleasant client, that I had continued to handle them directly and looked forward to my quarterly meetings with Mubarak and his people. I think the relationship with Mubarak went a little farther than contractor and client. We hadn't had any social interaction outside of our working together, but I felt like he was a friend and I was certain that the feeling was mutual. From the beginning he called me by my first name, thinking it was my last. I being unsure if it was one of his customs, called him Mubarak and so it remained Fletcher and Mubarak from then on.

The first, second and fourth quarterly meetings were only with the security personnel about general security measures and challenges. The meeting for that day was the third quarterly meeting, which for the first hour included all top management. It was in that meeting that new security equipment and concepts were introduced. It was a key meeting, held once a year. I did get a little done for that important meeting, but my mind kept straying to the Alfaro case.

At 6:30 a.m., feeling sort of in a nether world, I started down the stairs, planning to go shower and get ready for work. I met Linda on her way up to see if I was going to run with her. I was going to say no, but seeing her ready to run, I answered in the affirmative. We were both dressed for it, so we headed on out through the kitchen and did our normal run routine. I was glad afterward that I had done what I knew was best for my body and at the same time, it gave my mind a little respite from all the sorting and pondering. I knew I would be better for the day ahead after the run.

Over breakfast, I remembered to tell Linda that Friday was a holiday, that I should be able to be free from work, and that Eli had informed me that his girls didn't have school on Friday and that maybe we would want to change our Barbecue date from Saturday to Friday. Her answer was that Friday sounded fine and she would work it out with Amparo. After our conversation I thought, how easy it is to get stuck in a rut and quit communicating. If we hadn't done our little run and had breakfast together, it was likely that none of that conversation would have taken place and it might have been the first of many days of a breakdown in communication. I thought, *Am I exaggerating? No, it had happened before!*

Sometimes I am moving so fast from one scenario to another that I get disoriented. Fortunately at times, while I am in the middle of a lot, I get a brief respite that lets my mind drop off the beaten path where it can put things in order, moments when I am forced to stop thinking deeply. It happened that morning while brushing my teeth. All morning I had planned on going to the office, but as I thought about it, I came to the realization that I didn't have much going on at the office.

I decided that there were other things I could and needed to do, while monitoring the radio with Roberto on duty watching out for Raul. With our analysis of the case on Monday and Tuesday, I realized that the former junior pilot for Alfaro had nothing to do with the case. He was merely an immature pilot. I figured it was better to clear his name as quickly as possible. So instead of heading to the office, I decided to head over to the airport, talk to Brenda about Ortiz and check on the work ordered on the plane. I also decided it would be a good time to spend an hour at the practice range. I had only gotten in one practice day in the past month, due to my trip to the states.

I changed into my flight suit. Linda came in as I was pulling out my munitions and practice range equipment. I told her what I was up to. She just smiled and gave me a hug.

I first went by Mag to talk to Brenda. I told her that although we had not solved the case we were working on that we had gone far enough to know that her former pilot was not involved in any way. She was glad to hear that, since he had phoned saying he was coming in later that morning to see about flying again for her. I left feeling glad that I had not waited longer to tell her to forget we had ever doubted the man. I shook my head as I thought, '*how easy it is to mess with someone's future, on mere conjecture.*'

Ralph wasn't in, but the head mechanic told me that everything I had requested had been taken care of. He explained that on the seat it was more than lubrication. It had been necessary to change two of the track rollers and while working under the seat they had notice one of the braces was missing a rivet, which they replaced. I reflected on how an aircraft requires constant vigilance, how one rivet, one screw, or a slight tear in the metal can lead to greater damage, or even disaster. I was glad to have found a shop with conscientious mechanics and Ralph and his crew knew that I would never question them about repairing anything that required it. I didn't need to fly that day, but it was comforting knowing that I left my plane ready to go whenever I wanted.

I arrived at the gun range a little after 9:30 a.m. It had been a long time since I had gone to the range during the week. I usually went on Saturday afternoons. I had forgotten why I had decided to go on Saturdays until I arrived that day. There were a dozen vehicles and all of the slots in the pistol range were occupied. I started to turn and leave when a cornel that I knew walked up and shook my hand. He saw my demise and insisted I wait for just a few minutes. He explained that a couple of his men were just about to finish their allotted ammunition and I could take their slot. As it turned out, I had accidentally gotten there at a good time. If I had gone to the range before the airport I would not have gotten to practice that day.

My practice went quite a bit better than my first Saturday back in Guatemala. From the start, I was able to put sixty percent in the A section, and the rest in C. None had fallen outside of C. I was back in the saddle.

As soon as I stepped clear of the shooting area to exit, I received a call from Roberto on the radio. He asked if I had been in a meeting since he had called a couple of times without me responding. I explained that I was just then leaving the gun range and asked if everything was okay. He reported that he had followed Raul to the factory and was merely waiting a half a block from the factory entrance. He stated that Raul had passed him as he exited his home, and that Raul had smiled at him, so he figured that his father and he had been able to talk. I felt a little guilty for having been where I couldn't hear Roberto's radio transmission initially, but I drove back home feeling a lot more positive than I had started out the day. It was good news to know that Raul was aware of us.

Linda and the children were gone doing their things. I put up my gear, changed into shirt and slacks, and headed for the office.

Yaneth wasn't at her desk when I arrived around 11:30 a.m. As I walked back to my office, I saw her in the dining room. We both said hi. She came in as I was sitting down at my desk. She said she had heard Roberto's radio transmission and mine just fine. She said she had the salary and suppliers checks ready for signing if that was a good time for me to sign them. It was, so she brought them in. I finished signing at noon. When she came to retrieve the signed checks, she brought in all the folders for the meeting at Super Cajas. I looked over them and thanked her for a job well done.

I seldom ate hamburgers, but I decided to have a McDonalds hamburger before going to my meeting. I loaded the files in the trunk of the Audi and drove to McDonalds, which was only two blocks away, but I had to drive six blocks to get there on the one-way streets. I never did like the Big Mac because of the sauce. I really preferred a quarter-pounder with just mustard and pickle, but I had long before given up on placing a special order on the quarter-pounder. It never came the way I ordered it. I found the plain hamburger to be my next favorite, so that is what I customarily ordered at McDonalds. Even then, it was difficult to get their plain hamburger. Half the time it would come with cheese, but slipping the cheese off was not too difficult, so I adjusted to that little crinkle.

As I was leaving at one fifteen for the meeting at Super Cajas, Roberto called on the Radio to say that Raul was on the move, apparently to go have lunch and that all was normal.

Generally it was a twenty-five minute trip from Zone 9 to the area in Zone 12 where Super Cajas had their plant and offices. I decided to go through Zone 13 on 5th Street to Petapa and then South on Petapa. The traffic turned medium heavy just before transitioning into Zone 12. Then everything came to a halt between 3rd and 2nd Avenues, a block and a half from the rail crossing. I could barely make out a train maneuvering across the intersection. After sitting patiently in the car for several minutes I noticed in my rear view mirror that some cars were making a u-turn and exiting south on 3rd Avenue. It wasn't until I notice the cars taking 3rd that I remembered it as an alternative way to Petapa Avenue. I opened my door and stepped out to look ahead to see what was the problem. The train engine was just South of the crossing with several cars behind it blocking the crossing. Nothing was moving. I got back in the car and maneuvered to make the u-turn in order to head back to 3rd Avenue. I remembered that 3rd ended at a street that turned back west about four blocks South of 5th Street. I was meeting heavy traffic, but my lane was light and moving until I turned the curve towards the rail line. This time it was a bus in my lane whose rear end of the drive train had dropped out, about a half a block from the rail line. The two lanes were taking turns going around the bus with the bus driver's helper directing traffic and receiving insults. Since the traffic was heavier from the opposite direction, someone had come up with the formula that they should pass fifteen vehicles to our five. Anyway my fifteen minutes to spare turned into ten minutes late by the time I pulled into the parking lot at Super Cajas.

The attendees at the meeting had obviously observed that I was going to be late and had arrived at a unanimous decision on what to do about it. As I entered the conference room and walked towards my customary seat at the head table, they all stood and applauded. They were smiling and all I could do was blush and smile back. I had been the one that had insisted over the course of five years that everyone arrive on time to our meetings. It was as though I had crossed a cultural gap by arriving late. I didn't bother to explain to anyone about the train, or the bus. No matter how I explained it, it would have sounded very much like the excuses they had proffered when they had arrived late to previous meetings. So much for my 'organized gringo image!'

During the conference, we talked about new equipment for management, including a briefcase with a debugging device incorporated and we introduce improved equipment for the security personnel. They gave me a little bantering during the mid morning refreshment break, but it was all good-natured. In general, the meeting went well. We finished up at a quarter till five, but it took me fifteen minutes for the handshakes and 'abrazos'. Once I was out the door, I walked pretty fast to the car and turned on the walkie-talkie.

Before starting the car, I radioed Yaneth to see if she had heard from Roberto. Roberto came on before Yaneth could answer to say all was fine, that he was following Raul to Landivar and that he would report in once he arrived.

I told Yaneth that I would be monitoring the rest of the evening, that she could go on home, and don't forget to plug in the radio to charge. I drove on home from Zone 12. The traffic was moderate in my direction, but heavy in the opposite. About midway home, Roberto radioed to report that they had arrived at Landivar and that Raul was in his classes. Both of us could relax for approximately three hours. I told him about Silas and that if he ran into him to tell him that he worked for me.

With me monitoring the radio, it was awkward trying to fit into any normal family activity. I kept the radio turned on through supper, but

I didn't want to be a wet blanket for any of their evening activities, so I tried to find a place alone to read and monitor. The only place available was the bedroom. I sat in the wing-backed chair and tried to read. It was a halfhearted effort. Frequently I discovered I had turned several pages, but could not remember what I had read. I was sleepy, but I could not go to sleep until Roberto reported Raul safe at home.

Roberto radioed a little after 8:00 p.m. to say that he had met Silas and found him to be a pleasant and alert person. I had never related how I had met Silas, and made a mental note to do so when Roberto and I had some time together.

Roberto radioed again when they left the campus and again when Raul was safe in his home. That was around 10:00 p.m. It was time to hit the sack. I would be on duty the next day.

CHAPTER 17
Thursday, August 14

I slept through until 6:00 a.m. on Thursday. It had been awhile since I had caught eight hours of sleep. I had no more than brushed my teeth and washed my face when Linda came in to do the same. We said our good mornings and dressed for our run.

I had a pretty routine morning from that point and I was in the office by five 'til eight. Roberto was in the reception area talking to Yaneth when I walked in. I was glad he was there early and I was just saying hi to him and Yaneth, when Mike came walking out from one of the back rooms. I was surprised to see that Mike had gotten in so early from the Peten. I had Yaneth pass the PBX to my office and invited all of them to meet there.

As it turned out Mike had taken off from Flores at a little after 6 a.m. He said he had to climb through a Stratocumulus cloud layer over the Peten, but had a smooth flight above the clouds which extended to near Cobán and then clear skies from there to the capital. He came straight to the office from the Guatemala airport. I expressed my appreciation for that.

It was a rather fast meeting, but we got through the important issues. One of the first things we did was to bring Mike up to date on the latest developments in the Alfaro case. We discussed the case a little and theorized on some possible links, but didn't arrive to any solid conclusions. We determined that Mike would act as my backup for that day, while Robert tried to search out any leads we might have on the Alfaro case, and we decided that Mike would also be the backup during Roberto's turn as point man on Friday.

I was in place near the Alfaro home by five till nine. Raul and his guard came out of the garage at 9:30 a.m. I followed them to the factory in Zone 12, where I remained on the street until they came out to go to lunch. I followed them to a little cantina-restaurant on Petapa

Avenue near San Carlos University. While they ate their lunch inside the cantina, I spread my lunch on the trunk of the car. When I was on surveillance I preferred eating light. I didn't eat cold sandwiches very often, but enjoyed the once in a while changes from hot food. It had a sort of picnic feel to it. Linda had prepared three tuna salad sandwiches, chips, two cans of coke and a pair of the local version of Twinkies. I could only down one of them.

Raul and his guard were in the cantina for an hour. From there I followed them to the School of Engineering on the San Carlos University campus. His guard stayed in the vicinity of the car, while Raul entered the building.

He exited the building thirty minutes later and drove from there to Zone 1. I lost sight of his car twice on the way there, including just before getting to the Civic Center. I didn't know his destination, but I figured there was a good chance that it was one of the buildings in the Civic Center. I decided to check the parking areas around each of the government offices in the area, which included the Municipality, affectionately known as the Muni, the District Court Building, the Public Finance Building, and Social Security. I started with the first parking lot, which was the one on the North side of the Muni. I took a ticket and drove through the lot, row by row. Raul's car wasn't there, so I got in line to pay for parking, although I hadn't parked. There were three cars ahead of me. While waiting in line to pay, I radioed Mike about my predicament, not that he could do anything about it, but I wanted someone to share my frustration.

After paying I drove to the parking lot one half block South of the Muni. The lot adjoined the Social Security Administration, which was across the street from the Muni. I had just been handed my time enter ticket to the parking area and was going to start the isle by isle routine when I glanced across the street that ran between Social Security and the Muni. There was Raul's car stopped in a no parking Zone at the base of the steps in front of the Muni. His guard was by the car, ready to move it if ordered to do so. I drove on across to the parking lot to the exit, which brought me out beyond the Muni on Sixth Avenue. I quickly drove the eight blocks of one-way streets that brought me onto the street between the Muni and Social Security. I was sweating it, but happily, Raul's car and guard were still stationed in front of the Muni.

As I pulled up on the opposite side of the street across from Raul's car, a policeman crossed the street walking towards Raul's guard. While watching the action, I radioed Mike to let him know that I had found Raul's car and his guard. Meantime I watched the officer talking to Raul's guard with lots of hand and arm movement. I find it interesting how much more noticeable people's body language becomes when you can't hear them speaking. The policeman gestured towards Raul's car, then pointed towards a no parking sign, then with strong arm language pointed to the guard and then in a sweeping motion up the street, which I took to mean, take your car out of here. I soon had my interpretation confirmed when the guard got in and started the car and then drove off a little jerkily. He did not have much experience driving. I followed.

We made three slow trips around the block and back in front of the Muni, to discover that the policeman was not going to move from the spot. On the fourth trip, the guard pulled in to the curb as Raul was coming down the Muni steps, carrying a long tube, like those used for rolled building plans. I had the air-conditioning off and the window down on my side and Raul glanced up as he reached the sidewalk. We made eye contact. He smiled and waved at me and I waved back. I couldn't be sure, but it looked to me like a 'what took you so long smile?'

I began to feel more like an invitee than a tag along. We had arrived at a 'we' thing, instead of a 'them and me thing'. My job still was not as easy, or as effective, as riding in the same vehicle, but a lot better than being a reject, and there was always the hope that our relationship would continue to improve.

From there, we drove about ten blocks to the Industrial Bank corporate towers in Zone 4. I followed Raul into the parking garage. I was able to find a spot just one isle over from where he parked in the S3 parking level. Raul was headed towards the elevators by the time I got parked and out of my car. The guard remained by the car.

I pulled the two cold cokes from my cooler, dried them with a napkin, and stuck one in each front pocket. I walked on over to Raul's guard. I wasn't sure if I was stepping over a boundary by approaching so openly, but I figured there was nothing to lose. When I extended my hand to shake, the guard's hand met mine. I thought, 'how about that, by being bold, I had made a breakthrough in establishing diplomatic relations.'

Alejandro was ready for a coke. We chatted and drank for a few minutes. Apparently Raul had expressed some level of trust towards me and had not sworn his guard to secrecy. I was able to find out that Raul was merely dropping off some plans at the office of a client and from there was headed to Landivar. Alejandro's voice dropped off a little at the end of that last disclosure, as thought he had some second thoughts about whether he may have passed a line of discretion. I mentioned how nice it was to have a break in afternoon showers, trying to put him back at ease, as though the information was inconsequential. He relaxed enough to ask if I had a smoke. At that moment, I was almost wishing that I carried cigarettes, even though I didn't smoke, but I had to answer no, that I didn't.

I had originally planned to merely say hi to the guard and return back to my car, but I felt that I was in the middle of a breakthrough and decided to take it a step farther and wait for Raul. It was only a few minutes 'til Raul stepped from the elevator complex and walked towards us. We said hi and he asked in a friendly manner about my family and me. I did the same about him and his. I was feeling good about having established a level of communication and didn't want to prolong the encounter to a point of me possibly over-stepping Raul's level of confidence, so I expressed my pleasure that he and his were okay and reached out and shook good-bye and was turning to leave, when Raul said: "I will be heading to Landivar from here."

I said, "Thanks for the heads up. I really don't want to get in your way. I just want to help."

He answered, "I know. We will see you there."

It was all I could do to keep from jumping and skipping on the way over to my car, but I contained my pleasure, and walked sedately and professionally. Raul gave me time to get behind him before exiting onto Seventh Avenue. We cut across by the new Sheraton Hotel to reach Seventh Avenue, which took us to Second Street, which turned into Vista Hermosa Boulevard, once we crossed Reforma. He made it possible for me to keep him in sight all the way to Landivar. I had enough time at the traffic signal just before turning off of Vista Hermosa Boulevard at the softball diamond, to radio Mike to inform him that we were in Zone 15 on our way to Landivar and that all was well. I also told him I would radio again from Landivar. I asked him to acknowledge receiving my transmission. He did.

Silas Guzman was posted at the entrance to the Landivar parking lot. I waved hi as I followed Raul in. It was 6:45 p.m. when Raul entered M building. I went back to my car, sat on the trunk, and radioed Mike. I first told him where I was and that he could reply freely. I told him that I had been able to talk to Raul and his guard and was hopeful that we would soon be able to get back to a more direct protection mode.

As soon as I finished speaking, Mike replied, "Great news. If anyone could put it back together, you could. Any idea how soon we can return to a normal surveillance?"

Roberto showed he was also monitoring the frequency by interjecting, "Roberto here. I have been monitoring. Congratulations! This blind following is not only hard, but also not as effective."

I buttoned the radio, "You are right on that point, Roberto. To answer your question Mike, I don't know how soon we can sit down with Raul and his father, but I sure want to do it as soon as possible. I will phone him tomorrow, even though it is a holiday, although I doubt that we will be able to resolve anything until Monday. I will radio when we leave the University."

I had one sandwich left and nothing to drink. The sandwich didn't look very appetizing after a long day. The ice had become water many hours prior. I walked down to the stand and bought a pupusa, a grape soft drink, and some chips. I took them back to the car where I could eat while watching the area. It was 9:30 p.m. when Raul emerged from M building with some noisy friends. They all descended towards the parking lot. Once they reached the parking lot, most of them headed different directions supposedly to their own vehicles. Raul and two others, separated from the rest and walked towards Raul's car.

I was fifteen feet from Raul and his car when he said in my direction, "I am headed with some friends to Twenty Third Street in Zone 13, at the end of Las Americas."

I merely turned and walked on back to my car. While opening the door of my car, I noticed that the two friends were getting in a Toyota Celica next to Raul's BMW. I was starting my Audi as they backed out of their parking spaces. I was able to keep Raul's BMW and the Celica in sight all of the way to their destination on Twenty Third Street, which was actually only four blocks from my home. Las Americas Avenue ended at a half circle with a large cross in the middle of the circle at Twenty Third Street, which angled west to Hincapie Avenue. The street was only one block long. There were half dozen large homes, a fifteen-story apartment building by the name of Vista al Lago and a small university by the name of IFES operated by Opus Dei. I had supposed that Raul was headed to the home of one of his friends in one of the houses, or in the Vista al Lago building. I had forgotten about one other institution on that short street.

CHAPTER 18
Party Surprise

I was about one half a block behind the Celica, which was a couple of car lengths behind Raul's BMW, once we got onto Las Americas Avenue. A park that was fifty feet wide divided Twenty Third Street. The north side of the street consisted of one way lanes headed west towards Hincapie and the south side of the street had one way lanes headed east towards Las Americas Avenue. There was a crossover in the middle of the block that allowed traffic to cross from one side of the street to the other without having to go all the way to Las Americas, or Hincapie.

The IFES University occupied a half block on the North side of the Street immediately after exiting Las Americas Avenue. The rest of the north side consisted of homes and a small quick stop store. The South side of the street was dominated by the fifteen-story Vista al Lago apartment building, which was on the circle on the eastern end of the street that entered Las Americas Avenue. The rest of the South side consisted of homes and one other institution I had forgotten.

It wasn't until I turned onto 23rd Street that I remembered the house of prostitution on the South Side of the street. It finally hit me, where Raul and his friends were headed. Just in case, I stayed behind them down the Northern length of 23rd, then out onto Hincapie Avenue and back onto the South side of 23rd. The house of prostitution was the second house from Hincapie. There were lots of cars parked on the South Side, but Raul found a slot just beyond his destination right in front of the crossover to the North side of the street.

The rest of the South side looked pretty full of cars. The Celica turned into the crossover to the North side of the park, and I did the same. I didn't want to park beyond Raul's car. The Celica parked immediately on the North side. Once I entered the North side, I backed up a few spaces to park behind the cross over. That way it didn't matter which direction Raul chose to drive when he left, I would be in a position to easily fall in behind him. I was just beyond IFES. There were plenty of parking spaces on that side, since IFES classes were over.

By the time I parked and got out of my car, the two friends from the Celica were halfway across the park to catch-up with Raul. I did a short jog to the Southern edge of the park straight across from the house of prostitution. I remained in the shadows of the trees, from where I was able to observe Raul and his two buddies joining up about midway between his car and the house. They put the arms over each other's shoulder and walked on towards the house entrance. There were guards on either side of the entrance to the house. Raul and his friends changed to single file behind two other men that were ahead of them being searched for weapons. By the time they got to the door, there were others that got in line behind them.

Once they were in the door I glanced around the area. Raul's guard Alejandro was standing by Raul's car. As I looked around, it became clear that it was a high-end house of prostitution. There were numerous BMW's, Mercedes, Volvos and a host of Suburbans. It was a playhouse for the rich, accompanied by a small army of body-guards, some sitting in cars while others leaned against cars and trees and a few gathered in little knots.

My pupusa was doing what pupusas sometimes did to me. My stomach was rumbling and telling me that I better never eat another pupusa. Figuring that Raul would be inside for a while, I actually considered going home, but my logic took over my thought process and I was able to discard the thought. Instead I walked back across the park to the quick shop. It was five till ten and they were just getting ready to close up. I convinced the guard at the shop door that I would only take a minute. I went in, bought a coke and couple of packages of Lemon Sal Andrews. It served the same purpose as Alka-Seltzer, but tasted terrible. I had no choice since they didn't have Alka-Seltzer.

I asked the cashier for a cup of water. She brought me a cone cup of water. I knew it would be a challenge to prepare an antacid in a cone cup, but I had done it before. I carefully held the cup with my left hand while aligning the foil packets of antacid in my right hand, so that I could tear off a corner with my teeth. The tear was a little jagged, but I didn't spill any antacid. Next I emptied the contents into the cone cup. Of course it started to foam above the small cup, but I was able to drink the top off without any loss of liquid, except the shower of fizz that covered my hand. Once it calmed down, I drank it down. My gag reflex reacted so strongly that I had to shake my head to keep it down. It didn't feel good at the moment, but I knew it would later. I was just glad that I caught the little store before they closed. I had caused everyone a five-minute delay in their closing time, so I guess I deserved the dirty look that the guard gave me when I left. I stuck the coke in my pocket for later.

I walked back to about the middle of the park, where I could observe, but not draw attention when I transmitted and listened on the radio. I radioed Mike and told him my location and that all was normal. Roberto chimed in on the channel and asked if I wanted him to relieve me, or at least come and share the last part of the evening. I told him I was fine, and that he better hit the sack and rest up for tomorrow. I told Mike I would radio him as soon as we moved from the present location. During the last couple of sentences, I could only say a few words in between each loud burp. The antacid was working. I was already feeling much better.

I walked over and stopped under one of the trees on the Southern side of the park. Alejandro was not by Raul's car. I scanned up towards the house. That was where most of the guards were waiting for their charges. Raul's guard was not amongst them. I slowly moved my search down the street towards the Vista al Lago. About six cars ahead of Raul's car there was a Nissan Patrol. I could see a driver with his arm out the door and some guards standing on the sidewalk talking to Alejandro. I couldn't make out much detail, but I could tell it was Alejandro. I thought, 'Alejandro, what are you doing visiting so far from where Raul is, or at least where his car is located?' I was tempted to go tell him to get his ass back where it belonged, but then remembered that I had just recently become an accepted part of the equation. If I shook the boat, I might again become a reject. I decided to just continue being vigilant.

A half-hour later Raul exited the house. He was alone, so I figured his friends had decided to hang around longer, maybe they had taken longer to pick a princess. Raul walked over towards his car, while looking around for Alejandro. He glanced over my way and I stepped out from under the tree where he could see me. He nodded his head and turned to continue his search for his guard. When he got to his car, I could tell that someone, it looked like perhaps Alejandro, had called to him. Raul started walking towards the Nissan. I got a gut wrenching dread that brought me out into the open and I started towards the Nissan, but I was a hundred feet behind Raul. I wanted to shout to him to turn back, but I thought I was probably overreacting. I stopped for a moment and reached down and grabbed my gun.

When I looked up again, some of the men were hustling Raul and Alejandro into the Nissan. I started running towards them as the others started closing doors and getting in. I was around seventy feet away when I pulled out my gun and took aim, but realized I could not distinguish anything other than the car to aim at, and that I could accidentally strike Raul, or Alejandro. I turned and ran to my car and glanced back just as they were pulling out. I jumped in, dropped my gun in the passenger seat and started the car. I started to head into the cross over, but as I looked in their direction I saw the Nissan turn right beyond the circle. That meant they were heading south. If I was right it would be better not to cross and follow them, but instead to go straight ahead to Hincapie and turn South.

As soon as I turned the curve on Hincapie, I was pretty sure I saw their taillights starting to descend the hill about three blocks ahead of me. I knew my Audi would handle the curves beyond Santa Fe better than their Nissan. I held the pedal down and the Audi caught a little air as I broke over the crest of the hill to start the descent. By the time they reached the first curve at the entrance to the Santa Fe Cemetery, I had closed the gap to two blocks and I could tell that it was the Nissan Patrol. I managed to gain another half block by the time we reached the steel bridge at the base of Hincapie. I turned off my headlights, leaving only my parking lights. I decided to not try to close any more distance, as long as I could keep them in site. They were passing vehicles as was I.

Once we arrived a Boca Del Monte at the top on the other side of the ravine, I no longer had to be shifting, so while driving with one hand, I radioed Mike. "Mike, do you read me?"

"Yes Orv, go ahead."

"They have kidnapped Raul and his guard. I am following south through Boca Del Monte. Tell Roberto to try to contact his friends."

Roberto came on, "I read you Orville. Where are you?"

"Boca del Monte, but I have no idea where we will end up."

"I will see what help bzzzz…. static bzzz."

"You are breaking up, I can't read you."

"static…bzzz. bzzz."

The radio went dead. The antennae did not reach South of Boca. 'Crap!!!' Anyway it was getting curvy again, so I needed both hands and I had failed to pass the last couple of vehicles in a timely manner. The Nissan was pulling out ahead, I needed to concentrate. It took a couple of kilometers, but I was able to again get within a couple of blocks of the Nissan. I didn't know whether they had noticed I was following, but I figured they probably had. We were coming up on the descending curves just before Villa Canales, so I again needed both hands. There were several cars in the curves, which slowed them down and made it possible for me to continue without lights, keeping my bearing by watching the tail-lights and head lights of the cars ahead.

As we entered Villa Canales, the streets were lit, so I continued without headlights. I could see the street adequately and I could easily follow the Nissan's taillights. I knew when there was a speed bump coming up, when I noticed the Nissan bounce over them. I was trying to anticipate their possible destinations and came to the conclusion that they might be headed to Santa Elena Barillas, which was a ruffian community, on a mountain, about twenty kilometers beyond Villa Canales, from where I hoped to be high enough to make a radio transmission. That possibility was nixed when the Nissan veered right at the Southern Edge of Villa Canales, onto the road leading to Lake Amatitlán. The road we were on paralleled the railroad a couple hundred meters east of the rail line and ended at the Lake. The road at one time, was paved, but now consisted of water holes interspersed with pavement. The Nissan was doing a lot of up and down and dodging left and right around larger holes. I couldn't see well enough to dodge, so I was doing more up and down. About 3 kilometers after leaving town, they made a left onto a secondary dirt road, which was actually smoother than the main road, but with numerous sharp turns. Fortunately I could tell when a curve was coming by the Nissan's brake lights, but I had to slow way down in the curve, because I could barely see. As soon as I came out of a curve and could see their tail-lights I would accelerate to close the gap.

We had been on the dirt road for approximately a kilometer when all of a sudden I could not see! The Nissan's taillights totally disappeared. I quickly braked in a controlled manner and resisted turning on my headlights. I moved the gear stick to neutral. I sensed the road was pretty level, but stepped lightly on the parking brake anyway. I reached into the glove compartment and extracted the flashlight. I still didn't want to use any light, but figured I might be able to shield the beam and at least get some orientation. I closed my eyes for a few seconds to allow them to adjust to low light. I reached up and turned the dome light switch to the full off position, so it wouldn't light when I opened the door. I opened the door and stepped out. Once I was out of the car I realized that I could see without the flashlight, just not well enough to drive at the speed I was driving while following the taillights. There were no electrical lights anywhere near, but the pale moonlight through a thin cloud layer, did cast some shadows. The road was sandy and moist with tall heavy vegetation on both sides.

I listened intently, but did not hear the Nissan, or any other vehicle. There were dogs barking all around, and some distant voices somewhere off to my right. I felt exposed on the road. A car could come at any moment, one of their cars. I got back in the car. I pressed in the clutch, waiting a moment to make sure the transmission was synchronized before easing it into first gear. I didn't touch the accelerator. I only partial released the clutch so that it would move forward slowly without straining the idling motor. I drove it forward slowly about fifty meters with my head out the window, until I found a place that I figured would be okay to pull well to the right. I left the engine idling and again exited the car, merely pushing the door shut to the first latch. Then I walked on down a ways.

I would stop every few paces and listen intently. All the sounds were coming from further down and off to the right. It was sugar cane fields on both sides of the road. There didn't seem to be any activity anywhere to the left. The road made a turn to the right about 25 meters beyond where I stopped. That was where I had lost the taillights. As soon as I turned the curve, I could distinguish some structures off to the left about fifty meters farther down. As I got closer I could see that the buildings, or what remained of the buildings were probably the house and outbuildings of a small farmer. There was a barbed wire fence and a barbed wire stretch gate, called a "tranca" over what was once the vehicle entrance. I listened for a moment. *Still no sound in this area*. I lifted the wire off of the lead pole to open the gate and stepped through. I walked on in and did a reconnaissance of the area.

There were two buildings whose adobe walls still stood. The third had only one standing wall with the other three walls and the roof structure heaped towards the middle. They had been abandoned for some time. Their roofs were no longer roofs, just wood poles jutting into the moonlit sky. Apparently the new owners were using the place as a graveyard for worn out tractors, vehicles and machinery. I discovered a place where my car would fit snugly and pretty much out of sight between an old shell of a pick-up and a rusted out stationary harvester. I seemed to be pretty much alone, so I decided to turn on the flashlight to help me scour the area between them. It consisted of tall grass and weeds that grew tall except in the middle where it was bald, which made me think that a vehicle had recently been moved from it. I picked up a few machinery parts and threw them to the back.

I opened the gate wide as I left and walked swiftly back to the car. I drove it slowly down to the entrance without lights and my head out the window. When I got to the open entrance, I accelerated ever so lightly to assure that the engine would not stall. I definitely did not want to have to use the starter. I drove it on through the opening and over behind the first building where I had located the parking spot. I backed it in over the tall vegetation, then got out and examined my parking job. It was okay, so I got back in and turned it off.

I pulled the extra ammunition clip from the hidey-hole, and took a couple dozen additional rounds out of the box of ammunition in the glove compartment. I removed the car key from my key ring. I put the rest of the keys, the car papers, my agenda and wallet in the trunk and removed my hunting knife and scabbard from my canvas tool bag in the spare tire compartment.

I attached the knife scabbard to my right leg. The lower strap fit snug just above my ankle and the upper strap wrapped above the calf of my leg. I kept only the gun, ammo, the hunting knife, my pocketknife, small flashlight and car key. After I locked the car, I stepped to the front and as much as possible raised the grass and weeds I had backed over when I parked. I was able to stand most of it up pretty well. I stood back and admired my work. The Audi was pretty well hidden in the dark and might not be noticed immediately in the daytime.

I walked to the corner of the building and stepped alongside it for a measured three paces, where I deposited the car key in the grass next to the wall. The whole operation had taken about fifteen minutes. I pulled the gate closed as I left and started walking quietly on down the road, towards where I had heard the dogs and people.

An eight-foot block wall started on my right, and about twenty-five meters beyond where I had left my car. Another twenty-five meters farther down, the road started a gently decline, but the wall remained level on top which made it higher from ground level. I heard talking and stopped to listen. It was coming from a little beyond where I presently stood under the shade of some trees whose branches extended from inside the wall. I crossed over to the left side of the roadway and walked a little more deliberate. There were more trees and less moonlight. My vision was impaired, but I could make out an entranceway through the wall a little farther down. They were still talking. I decided against continuing ahead.

As I turned to go back the way I had come, I scuffed some pebbles with my foot. The talking stopped and then I could hear some latches being withdrawn. I ran about ten meters back under the shade of some trees, where I had seen a boulder beside the road. I quickly and quietly reclined myself in a depression behind it. Within a matter of seconds of lying down I saw a light beam pass above me. My head extended beyond the boulder and I was sure my feet did the same. My hands were extended into some weeds out in front, the flashlight in my left, the gun in my right.

I could hear him walking towards me and I could see the light beam swing back and forth. I flipped off the safety on the gun and waited. The adrenaline had my heart pounding in my ears, part from the little sprint, but mainly from what I was anticipating. My legs and arms felt like springs, ready to release. He stopped walking. I couldn't see him, only the light as he played it to the opposite side of the road, then back to my side, then over me as I tried to melt into the soil. The light stayed over me for several seconds. I heard some clothes shuffle. 'Is he coming closer?' Then two shots. *Not so loud. Am I hit? I don't feel hit.* I could still see the light. *Am I dead, or in between life and death?'* Then the light left me, and he said, "No hay nada por acá."—There is nothing up this way.

I could barely swallow, as I heard his buddy repeat the same message from farther on down the road. After a couple of minutes, I heard them close the gates and resume conversation. I realized that the shots had come from inside the compound. That was better than being dead, but still not good news. I continued to lie beside the boulder for several minutes; feeling like my bladder was about to burst. I had just urinated after parking the car, but for some reason my bladder had not gotten the message. Finally I eased away from the boulder and onto my hands and knees. My bladder immediately felt better, but I was pretty sore on my front lower abdomen. I felt around by the boulder and discover my bladder problem. A large piece of tree root protruded from the ground just under the curve of the boulder. I must have been hugging it pretty tight to cause that much discomfort. I carefully walked back towards the corner of the wall, making sure I didn't make any sound and frequently looking back towards the guard post to make sure there was no more action from the guards. By the time I got back to the corner, the pain in my abdomen had pretty well worked itself out.

When I got to the corner of the wall, I crossed back over to the wall side of the road. The area was pretty dark with trees blocking out the little bit of moonlight that filtered through the clouds. To reach the wall corner, I had to climb up a four feet bank of clay soil that had eroded from around the wall, exposing a foot and a half of the footer that supported the wall. From there it was another yard up to reach ground level on the part of the wall that went from the road back into the fields. I had to pocket my gun to climb the last part of the bank with both hands. I was glad I was a ways back from the guard post, because I slipped twice quite noisily. Each time I stood very still afterward to make sure no one had heard, or was disturbed if they had heard. Finally I was along the field side of the wall. I was in the edge of a sugar cane field which was planted to within ten feet of the wall. From the edge of the planting to the wall was filled with grass and weeds which grew to about waist high in open areas and shorter wherever trees extended over the wall and blocked the sun.

I started walking down the along the wall. I could hear small animals scurry away as I walked and stopped to survey. I came across a couple of trees between the wall and the sugar cane, but there were considerably more trees inside the wall. Not a forest, but plenty of trees. Every now and then fallen limbs would block my path and I would have to walk around through the sugar cane, which was dense and taller than me. I had covered about two hundred meters along the wall and was working my way around a fallen tree, when I discovered the wall made another ninety degree turn just beyond the fallen tree. I had traversed the length of the wall on that side.

To continue walking alongside the wall from there would be quite challenging since the terrain looked totally uneven and loaded with prickly scrub trees. I surveyed the fallen tree. It had originally grown by the wall and was recently cut down. The eighteen inch stump remained about a foot from the wall with the trunk and tree lying sort of lateral to the wall fallen in the direction I had come from. Some of the larger limbs had been axed off, probably in the process of becoming firewood. I looked up at the wall. I could see some strands of barbed wire along the top. I looked around the felled tree and spied a rather large limb that had the vegetation cut off of the smaller extremities. Apparently the firewood gatherers had completed their load and left the limb partially worked for the next day.

I grabbed the big end of the limb and drug it over by the stump. It was about eight inches diameter at the base and looked to be about twelve to fifteen feet long. I stood upon the stump and pulled the base of the limb up over me towards the wall. I was really huffing by then. I turned while under the limb, so that I was facing the wall with about three feet of the butt extending above my head towards the wall. I let it settle on my shoulder, just to catch my breath. Then with me under the limb, I left one foot on the stump and reached out the other foot to rest against the wall. I gave it my all, pulling the sturdy limb up over my head and was able to prop the base of it about a foot and a half from the top of the wall. There was a light thud as the base thunked up against the wall, but the loudest part of the operation was my huffing and puffing. I sat down on the stump for a breather.

After a few minutes I stepped away from the stump to survey my handiwork. I had erected a ladder of sorts. It looked pretty stable with the minor limbs spread out on the ground supporting the base up against the wall. I looked at it and thought it would be better positioned a little higher and more vertical, so I again climbed up on the stump and position myself a little lower under the limb for another lift. I had my back and my legs bent ready to shove the limb up another foot higher on the wall. I breathed deep and put my body in gear, but I couldn't budge the limb. Either it had gotten heavier, or I had gotten weaker. I sunk back to sit on the stump to get my breath. Oh well, I would have to use the limb as it stood. My legs and arms were trembling from the exertion on the limb and probably a little dehydration. I was wet with sweat and wondering why I hadn't thought to bring water. Fortunately there was a steady breeze.

I was tempted to go back the way I came. I was convincing myself that I should go for help, I wouldn't be able to accomplish anything alone, but then I stood and determined that I had to get on the other side of the wall and see what I could do. Maybe Raul was dead anyway, but if not I had to do my best to get him out and the time it took to go get help could be the difference between life and death. It was my day, it happened on my watch and there was no one else to solve it. Tired, or not, Orville Fletcher was the only guy on the front line tonight. I stood up and shook off the glum that had tried to invade me. I stepped back, looked at my improvised ladder and reached up for the first handhold.

It took about ten minutes of careful climbing to reach the top of the base against the wall. The limb turned out to be pretty secure, settling only five or six inches below where I had placed it against the wall, but it was farther from the top than I had estimated from below. When I stood on the base, the top of the wall was about waist high above me. The barbed wire was sort of flattened out on top of the wall, and there was a three-inch limb that would have extended out over the wall, but had been cut off just inside. The limb was within easy reach. I was just stretching to grab it when I heard voices. I shrank back to my side of the wall and down as low as possible while keeping my balance on my precarious perch. The voices did not seem to be getting any closer. I ventured a peak above the wall. I saw a cigarette brighten about fifteen meters off to my left, more conversation. A dog barked beside the cigarette. I watched silently as the one with the dog continued walking on up the wall away from my position. I could hear the other person move away, but I couldn't tell which direction, but it least it was not back my way.

I again reached across to the limb with my right hand and discovered a hold for my left hand on the root limb. It was a stretch, but I had a good hold. I tensed my arms putting a good portion of my weight on them. The limb was holding well, but my upper torso was feeling about the same as it did after three rounds of racket-ball with my boys. It was all I could do to support myself while vertical walking my feet up the wall to where I had a perch on top of the wall. My handhold was now nearly at waist level. My toes were under the three strands of barbed wire and my legs were pressed against the wire. My right shin must have been pressed against a barb, because something was sure hurting down there. I got my balance and moved my right foot back an inch, which relieved the pain, but left me less firm on the wall.

I decided to go ahead and make the crossover. From my higher position, I was able to get my upper torso into the limbs and not have to hold my weight with just my arms. With some effort I pulled my right leg free. Apparently the barb was still lodged in my pants leg, because it came free with a rip and then a jerk and a pretty loud snap of the wire, as I got free of it. *So much for my new pants.* I held still for a moment to see if I had attracted any attention. I decided to get my other leg across immediately, afraid the guard might head back my way any moment, and I was in no position to do anything, but smile. I got a foothold with my right heel on top of the wall inside the fence and proceeded to extract my left foot from the other side of the wire. With being able to bear some weight on my right heel I was able to cross the left foot over much easier and silently. By again supporting my weight with my upper torso, I was able to swing my legs down and around the large limb, and from there I shinnied down the limb toward the trunk, orangutan style, but not orangutan smooth. I was definitely not as well equipped for the job. I made it to the trunk where it was only a two-foot drop to the ground, but my hand over hand descent on the limb sure did a number on my wrists. I landed in a bunch of vegetation, which fortunately absorbed some of the sound.

I quickly surveyed my surroundings and decided to head to my right away from where the man and dog had walked. I surmised they were watching this outer wall and could come back my way at any moment.

CHAPTER 19
Friday, August 15

Ｍy watch gave a little beep. Since I was pretty well hidden by the vegetation, I pressed the light on my watch and confirmed that I had just crossed to the other side of midnight, at least a couple of hours beyond my bedtime. I had a fleeting wish that I would soon awake and discover that my predicament was just a long nightmare and not truly the middle of a lousy night that didn't look too promising.

I un-holstered my gun and headed off to the right and soon came upon the perpendicular section of the wall I had seen from the outside. To continue into the property I needed to turn left and follow the wall, or diverge even farther left into the vegetation. It was hard to see much since I was mainly in the shadow of low trees, which grew pretty close to the wall, but I was on a slightly worn path, which made walking pretty easy. I decided to stay close to the wall for the moment. The terrain was descending and there were some large boulders along the way, some large enough that the path had to go around them. About a hundred yards further down I came upon a small clearing, which was bathed in moonlight. With the moonlight, I was able to determine that the thick undergrowth consisted of unattended coffee plants. I was walking through an un-kept coffee plantation.

I stopped a moment to listen and survey my surroundings. I could hear some talking off to my left and further down. The path led out into the open moonlit area, and I was trying to decide whether to continue out into the clearing, or to skirt it in the shadows. I would be exposed in the moonlight, but going around would be harder, more time consuming, and probably noisier.

I decided to stay on the path, in the open, but with a lower profile. I knew the ankle holster wouldn't work well for what I was about to do, so I place my gun in one of my pockets and dropped down on my hands and knees. The path was sandy soil and I was able to move across the clearing rather easily on my hands and knees. I had made it to the shadows on the far side and was just starting to shift all my weight to my legs in preparation for standing up, when I placed my left knee rather heavily onto sharp stone protruding through the soil. The stone got me in the soft tissue right below the kneecap and I felt like a sharp hammer had hit me. In my zeal to get off it, I ended up on my side. Besides hurting like hell, my lower leg took on a burning-numb sensation like when one strikes their elbow just right. I remained lying there for a couple of minutes until the numbness subsided, leaving me only with a throbbing localized pain. Finally I carefully got up on my feet, took my gun from my pocket, and hobbled on down the path.

I heard a dog bark about fifty yards behind me and decided I had better pick up the pace, which meant a faster hobble. The dog had probably picked up my scent where I had crossed the wall. The dog barked again and then other dogs farther down and to my left barked back, and then it became a continual chorus of barking. Initially it made me feel vulnerable, but as I continued moving I began to think that all the chorus of barking gave me some cover. In Latin America, only the first dog knew what he was barking about and once a group of dogs joined in on the barking, even the first dog forgot what he started barking about and they all just barked for barking sake.

The tree cover and coffee plants ended about two hundred yards down from where I had entered the compound. The ground became rockier with high grass in between. The clouds were again blocking most of the moonlight. I stopped again to listen and look around to get my bearings. The barking was pretty continuous, so it was impossible to pick up any sounds other than the barking. I could see some lights and building shapes off to my left, but it was totally dark straight ahead. I detected a little movement over by the lights so I decided to venture straight ahead, remaining parallel to the buildings and lights.

I was moving around some bigger boulders when I stepped into knee-deep water. I was so surprised that I almost lost my balance. I realized I was on the shore of Amatitlán Lake. The wind was blowing from the land to my back, so there was next to nothing in wave action. I pocketed my gun and reached down to get a little water in my hand. It tasted a little brackish, but palatable. I drank several handfuls and then bathed my head and arms. The drink, and the cool breeze on my damp head and arms restored me. I dried my hands on my shirt and again took my gun in hand.

I decided to move to my left staying along the shore and in the water as long as possible. I was about a hundred yards from the lights and as I looked towards the lights from out in the lake, I could see the reflection of the lights on the water and distinguish the shoreline pretty clearly. There were a couple bumps along the shore that could have been boats but I wasn't sure from that distance. I continued feeling my way about four or five feet from the shore where the water remained between ten and fifteen inches deep. I came upon a boat in the water and decided to go around it on the shore side rather than go deeper in the water.

I was about ten feet beyond the boat on the shore when I decided to return to the boat. I had the beginnings of a possible plan. I went to where the rope was attached to the boat and checked the knot. It was a standard knot but loose enough to untie, so I untied it and retied it with a slipknot that would permit a fast release when needed. I checked inside and there were a couple of oars lying on the middle bench seat. I continually checked where I had come from and the route where I was headed. I moved on down the shoreline towards what appeared to be another boat that was on shore about twenty feet straight out from an unlit wooden building. As I got closer it appeared that there was a tarp or some other soft object lying on the stern. As I got closer I figured it was someone that had slumped over asleep. I changed my gun to my left hand and pulled my hunting knife from its sheath on my right leg.

As I approached I pocketed my gun so as to have my left hand free. His back was to me as he slumbered resting on the gunwale of the boat. I remember thinking he looked uncomfortable. I grabbed him by the hair of his head with my left hand and slipped my knife around to his throat in one swift movement and said, "Don't make a sound, or I will kill you."

He felt strange in my hands. I spoke again, "Shake your head if you understand me." Nothing. I detected he was lifeless. I continued with my knife in place but brought my face closer to see his face. I decided he was either passed out or dead. I put my knife back in its scabbard and pulled my penlight from my pocket. While shielding the beam with my other hand, I gave a quick shine into the man's face and then turned it off. *Oh, crap. It was Alejandro. Dead, a shot in the center of his forehead.* I held the light over the gunwale, within the boat where the light would not illuminate outside of the boat. I flipped it on and looked over Alejandro's body, discovering he also took a shot to the chest, probably accounting for the two shots I had heard earlier. I shined around the inside of the boat, expecting to discover Raul's body too. *Whew!! Relief!!. Only the guard.* As I shined the light onto his lower extremities, I saw that they had tied three concrete blocks to his legs, probably planning to dump his body in the lake sometime before sunrise.

I saw a flashlight beam come out of the woods close to where I had emerged. I quickly moved to the opposite side of the boat and knelt behind it, retrieving my gun from my pocket in the process. I saw the light beam swing over the boat and strike a boathouse just beyond my boat and what appeared to be a pontoon flat boat pulled up on the shore beyond that. Then it swung on to the left and touched the main house and some smaller buildings about fifty yards from the shore. The light illuminated a guard just outside the main house cluster. The barking chorus had somewhat subsided, but started up again.

Someone from over by the house, probably the guard shouted, *"Todo bien Pedró?"*–Is all well Pedro?) Pedro answered, *"Todo bien Jacobo. Y por tu lado?"* (Everything's fine Jacobo. What about your side.) Jacobo answered, *"Todo Normal. Hasta la vuelta."* (Everything normal. We'll see you on your next round.) Pedro, his barking dog, and the light beam turned back towards the trees and began walking back the way they had come.

Jacobo exchanged a little conversation with someone else, probably another guard that I couldn't see. I scanned the area between the beach and the house and decided that I wanted to move a little farther down the beach to a point straight out from main buildings. It would bring me a little closer to the main buildings and a little less in the line of vision of Jacobo. I still didn't know where the other guard was but suspected he was on the far side of the buildings.

I began working my way over towards the pontoon boat, which I estimated was pretty close to straight out from the end of the buildings. I wanted to walk carefully, but not slow enough to keep myself over exposed. I was moving bent over ape style until I got to the far corner of the boathouse. The moon was pretty well hidden by clouds then, so I thought of taking advantage of the dark and making a swift passage to the pontoon boat, which I could barely make out in the dark. Then I thought better of it and decided it was too risky. I could trip over some unseen object and numerous other scenarios that could blow any chance of successfully rescuing Raul. I decided to plod on slowly and carefully as I had been doing. After passing the boat house the shoreline became slippery and tricky walking due to roots and rocks. I had to do a little balancing while walking, so I put the gun in my pocket.

It took me about ten minutes to make it to the pontoon boat, but I had made it unnoticed. Things had become quiet up by the main house. With the moon hidden by clouds and Jacobo backlit, I could see him in his chair leaned back against his building. I was glad the moon was hidden, because otherwise I would have been very visible. I had to watch where I placed my feet, but after ever step I looked to the main buildings to see if anyone was in a position to see me. My theory looked to be true. The Pontoon boat was pretty well straight out from the buildings. Although it was vague, I could make out some cars parked a little farther along and closer to the buildings. I decided to go around the front of the pontoon boat so as to make my advance towards the main buildings a little closer to the parked cars, just in case I needed quick refuge amongst the cars.

I took one step beyond the opposite side of the pontoon boat, and looked towards the main buildings and then I was covered with hands and shoved very hard to the ground. My head struck something and it either knocked me out, or I blacked out momentarily. I don't know for how long, but as I was coming around I could hear and see a numerous host of camouflage legs trudge by me as I awoke and began to struggle. Hands grabbed me again and a towel, or something towel like, was shoved against my mouth and someone whispered in my ear in heavy accented English: "Mr. Fletcher, please be quiet. We are on your side. We are taking our hands off of you, but you must remain quiet."

I stopped struggling and they removed their hands and then I asked, "Who the hell are you, and how do you know me?"

He again leaned close and said, "You must quiet down, please do not speak anymore. We are in the middle of an operation. I will explain a little later."

I couldn't see well in the dark, but it dawned on me that I recognized the voice. It was the German, Jan something. There was another soldier there with him. They both had on ski masks. Apparently the rest had moved past us. I sat up and began looking in the direction he was looking towards. He was scanning between the main buildings and the vehicles. Some of that area was getting intermittent moonlight and from our side I could make out some of the troops' heads bobbing around amongst the cars. They were doing a pretty good job of keeping the cars between them and the buildings they were approaching.

Then I heard someone yell in pain up by the house and a second one yelled similarly within seconds. There were several shots fired, I couldn't be sure, but they all seemed to be in the area of the main buildings, and then the second story balcony lit up with an explosion and what appeared to be smoke grenades went through some first and second floor windows. After that there were shouts and shots ringing from all directions up around the main house complex. The officer squatted by me started receiving walkie-talkie transmissions in Spanish, which he answered back to. Apparently, the man was the official in charge of the operation and he began to get numerous reports from several of his troops. They had taken control of the smaller buildings and were in the process of assaulting the main house.

I turned to Jan; "I guess its okay to talk now with all the noise. There are at least two men back in the plantation and two at the main gate about one hundred fifty yards to the right of the vehicles and main house."

Jan answered, "Thanks I will tell the captain about the men back in the plantation. He already has men assigned to securing the main...."

Suddenly we heard a loud 'fwhooom', a sort of muffled explosion. The front part of the first floor of the main house was engulfed in flames. There wasn't anyone coming out of the doors, but a few started hanging and dropping from a balcony near the rear of the house. It was eerie, finally seeing the details of structures I could barely decipher moments before in the dark. The blaze served as a dancing backdrop for the surrounding trees, people and the other buildings.

People were shouting and running and then we heard shots from the direction of the main gate. The captain was standing and asking about the fire and specifically if any of his men had been hurt by the fire, or explosion. The answer from his team leader was that it was too chaotic to know for sure at the moment, but that to his knowledge, none of his men had entered the house before the blast.

Jan tapped the captain and relayed my message about the men up in the plantation. The captain relayed the message to his team leader. We stayed by the pontoon boat while the operation continued. I looked back at the lake and was able to make out several rubber motorboats, the kind used by Special Forces.

Jan turned and asked, "Are you okay? Did you get hurt when our men took you down?"

I rubbed my forehead and said, "Nothing serious, just a couple more knocks to add to others I gave to myself tonight. I am amazed that you guys could put together such an operation on such short notice."

"What do you mean such short notice?"

"Well I didn't start following Raul's captors here until around two hours ago."

"This operation was not put together for you, or your client's sake. We have been working on this one for some time, but started finalizing it this past week. The pictures and the registration on a pickup you sent with your man Rosales gave us a confirmation of who we were after."

"You mean, your showing up here tonight has nothing to do with Roberto talking to Lieutenant Malvo about the kidnapping of our client?"

"No! We were already in the field, executing our operation when Lieutenant Malvo informed me by walkie-talkie of your situation. We had no way of stopping our operation, but it is good that he told us to be on the lookout for you. Otherwise you may have been deemed one of the enemy."

"Coincidence or not, I am sure glad you showed up. I was beginning to wonder what if anything I was going to accomplish alone."

"You mean you were planning to go up there alone?"

"Well as far as I knew, I was the only one here, and the only one that knew I was here. I had no way of knowing if Roberto had been able to contact anyone that could help and even he had been able to make contact, he had no knowledge about where I am. How did you know where to come to?"

Like I said, "We didn't know where your client had been taken to, but we had already planned a raid on this.."

The captain interrupted us to ask where I had seen the men back in the plantation. I explained that one was patrolling the perimeter on the left and I thought the other was patrolling on the right. I explained that I had only heard the one on the right side for a few moments when he was conversing with the other.

The captain relayed the information to his team. They answered back that they had the one that patrolled the left sector and were searching for the other. They also reported having control of the gate guards. There were three. The captain asked how it was going at the main house to which his team leader reported that eight had been captured and they were in the process of securing the main house.

Jan continued, "Like I was saying, we had no way of knowing where your client would be taken, but since we knew the gang was here, this was a logical destination. Are you sure your client is here?"

"Well I haven't seen him since we left Zone 13, but I followed the vehicle used for the kidnapping to this farm, and his guard is dead in a boat about one hundred yards back that way." I pointed back the way I had come.

"So how did you get in here?"

"I came over the back perimeter wall near the corner about two hundred yards to the back of the property. I worked my way down along a path inside the wall that comes down to the lake."

"And you were going to try this alone?"

"Well I hadn't come up with any alternative. I figured my client was in danger and yes, I guess I was winging it. I am glad you guys showed up and I hope my client is okay. So may I ask you Jan, what is your relationship in all this?"

"I can't tell you much, or I would have to kill you." He gave a dry laugh. And said, "Just kidding. Suffice it to say that Uncle Sam has a lot of interest in making the new Guatemalan democracy work. These rascals that we are rounding up tonight are one of several gangs that have been running guns and other military equipment left over from the wars here in Guatemala, and Nicaragua. This gang consists mainly of former Nicaraguan Contras and Guatemalan mercenaries. In addition to the illicit arms, they have branched out into kidnapping and extortion as well. Besides being a destabilizing factor for the new government, I think their working outside the normal trade channels on military equipment cuts out the Guatemalan generals and Uncle Sam and we can't have that."

"So do you work for the Guatemalan Military, or the U.S. government?"

"I don't work directly for either, but indirectly for both. I am sort of an in between that can do things without a bunch of paper trail. I am neither American, or Guatemalan, but I can probably get in...."

He stopped talking to listen to the team leader report that all was under control. The team leader continued: "Tenemos echo casas y dos soberanos hechos, nada serio."

The captain turned to Jan to say he was going in and for us to remain there. He radioed his man to tell him to meet him at the front of the first building. He handed Jan his radio and told him to monitor it in case he called.

We watched the captain walk up towards the house and saw a flashlight coming towards him, but we could not make out anything other than shapes of men moving around, except up near the main house where the flames still burned with lessening intensity.

I turned to Jan and asked, "What were they reporting to the captain?"

Jan said, "The team leader says they have three enemy casualties and two of our men wounded, but none seriously."

I then asked, "What were you saying before the radio transmission?"

"I was merely saying that I can probably get in to meet with some colonels and generals of several countries easier than many of their own officers, but having said that, if something went wrong, or some of the things I do became public, no one on either side would remember having met me, and that's all I am going to say about my line of work Mr. Fletcher."

The radio came on calling with Delta one calling Horacio. Jan picked it up and answered, "Horacio listening."

The caller, which sounded like the captain, said, "Tenemos dos neutrales, que hacemos con ellos?"–We have two neutrals, what do we do with them?

Jan asked, "Están bien y en que condición se encuentren?"–Are they okay and what condition are they in?

The Captain, "No los hemos tocado, ni hablado, no hay sangre y no parecen golpeados, están acostados en camas con sus ojos cubiertos. Uno está en la primera casita y el otro en la segunda."–We haven't touched them, or talked to them, but they are on beds with their eyes covered. No blood, no apparent injuries. One is in the first out building and the other in the second.

Jan answered: "Dejenlos, tengo un idea de como manejar ellos después que terminamos nuestra operación."–Leave them, I have an idea on how to manage them after we finish up our operation.

While Jan sat silent for a minute, I heard a couple of big military trucks come from the direction of the gates. I could tell they were military trucks because of the unusual whine of their turbo diesel engines.

Jan turned to me and said, "There are two hostages and your dead guard. Here is the plan. Hostages are always a complication for us. It will be better for us if they don't know anything about us. We have to load up the arms that were stored here and then we will to take the guard's body and our captives back with us across the lake, the same way we came. You will be responsible for the hostages. The hostages have not seen us and we will leave it that way. Where is your car?"

"I left it hidden in an abandoned homestead up the road."

"Okay, I will tell our men that you are exiting the main gate. Go get your car. Give us about forty-five minutes to load the trucks and clean up. You will know we have finished when the trucks drive past you. Then you can drive back, pick up the hostages and leave. You get to be a hero tonight, just leave out the details. Your client's guard will be at the city morgue by tomorrow evening. The report on where he was found will not be close to this location. I don't know how you would have gotten out of here alone with your client, but I get the feeling that if one man could have done it, it would be you."

He looked at his watch and declared, "It is 3:45. I estimate that it will take us until 4:30, but if the trucks haven't passed, wait until they have."

"Thanks Jan. I don't doubt that I was in over my head. I am sure glad you showed up and I owe you a big one. I hope we meet again in a more relaxed setting."

I reached out my hand to shake his, but instead he raised his hand in a salute, and then shook my hand. I walked on over through the cars towards the gate. The little blue Datsun pickup was amongst the cars. The front gates to the complex were open with one lying over to the side of the gatepost, apparently ripped from its hinges. There were four camouflaged military men, one on each side of the entrance. They saluted me as I walked by them. I saluted back and headed on up the road.

It started to rain. It wasn't heavy, but I was pretty wet by the time I reached the car. I retrieved the key, started the car and I pulled it out near the gate to the road. I checked my watch. It was a quarter after four. Daylight would break in an hour and half. I still had fifteen minutes to wait. I shut it down and got out. I relieved my bladder, and then opened the trunk to retrieve the belongings I had left there. I kept shaking my head in wonder about all that had happened in the past twelve hours and then I felt chilled and got the shakes. It was a little chilly, but I knew that it wasn't the cold that was affecting me. I had survived other close encounters with death and it always gave me the shakes. I couldn't help but rehash the incidents of that night while I waited for the trucks

By the time the trucks went by at 4:25, I had overcome the shakes. I started the car and drove back to the compound to get the hostages. The fire had either died, or been put out. Someone had doused it with water, probably after it had spent its energy. The fire had pretty well remained in the one front room. That is the way a fire burns in a concrete house. I didn't inspect it closely, but surmised that the room had been a kitchen. The cabinets, table, chairs and anything else wooden were heaped in ashes around the room and the stove was barely recognizable as a stove. It appeared that a small propane tank had exploded. Its charred remains were lying against the wall opposite the stove.

I found Raul in the first out-building. He was somewhat awed that I could carry out his rescue and scare off everyone. I didn't offer any explanations, except to say that I had help.

I found the other hostage in the second building. He was Juan Sierra, the twenty-year-old heir of the sugar cane Sierras. He was as happy as Raul to be freed from captivity and twice as talkative. I thought I would solve the problem by putting him in the back seat. Wrong, it just meant he had to talk louder. He recognized me as a gringo, so he told me all about all the places he had been in the U.S., which included both Disney parks, the Grand Canyon, Houston, New York and a dozen other places, many of which I had not been to. He couldn't believe that I hadn't been to all those places, me being a gringo and all. He also told me what a great family he came from and that his dad would handsomely reward me and that I should come to work for his dad, and..... I got the feeling that he thought I was unemployed. I recognized that it was nervous chatter. He wound down after about ten minutes and fell asleep.

I thought it best that I break the news about Alejandro's death. I said, "Raul, you need to know that I found Alejandro dead."

Raul Answered, "I know. He was killed in front of me soon after we got there, before they put me in a room. I couldn't see anything because they had a sack over my head, but I could hear. Alejandro knew a couple members of the gang well enough that he was calling them by name. He was begging them to forgive him of something that had happened in the past. I don't know what it was, but I got the feeling that it had happened some time ago. It was horrible hearing him beg for his life and then to hear him die right in front of me. I was sure they were going to kill me next. I am convinced that their killing him had nothing to do with me.

My adrenalin had all been used up. I drove slow and deliberate. I kept trying the walkie-talkie, but I didn't get in line with the relay antennae until I was in Boca del Monte. I radioed Roberto and Mike. I figured one of them would be monitoring. They both were. They too had been through a long night. Both had stayed close to the phones in the office. I told them where I was and that I was headed for the office, and that one of them should phone Alfaro and tell him that his son was safe and to meet us at the office. I relayed Juan's phone information and told them to give his family the same message.

I had just finished issuing the last instructions, but reconsidered. I buttoned the walkie-talkie again and told them to only phone Raul's family, we would contact the other family when I got to the office. The Alfaros knew us, whereas the Sierra family did not. It would be better for young Juan to phone his family once we arrived at my office. Otherwise his family could logically suspect that our call could be a trap, or part of the shakedown. My transmission awoke Juan, and he talked non-stop the rest of the drive to the Etisa building.

It was 5:15 a.m. when we arrived at the Etisa parking lot. Roberto and Mike were waiting and Jorge Alfaro pulled in just as we were parking. I sent Juan up to my office with Mike, so he could phone his family. I didn't try to explain much to Jorge and he seemed fine with that. I merely told him that the gang responsible had been effectively disarticulated and that his family should be safe from any more directed threats. He thanked me and said he would phone me later in the day.

The Sierras showed up a half hour later with two carloads of family and two carloads of bodyguards. The whole family couldn't thank me enough. The father assured me that he would be in touch with me on Monday.

The sun was just starting to peak over the mountains to the East when I arrived home at 6:15. Linda woke up while I was toweling dry from my shower. She first noticed my bruised knees, then she did a closer inspection and found a few other gouges and lumps.

Her comments were, "Poor boy! Looks like you've had a rough night. Are you going stay home and lick your wounds, or go jog with me?"

I felt somewhat rejuvenated after the shower, so I accepted her invitation. She was full of energy, which I wasn't, so she stayed in the lead during the run. She would look back and smile every now and then. I began to feel motivated, watching her spunky little body jog in front of me. Hmmm!!!! Maybe I won't just rest when we finish the run! It felt great to be alive and I thought, holiday or not, today did turn out to be my **PAYDAY.**

EPILOGUE

I was able to catch a three-hour nap before going to the barbecue at the Navarro's home, so I was in passable condition for the afternoon barbecue and games. I must admit that there were a couple of times that the croquet mallet was holding me up instead of me holding it up.

Few cases are totally solved. Some things remain a mystery, like the gang that was disarticulated that night. Lieutenant Malvo did tell Roberto that Raul's former guard had a connection with three members of the gang. Alejandro counted one of the members as a friend, without knowing what he was up to. As to the two others, they had met at a previous job and there had been bad blood between them. Although Alejandro had no part in Raul's kidnapping, he was an intended victim, and unknowingly an important element in their being able to track Raul.

As to the Alfaros: The wife and daughter took their vacation with their relatives in the U.S. Jorge gave us a very handsome bonus and contracted us for security consulting on a retainer basis.

As to the Sierras: In addition to verbally expressing their gratitude for rescuing their son, they also expressed it in a monetary manner. It was, shall I say, 'symbolic', an extremely small fraction of the ransom they saved. Perhaps it was the head of their security, the ones that had allowed the son to be kidnapped, that had recommended how much of a reward would be appropriate for the services of a small firm such as ours. *The thought crossed my mind that I should have left their son tied to the bed for them to rescue. An unkind thought! Dear Lord, scratch that last thought and forgive me for having had it! Hmmm! I think it is time to let my brain rest for a while!!!*